LIKE YOU KNOW

DEVILBEND DYNASTY: BOOK FOUR

KAYDENCE SNOW

Cover design by Sonder Publishing

Editing by Kirstin Andrews

kaydencesnow.com

PROLOGUE

THE SPLASH OF CRIMSON ALL BUT GLOWED AGAINST THE white beading of my designer dress. If I weren't standing in a dark alley, staring in disbelief at the bleeding uniformed policeman on the ground, I would've thought it was an edgy fashion statement about privilege in America.

The policeman groaned and screwed up his eyes in pain, his hands pressed to his hip where he'd been shot.

I'd been standing so close to someone when they got shot that their blood splattered on my dress.

I started to shake. Why was I shaking? It was a warm night; summer was practically here.

The sharp screech of tires rounding the corner cut through the night and my shock. I let out a pained, desperate cry and started to go after them. That couldn't be the last time I saw her.

"Amaya!" Jet's voice stopped me in my tracks. "Stay with me."

He was crouching by the officer's prone form, holding his shirt over the bullet wound as the poor man writhed in pain.

"They're gone." His tone softened, and his dark eyes

turned gentle. "I need your help. I need your help with this. Please."

I didn't want to help Jet. I wanted to run. But he had a point—there was no sense in running after a speeding car, and the man on the ground was in real trouble. His arms hung limp beside him, and he'd gone really pale.

I dropped to my knees next to them, and Jet took charge, guiding my hands to take over from his and press into the wound. The shirt was soaked, and my fingers felt disgusting in the warm, slippery blood.

It was kind of fucked up that I already knew what to do in case of a shooting—that this wasn't my first.

"We need to call 911." My voice shook.

But I had no idea where my phone was, and I needed both hands to lean all my body weight into the bullet wound. Jet would have to call.

I looked in his direction, but he'd already turned away, giving me his back.

He was going to leave me here, elbow deep in a dying man's blood. I just knew it.

CHAPTER ONE

IT WAS A BRIGHT, SUNNY MONDAY THE FIRST TIME I LAID eyes on Jet. I'd been hearing whispers about him all day. Fulton Academy wasn't a massive school—exorbitant fees made it out of reach for many. Most of us seniors knew one another, and I made it my business to know the latest gossip. Since before school even started that day, I'd been hearing about the new guy. His name was Jet, and he was hot. That was about the extent of it.

I was a sucker for a mystery. That was the only reason I looked up when I noticed someone unfamiliar walk by.

The final bell had rung ten minutes ago, and I was the first one out. I'd been leaning on the hood of my purple Jaguar F-Type, waiting for the girls, sunglasses on, enjoying the sun on my face as I read a romance novel on my phone. He came striding past, curious looks and secrets trailing in his wake.

He wasn't even carrying a backpack. He had his left hand in his pocket, and his right gripped a helmet and a leather jacket. No one had picked up that the new guy rode a motor-cycle? At least they'd gotten one thing right. He was hot.

His hair was shorn close to his head, and he had a body I could only describe as "solid." Not super tall or overweight, but the fit of his school uniform hinted at strength. Despite the helmet and leather, or maybe *because* of it, he looked innocent. He had a round face that somehow fit with a square jaw and full lips. Kind of a baby face.

When he glanced over, he caught my gaze and flashed a lopsided grin. He even had dimples. I nearly smiled back, nearly gave in to the giddy, amused feeling in my chest. He was a walking list of contradictions, and that intrigued me.

I held it back though, dropping my gaze back to my screen as if I hadn't even noticed him. Better to keep a distance from people until you could figure them out. Less chance of giving them power over you. Out of the corner of my eye, I caught how his grin widened before he turned away.

I tried to go back to my book. The main characters were arguing, and I could tell they were about to have rage-sex. But even enemies-to-lovers couldn't get me to focus. I bookmarked my spot and navigated out of the app.

A motorbike engine came to life somewhere behind me. It had to be Jet. No one else at Fulton rode a motorbike— they all preferred luxury cars to show off their privilege. Not that I could judge anyone, considering the car I was sitting on.

Everyone looked in his direction, the girls and some of the boys practically drooling at the prospect of a mysterious new student who was a bit of a bad boy. If romance novels had taught me anything, it was that bad boys rode motorbikes and would break your heart.

Once again, I refused to look, but resisting the urge to turn around was almost painful. So I compromised with myself, opening the selfie camera and striking a pose. I took several shots but didn't even look at myself. I was watching the bad boy in the background as he zipped up his leather jacket and glanced around before securing his helmet.

As he rode off, the engine making an obscene amount of noise in the tranquil grounds of the school, I lowered my phone and flicked through the photos. I zoomed in on him over my shoulder. In one pic, it looked as if he was staring right at me. I zoomed in even more. Was he smiling again? But the image was too fuzzy this zoomed in. I pulled it back a bit. His ass looked great in the gray slacks of the Fulton uniform.

I bit my lip, shamelessly perving on photos I'd taken secretly like a grade-A creep.

"Whatcha doin'?"

I jumped and nearly dropped my phone. Mena was suddenly by my side, perched on the car and leaning in to look at my screen. She laughed as I fumbled and shoved the phone into my pocket.

"Bitch, you gave me a heart attack!" I shoved her shoulder, then pulled her in for a side-hug.

"I called your name, like, three times." She laughed, her pale blue eyes sparkling. She'd done her eye makeup perfectly, making them pop even more, but she'd left the foundation and cover-up off today. Her port-wine stain birthmark was clearly visible on her nose and cheek. She was beautiful, regardless of whether she wore makeup or not.

I slid my sunglasses on. "I was just trying to get info on the new guy. No one seems to have any dirt on him."

"By staring at a picture of him?" Mena gave me a teasing look.

"Research?" I shrugged, and we both chuckled. She'd seen me checking his ass out like a stalker. If it were anyone else, I would've been embarrassed.

Hendrix and Donna walked up, hands clasped, both their

bags over Hendrix's shoulder. He dropped them both onto the ground as they stopped in front of us.

"How much longer?" he groaned.

Mena checked the countdown timer on her phone. We all had the same one. "Thirteen days, sixteen hours, forty-nine minutes."

Hendrix groaned again, and Donna pulled her own phone out. "Is that it? I was hoping to squeeze in a few more practice exams, but with tennis and pottery . . ."

The only thing Donna loved more than overachieving was Hendrix. Which was a good thing, because he helped her stay balanced. Her tendency to be extremely hard on herself had come to a head a few months ago, with some messy consequences.

"I'm sure you can find a corner to do some study while we're away, babe." Hendrix was only half teasing.

"I wonder if the resort has a business center," Donna mused.

"No!" I slapped at her phone, and she twisted out of my reach with a frown. "No studying on spring break."

In the past, we'd usually spent spring break hanging out by the pool, shopping in San Francisco, going to parties, and relaxing. But this was our senior year, and we'd decided to take a trip—one last Devilbend Dynasty party before we had to take exams and think about our futures. We were heading to the Bahamas on a private plane, courtesy of our friend Nicola. Most of our parents could've afforded to do the same, but Nicola's mom was a movie star and felt as if she had something to prove to the old-money crowd of Devilbend. No one was complaining though.

"Come on, babe." Hendrix picked the bags up again and headed for his Tesla, parked two spots down. "I wanna hit the gym. Turner's meeting me there."

Turner was Mena's boyfriend and worked at the gym. He went to a different school.

"You coming with us?" Donna asked Mena.

"I can drive you," I offered. I really didn't want to go home yet.

We said our goodbyes, and Mena jumped into the car with me.

"You can just drop me off at the bus station if you want," she said as I backed out of the spot.

"I don't mind driving you home." I shrugged, pulling up behind a Maserati and waiting to turn out of the school gates.

Mena gave my knee a squeeze but didn't say what we were both thinking. I kept nothing from my friends; they knew exactly what my mom was like. But Mena knew I didn't want to talk about it all the damn time either. Like the caring friend she was, she cranked up the music instead, and we jammed to Doja Cat all the way across town to Devilbend North.

I pulled up outside her apartment building and turned the music down. Mena lived in the bad part of Devilbend, in an apartment complex that had several entrances and thousands of people living on top of one another. The elevators were out of order half the time, the pavement cracked. Donna and Harlow were her cousins, and after we'd all found out she was being horrifically bullied at her old school, her aunt and uncle decided to pay for her to attend Fulton Academy with us. Best silver lining ever. I loved having her around every day. She reminded me not to be such a bitch all the time, and I had a feeling I reminded her not to take people's shit.

"You wanna come in for a bit?" Mena asked. "I have to get ready for work soon, but we could do homework for half an hour or just hang out."

"It's all good." I gave her a smile. "Go have a nap before you have to be on your feet for four hours straight." She worked at a diner, and while I'd never had a job myself, I knew how hard Mena worked, how precious her time was in between all her commitments.

"OK, well, make sure—" The roar of an engine cut Mena off mid-sentence. We both looked to the right and watched the new guy come tearing around the corner and into the parking lot of the building. He parked his motorbike, took the helmet off, and pulled his phone out, tapping away at it while still astride the bike.

"What the hell is he doing here?" I mumbled.

"People do live here, you know." Mena chuckled.

I gave her a withering look before turning back to Jet. "Do you think he lives here? Or is he visiting someone?"

"Dunno. Does it matter?"

"Not really, I guess . . ." It bugged me that no one had any good goss on this guy. And I couldn't stop wondering what it would be like to be on that danger rocket with him as he took that corner a little too fast, my arms holding on tight. He got off the bike and started walking toward the building entrance next to Mena's.

My friend gave me a kiss on the cheek and opened her door to leave.

"Wait." I grabbed her arm.

"What?"

"Follow him," I blurted. "See where he goes, what he's doing here."

"What?" Mena gave me an amused look. "What has gotten into you? No. I have shit to do. If you want to stalk some poor guy, do it yourself."

"I thought you loved me," I joked, pouting.

"With all my heart. Which is why I can tell you that you're acting batshit crazy. I have to go. I'll see you tomorrow."

I gave her a wave and watched her disappear into her

building. After another few minutes of looking at the entry next to hers, seriously considering taking a casual walk past there, I decided to put the guy out of my mind. He would've been long gone anyway, so it wouldn't have achieved anything.

I started my car and drove away. It wasn't even four yet, and I really didn't want to go home, so I headed for the hills. The winding road up was fun to navigate, and the concentration required to do it safely kept my mind off my mom.

I turned onto an unmarked side street. It looked more like a paved driveway, so if you didn't know to look for it, you'd miss it, which meant I was on my own when I rolled to a stop at the lookout. I lowered the windows all the way and killed the engine, then took a deep breath and let the sweeping view soothe me.

The edges of Devilbend were visible below, but straight ahead it was hills and valleys, and in the distance, San Francisco looked like a tiny model of a city. On really clear days, like today, you could even make out the hint of water glistening beyond.

I sat in my car and just stared, trying to focus on the clear blue sky and the vastness of it all. I was just one tiny human, barely a speck of dust in the universe. My problems were insignificant in the grand scheme of things. But that didn't stop my chest from tightening when I thought about going home. It didn't stop the empty feeling in my stomach when I thought about messaging one of my friends, then decided against it, convinced they all had better things to do.

Having had enough of my own damn thoughts, I grabbed my phone. I had some stupid number of Instagram notifications. Going through them all would be a good distraction, but I didn't know any of those people, and I couldn't be bothered. Instead, I navigated to the reading app and lost myself in a book.

I'd gotten through more than half of it by the time dusk

began to settle around me. The view had changed significantly, the sky a moody blend of colors as the setting sun painted the landscape a soft, warm orange.

I snapped a few pics for Instagram, got out of the car and took some selfies, then drove back down the windy road and reluctantly went home.

I wondered if my mom would be home or not. I'd had to endure her having parties and men over since I was eleven— since not long after my dad died. But this past year or so, she must've noticed I could take care of myself. She didn't need to pretend to parent, so she'd been going out more. Sometimes for days at a time. Wherever she went, she made sure to pay the bills, because the utilities stayed on and the cleaners kept showing up. I just never knew anymore if she'd be home when I got there.

It was almost worse than assuming I'd walk into chaos. At least then I'd know what to expect.

The garage door lowered slowly, and I sat watching it in the dark. Mom's Bentley was in the garage, but that didn't mean anything. It had been there the past two nights, and she still hadn't been home. Eventually, I got hungry and made my way inside, wondering if the Thai place would judge me if I ordered the same meal for the third night in a row.

But my thoughts evaporated when I walked into a lit-up house. The smell of cooking food came from the kitchen, and the sound of voices wafted to me on the aroma. At least there was no music blasting.

I rolled my eyes and followed my nose and ears. The urge to just go upstairs and lock myself in my room was strong, but better to know what I was dealing with.

"There's my beautiful girl." Mom beamed at me from behind the counter. It was always my *beautiful* girl. Never my *smart* girl, or my *brave* girl, or my *strong* girl. Was she cooking?

But no, she was uncorking a bottle of wine. It made a pop, and then she poured two glasses.

A man stood at the stove, his back to me. He was average height with brown hair, wearing gray slacks and a white shirt with the sleeves rolled up. At the sound of my mom's voice, he looked over his shoulder and smiled. I didn't recognize him. I rarely recognized them. It was worse when I did, because then I'd find myself face-to-face with the father of a school friend or the guy who'd served us at the mechanic or some C-grade actor she'd met through Nicola's mom.

"Hey, Mom. Haven't seen you in a few days. Good to know you're alive."

She laughed before taking a sip of wine. "Of course I'm alive, silly! Come meet my friend." She waved me over enthusiastically as her "friend" turned off the stove and started plating up what looked like pasta.

I moved forward but kept the island between us, eyeing them both warily.

"Sweetie, this is Cal. He's cooking us dinner." She bugged her eyes out and grinned, as if the idea of a man doing something for her was revolutionary. "Cal, this is my beautiful daughter, Amaya Ann."

"Cooking us dinner?" I crossed my arms over my chest.

"Well, of course!" Mom sipped her wine.

"I've heard so much about you, Amaya," Cal said, all friendly and shit. "It's a pleasure to meet you."

"Let's sit at the dining table." Mom grabbed her bowl of pasta and sauntered over to the table that had not been used for dining in I didn't even know how long.

"Yes, let's." Cal smiled. "Can I get you something to drink?"

This motherfucker—literally—was offering me a drink in my own damn house.

"No thanks." I gave him a tight smile, then turned to my

mom. I'd seen enough. "You should've checked in at some point over the past three days. Then you would've known that I was busy tonight." I grabbed the bowl of pasta. I was hungry and not about to say no to a home-cooked meal.

Without another word, I made my way upstairs to lock myself in my room, eat alone, and read until I couldn't keep my eyes open.

CHAPTER TWO

THE NEXT DAY, I DIDN'T SO MUCH AS CATCH A GLIMPSE OF Jet until lunch. I had just packed my books into my locker, and when I closed the door, I found him casually leaning on the locker behind it, hands in pockets, the tie of his school uniform askew.

He'd clearly been hoping to startle me, sneaking up like that. I didn't give him the satisfaction. Instead, I looked past him as if he weren't there and made to turn away.

"Amaya, right?" He flashed an amused grin. He had dimples. He had that baby face that made him look as if he was too young to be a senior and that tight body that suggested he was too old to be in high school.

I sighed and decided to indulge my curiosity. "Yeah?"

"Do you make it a habit to stalk all your classmates? Or am I a special case?"

"I have absolutely zero idea what you're talking about, and the fucks I have to give are in the negative." Had he seen me parked at Mena's building? He hadn't even glanced in our direction.

"The F-Type has a custom exhaust system with valve

control, twenty-inch gloss black wheels, and probably a whole lot of other custom mods I couldn't see from a distance. It's one of my dream cars. I'd recognize it anywhere, even without the purple custom paint job. You drive a distinctive car, especially for that neighborhood. What were you doing there?"

"That's none of your business, but rest assured it had nothing to do with you." I crossed my arms. Who did he think he was, accusing me of stalking? Never mind that I'd been on the verge of doing exactly that.

He dropped the teasing smile and stood up to his full height. He wasn't that much taller than me, but he had strong shoulders and really good posture. Still, I refused to be cowed by any man.

"If you want to know something about me, just ask," he said matter-of-factly. "I don't appreciate being spied on any more than I'm sure you would."

I snorted. "You wish. I was dropping off a friend who lives there, OK? And I've had enough of this."

I turned and walked toward the cafeteria.

He caught up to me in a matter of a few paces, his gait easy, relaxed. "So . . . I may have jumped the gun a bit there." He rubbed the back of his head.

"Whatever. I'm used to men assuming the world revolves around them."

He laughed, and it was such a free, genuine sound it almost made me crack a smile. "We started off on the wrong foot."

I gave him a withering look.

"And that's my fault," he rushed to add. "So can we start again?"

Before I could respond, he jumped in front of me, blocking my way just feet from the cafeteria and my sushi lunch. "Hi. I'm Jet. What's your name?"

He held his hand out, smiling at me like an eager puppy.

"What kind of name is that? Were your parents aircraft enthusiasts or something?"

"Actually, my mom was an *NCIS* enthusiast. Full name is Jethro." He chuckled as if he'd just told a great joke.

"What?" I had no idea what this weirdo was saying.

"Never mind." He waved it away and stuck his hand out farther.

I was so damn hungry I just chose the path of least resistance: I took his hand and shook it. It was warm, his grip firm but gentle. I left my hand in his a moment longer than necessary as a sudden urge to lean forward and hug him overwhelmed me. I wondered if his hugs were as comforting as his handshakes.

"There. We're good. Now, I'm going to eat." I shook myself out of it and walked away, avoiding eye contact. I got my sushi and an iced tea, so wrapped up in trying to figure out what the hell had come over me that I didn't notice him following until I walked up to our table.

My friends were already there, joking, eating, a spare seat saved for me next to Donna. They threw curious glances over my shoulder, and only then did I realize Jet was still with me, holding a tray piled high with food. All kinds of food that didn't go together. Pasta and fries next to a sandwich and stir-fry and sushi and a burrito bowl. No way in hell could he eat all that on his own.

"What the hell are you doing?" I asked, not sure if I was referring to his disgusting lunch or the fact that he was still following me around.

"We're friends now." He shrugged. "I'm joining you for lunch."

"No, we're not, and no, you're not." I frowned as I took my seat. My friends had all gone silent, watching the exchange.

"Oh, come on." He smiled and pulled over a spare chair. It made an obnoxious scraping sound as he wedged it between Nicola and Drew. "I'm new here. I don't know anyone. Introduce me to your friends."

I rolled my eyes. "Jethro, these are my friends. Friends, this is some asshole that's decided to follow me around."

I then promptly started eating my sushi, my other hand checking my phone as I ignored him.

He was ballsy, I had to give him that. People didn't just *invite themselves* to our table. It wasn't some pretentious rule or anything, but a lot of the other students were too intimidated to approach us. Jet was new though; he probably hadn't figured that out yet, and my standoffish attitude hadn't put him off. He was either that confident or stupid.

He didn't strike me as stupid though . . .

My friends were much more welcoming, apparently charmed by his easy attitude and dimpled smiles.

"Hey, bro!" Drew clapped him on the back. "I'm Drew. Welcome to Fulton Academy. And don't worry about Amaya —the fact that she's calling you an asshole is practically an endearment. She must like you."

"I do not," I stated calmly, keeping my eyes on my phone.

A few people around the table laughed, and everyone pretty much got back to their lunches and conversations. It didn't take long for Nicola to start flirting with Jet while Donnie threw them glares from the other side of the table. Those two had been on again/off again since junior year. They were currently off again as of yesterday.

In record time, Nicola threw her hair over her shoulder and asked Jet out on a date. I nearly rolled my eyes. Everyone at that table knew damn well she'd be back with Donnie within the next week and she was using Jet to make him jealous.

"Someone should tell him," Donna whispered in my ear, chuckling with amusement. "Poor guy."

"Not it," I rushed to say. "I have a feeling he can handle himself anyway. Plus, more fun for us this way." I grinned at her, letting an edge of mischief enter my gaze, and we laughed.

"What are you two laughing about?" Mena leaned around Hendrix to ask.

"Tell you later," Donna said and changed topics.

I glanced at Jet and Nicola, still flirting, heads bent together as they planned their date. I had a sudden urge to get to my feet and tell him it wasn't going to go anywhere with Nic. I wanted to call everyone out on their bullshit almost daily. But I kept my mouth shut. It was more powerful to know things about people than to expose them.

He glanced at me, and our eyes connected across the table for a fraction of a second. And for that fraction of a second, I almost felt as if he knew what I was thinking. There was definitely intelligence in that gaze, an understanding that spoke to life experience. Jet had been through some shit. It was that same restrained look I saw every day in the mirror.

I picked my phone back up. I absorbed not a single word of the page I'd tried to read several times now, too distracted by the new guy who was still too much of a mystery for comfort. Instead, I texted Harlow.

A: New guy update. He's pushy and annoyingly confident. Straight-up followed me to lunch today and just sat with us.

Her response was immediate.

H: The audacity!
    A: I know right?! He's currently in the process of planning a hot date with Nic.

H: Baahaha! Someone should tell him.
A: He'll figure it out soon enough.

I snapped a pic of them surreptitiously, *just* tilting my phone to get the right angle while still pretending to type. I was a master of the low-key snap. I sent it to Harlow, hoping I wasn't interrupting her time with Easton too much.

Harlow was Donna's sister and had decided to quit school just last week. What was it with people leaving and arriving with barely a few months left in the year? Very inconvenient for me. But Harlow had a good reason. She'd never been any good at school and only managed to scrape by with the help of her crazy-smart sister and her crazy-influential parents. After being blackmailed and going through hell, she'd decided life was too short and got herself a job in tech—one thing she was exceptional at.

Maybe I should ask her to dig up some info on Jet. Because I couldn't think of a reasonable explanation for him starting at Fulton this close to the end of the year.

H: Oh damnnnnn! New guy is HOT!
A: I'm telling Mr. Monroe you're perving on other guys while he's incapacitated.
H: His name is Easton. He's not a teacher anymore!

Harlow was in a serious relationship with Easton—who used to teach at Fulton. He'd been shit at it, so it was a good thing he quit anyway.

A: The man took a bullet for you and this is how you treat him?
H: Shut up. Why are you deflecting?
A: What? LOL! I'm not.
H: Yes you are!
H: OMG! You have the hots for new guy!!!

A: I do not. He's not my type at all.
H: We all know you don't have a type.

She wasn't wrong. There wasn't a particular look I was attracted to. I'd never been in a serious relationship, but I'd casually dated and hooked up with all kinds of guys and girls. From ripped fitness influencers I met on Instagram to shy nerdy girls. I went for personality and energy more than anything else. I liked interesting people—but I also tended to lose interest pretty fast.

A new text notification popped up. Harlow had texted our group chat, and it wasn't long before Donna and Mena were throwing me secret looks as they all teased me about my "crush."

Please. I didn't have crushes. I had fascinations. And the jury was still out on whether Jet would be one of them.

CHAPTER THREE

JET AND NICOLA WENT ON THEIR DATE THAT WEEKEND, immortalized in several pictures posted to social media. As predicted by literally everyone, it didn't go anywhere. By Wednesday of the following week, she was back with Donnie.

"You know, sometimes guys just need to see what they've lost before they can appreciate what they had," Nic told me wisely in English. We had seats in the back, and Ms. Murphy was pretty easygoing as long as we did the work, so most of the class chatted while pulling quotes to memorize for essays. "And I kid you not, Donnie was at my front door waiting for me when I got back from my date with Jet."

"Mm-hmm." I nodded. We'd all heard some version of this story countless times. The date pics had clearly been a strategy to get this exact result. Those two were addicted to the drama and heartbreak and emotional reunions of their push-and-pull relationship.

We couldn't be more different. When I was done with someone, I was *done*.

"Not that Jet isn't great. We're just not right for each other. And honestly, I was probably not in the right headspace for dating so soon after my breakup. But Jet was *so* sweet. He was super understanding, and he still made sure I had a good time. He's so easy to talk to. And he's funny! And you know, I feel bad about how things went down between us, so I told him—I said I'll set you up with someone. But he already has another date lined up with Tess! That's exactly who I was going to set him up with too. He's totally fine, which makes me feel better because . . ."

Nicola droned on through the rest of class, with very minimal input from me. She told me in detail why Jet and Tess would make the perfect couple and about what a gentleman he was on their date and how he hadn't even tried to kiss her. She was convinced he was being sensitive to her situation with Donnie. I was pretty sure he just hadn't been able to find a break in her constant talking.

As I headed to equestrian, I wondered why he hadn't asked me out. Why Tess? Not that I'd have said yes. Although I might have—just to dig underneath that layer of unaffected casual cool and figure out what his deal was.

But as I passed through the hall where all the senior lockers were, I saw him walking by with Sara. They were clearly flirting. So was he going out with Tess or Sara?

I momentarily dropped my guard and frowned. Jet caught my eye over Sara's head and winked.

I shot off a few texts as I got into my horse-riding gear. Harlow had been in this class with me, and I found myself checking the door to the locker room, waiting for her to walk through it, before I remembered she'd quit. I missed the little troublemaker already.

Riding Harriet—Harlow's favorite horse before she went and abandoned me—and running through drills and tricks in the sunshine and fresh air for a double period helped get my mind off everything. When I checked my phone after, I had the answers I wanted.

A few junior girls had found out the gossip for me. Turned out Tess had asked Jet out and not the other way around. But apparently Sara had been planning to, and her friend got in first. They both liked him, and it seemed to be putting a wedge in their friendship.

I snorted and finished changing. Whatever happened to girl code? I would never ever let a man come between me and my girls. No dick on the planet was worth risking that.

Speaking of girls, I smiled with my whole face—and maybe even a little bit with that thing in my chest that occasionally pumped emotion through my body—when I spotted Mena and Donna making their way to lunch. I sped up to catch them and wrapped my arms around their necks.

I was feeling extra grateful for my friends. We'd been through a mountain of shit together.

They greeted me warmly, and we walked into the cafeteria with our arms around each other. Nicola and Donnie were making out at our table. Drew and Hendrix were in fits of laughter over what almost certainly was a dirty joke.

Jet was not there. Before I could stop myself, I scanned the room.

Even with every single person in the cafeteria wearing the exact same uniform, I spotted Jet easily. There was just something about his confident energy. He was sitting backward on a chair with the lacrosse team, having a quiet conversation with Oliver.

Once again, I wondered what his deal was.

He'd sat with us a few times during lunch, but he'd also sat with pretty much everyone else in the senior class. I'd even seen him sipping on a smoothie with the cheerleading team after practice the other day.

It was as if he purposely didn't fit anywhere yet slotted in seamlessly everywhere. I grudgingly admired him for it. High school had been nearly four years of figuring out who we were and where we belonged. To actively go against that was either deranged or genius. Especially in a place like Fulton Academy where everyone was *someone* or the child of *someone*.

I did my best to put him out of my mind for the rest of the day, focusing on my friends and my classes. Donna dropped Mena off at the bus station, so I pulled out of the parking lot on my own, my gaze snagging on the infuriatingly confusing new guy as he swung his leg over his bike.

He had a good ass. I had to hand it to him.

I thought about taking my homework to the library or the lookout and doing it in the car, but I decided to go straight home. I needed space to lay out all my books and notes to finish off an assignment.

When I walked into the house and heard voices coming from the living area, I sighed but wasn't surprised.

Mom had been home for the longest stretch in over a year. But so had Cal. Every single night, for a week straight, I'd come home to the two of them in the living area talking, or in the kitchen cooking, or in the media room watching an old movie. It was so fucking domesticated it made me feel sick. It was fake fake fake! Vivian Ellis didn't have a domestic, parental bone in her body, and Cal wouldn't be the first or the last asshole to try to play the husband role to get to her money.

She can pretend with him but can't even try to pretend with her own daughter? I thought bitterly as I followed the sound of chatter and laughter, my teeth clenching harder with each step.

The two of them sat on the veranda off the living room, the bifold doors open all the way, the sky sickeningly blue beyond. Lounging on designer outdoor furniture, cocktails in hand, they were the picture of laidback #CoupleGoals. More like #LiesAndDenial

I did not want to talk to either of them. I could hardly

even stand to look at them. But I was never the sneaking type, and I refused to pretend I didn't exist in my own home, so I didn't give a shit about the sound my keys made as they hit the counter. I didn't rush to get away from them or stay silent. I took my time pouring myself a glass of icy water and chugging it down.

Staying hydrated was the key to good skin, and I had been slacking on my H_2O intake today. Mom came flitting into the room just as I slammed my empty glass down on the counter.

"There's my beautiful girl." She beamed at me, pouring herself another cocktail from the pre-loaded shaker. "Where have you been all day? It's so nice out."

"At school." I let the contempt I felt show in my expression.

"Oh right, of course." She waved me off, ignoring the WTF look I gave her. "We're going out to dinner tonight. Cal booked us a table at that nice place on the top floor of that tall building downtown. It's not for a few hours yet though, so come sit. Have a cocktail with us. Tell us about what boy has your attention." She wiggled her eyebrows.

"Can't. Busy." I turned on my heel and walked off. I would rather have ripped out my own nails than spend an entire night with that excuse for a mother and her creepy boyfriend. To think I'd spent weeks hoping she'd just come home. It was worse having her here, with him. Dealing with her every damn day just shoved in my face that I had no one to rely on. It was easier to pretend when she wasn't here.

I guessed we both liked to pretend—apples and trees. I may not have fallen that far from the shit-show tree that birthed me, but I was determined to roll as far away as I could.

"Amaya Ann Ellis-Lahari." Mom's angry tone made me pause a few steps up the stairs, and I turned to face her, eyebrows raised. "You come back down here this instant."

"Or what?" I scoffed. What was she going to do? Bend me over her knee for a spanking? I'd like to see her try.

Cal walked up to join her, a worried expression on his stupid face.

"Don't take that tone with me. I am your mother, and you will show me the respect I deserve." She was nearly shaking with frustration. Cal gently wrapped an arm around her shoulders, and some of the tension actually left her body.

"Are you?" I cocked my head. "You sure don't act like it. You haven't even tried to pretend you're my mother since Dad—" I cut myself off. Nothing could make me cry at the drop of a hat like talking, *thinking*, about my father. And I refused to cry in front of them. "Ugh. Not worth it." I started climbing the stairs again.

"Don't you walk away from me!" Vivian screamed after me.

I flipped her off over my shoulder, not even looking back. If she didn't want me walking away from her, she shouldn't have done the same to me over and over.

I heard Cal's deep voice speaking low and calm but didn't try to work out what he was saying. I resisted the urge to slam my door so hard it would bring the house down, closing and locking it instead. Good thing I did too, because barely a moment later, footsteps thudded on the stairs and my door handle jiggled.

"Open this door!" Mom pounded on it.

I ground my teeth, rushing into my walk-in and changing into activewear. I really didn't want to go out the window, but I would if I had to.

Cal's irritatingly calm voice said something to Mom as I gathered my shit and slung my gym bag over my shoulder.

A soft knock sounded on my door, then Cal spoke to me. "Amaya? Could you please open the door? Your mom has gone downstairs to cool off. I'd just like to have a word with you."

He'd like to have a word with me? Fuck that. And fuck going out the window. Fuck them both!

I marched to my door, unlocked it, and opened it. Cal stepped out of my way reflexively as I barreled through, giving him my back as I made sure to lock my door from the outside.

"Listen, I know that you and your mother——"

"You don't know shit, Cal." Without waiting for a response, I jogged down the stairs, snatched my keys, and peeled out of there, my tires giving a little screech as I took off out of the garage.

I drove straight to the gym, forcing deep breaths down my throat the whole way so I wouldn't crash and die from rage-driving. Once I parked, I leaned against the car and lit a cigarette, hoping the death stick would calm my nerves, but I only got halfway through. It was doing nothing to stop the frustrated energy coursing through me, so I put it out and headed inside. I needed to thrash this out on some gym equipment. Then I'd call the girls and bitch about it. Then I'd have some ice cream, and everything would be right with the world again.

I spotted Jet on the bench press as soon as I walked in, and I sighed, pinching the bridge of my nose. Either this would make my night a hell of a lot worse, or it would be just the distraction I needed.

Half an hour into my workout, I still wasn't doing any better. If anything, I was even more frustrated, because Jet followed me around the gym like a bad smell. I'd changed machines three times, going from the treadmill to the cross trainer to the rowing machine without completing any semblance of a proper set.

"Hey, Turner." I abandoned the rowing machine and

darted up to grab Mena's boyfriend as he passed. He'd been moving about the equipment with a spray bottle and a cloth, wiping everything down between answering the phone at the front desk.

"Wassup?" He spun the spray bottle on his finger like a gun.

"Can you kick that creep out or something?" I huffed, glaring in Jet's direction.

Turner followed my gaze. "Jet?"

"Yes. Jethro," I gritted out. "He's been following me around since I got here."

"Amaya, you're the one that's used half the machines since you arrived. He's stayed in the weights section this whole time."

"Yeah, well . . . ," I spluttered. Technically he was right, but I'd made eye contact with Jet several times, and no matter which machine I was on, he seemed to be positioned so he could see me. "He's just . . . he's . . . he's looking at me too much. It's distracting."

Turner raised his brows and pointedly looked over his shoulder. "He's not even facing you."

He wasn't, dammit! He was doing lunges with a weight in each hand. His shorts tightened around his ass with every lunge in the most delicious yet infuriating way.

"It's . . . he's . . ." I sighed. "His very existence is an affront."

"Okaaay . . ." Turner frowned. "Are you all right?"

"I'm fine." I did my best not to let it come out snappy as I rubbed my temples. He was going to push me for more—he didn't believe me, I could tell. But then his coworker called him over to the reception area. Turner reluctantly rushed off, saying he'd be back as soon as he could.

There was nothing between me and Jet now, nothing to distract me from his inconvenient presence. He'd finished his lunges and shook his arms out, took a drink from his water bottle. Then he removed his sweaty T-shirt.

I barely resisted the urge to roll my eyes. Who did he think he was to just take his clothing off like that in public? The nerve of this guy, showing off his—admittedly pretty tight—body. I mean, his back was so damn smooth and defined it was downright . . . insulting!

And because he was clearly an asshole, he jumped up, grabbed the pole above his head, and started doing pull-ups. *Pull-ups*! The audacity! I mean, how was I supposed to focus on my own workout when he was over there, clenching every muscle in his back and arms and shoulders? His movements were smooth and practiced, his feet crossed at the ankles, his flesh dancing under all that smooth skin.

He finished a set and jumped down, making me realize I'd been staring at him this entire time—like the creep I'd accused him of being. With a huff, I sat my butt back down on the rowing machine, determined to focus.

Jet did a few stretches, checked his phone, then glanced at me over his shoulder. I caught his smirk just as he turned away. Why was he getting under my skin so badly? That little satisfied smirk made me grind my teeth.

When he jumped up onto the bar again, he didn't do another normal set of pull-ups. Instead, he lifted his legs so they were straight out in front of him—as if he were sitting down. Then he started pulling himself up and down again. He was clearly showing off.

Before I knew what I was doing, I'd jumped to my feet and marched over. I stopped in front of him and off to the side and . . . got completely distracted by his abs. I mean, there were *eight* of them, and each one popped out with the effort required to hold his legs up like that. It must've hurt, but he just powered through it with barely an occasional grunt. His front was just as defined as his back, and this close,

I could see the veins bulging on his arms. All of it glistened with a sheen of sweat.

He chuckled, the cocky sound grating on my nerves and pulling my attention to his face. I followed his amused expression with my eyes as it moved up and down slowly.

"You're disrupting my workout," I stated, lifting my chin haughtily. "Please leave."

Jet paused at the top of the bar, his arms holding him in place, his legs not even shaking a little.

"Hey. Amaya, right? From school?" he said with a slight tilt of his head.

"Hey, Jethro." As if he didn't remember who I was. I didn't look that different out of my school uniform with my hair up in a braid. Did I? I resisted the urge to adjust my leggings a little higher over my belly. "Stop playing dumb and leave me alone."

"*You* came over to *me*." He lowered his body and dropped from the bar.

"Yes, because I can't fucking focus."

"I was here first, which I know you noticed, and I haven't come near you or said a single thing to you."

"Yeah, well, you keep looking at me. It's disturbing."

"No more than you're looking at me." He flashed me a grin. Jerk. He had a point, but I wasn't about to tell him that. "And I don't know what you're complaining about. It's taken your mind off whatever had you in such a foul mood when you got here."

Whatever snarky response had been on the tip of my tongue fizzled out. I was stunned he'd noticed I was upset in the first place. I was even more stunned to realize he was totally right—I hadn't thought about the shit show at home for a good half hour. I may have redirected my ire at him, but I had stopped obsessing.

"Your face will freeze like that if the wind changes," Jet teased before taking a drink from his bottle.

I snapped my mouth shut and glared at him. He wasn't even remotely bothered by it.

"Come on." He tugged on my hand and immediately released it as he walked past. "Let's see if we can get you to stay on the same machine for longer than five minutes. I need to do cardio anyway."

Like hell he needed to do cardio. I'd never seen someone so fit, and I spent a lot of time in gyms. I still found myself following him over to the treadmills though, my thumb rubbing the spot on my fingers he'd touched. So weird.

Wordlessly, we got started on treadmills next to each other. They faced the windows, and I watched the people of Devilbend walking past on the street, on their way home from work or taking their dogs for a walk. The view and the steady repetition of putting one foot in front of the other were no different from when I'd first arrived. But something about having another person next to me, matching my pace, had the effect I'd been hoping for when I came here. My mind settled, my legs started to feel a pleasant burn, and my lungs and heart worked harder—I felt more in my body and not so much all up in my ugly emotions.

Jet didn't try to make conversation. He just jogged alongside me, his eyes trained forward. I snuck a look at his treadmill and confirmed my suspicion that he'd set his to the exact same speed as mine. It should've been distracting having him right there, shirtless, all that smooth muscle moving rhythmically. But it wasn't. If anything it was . . . comforting. There was something disarming about this guy, and that in itself should've worried me. But in that moment, I was just glad he was there, that he wasn't being an asshole like I'd been to him, that I didn't have to be alone.

"Wanna tell me about it?" he asked. "Or should we just crank up the speed and sweat it out?"

Reflexively, I reached for the controls. There were exactly three people on this planet I let myself be vulnerable with. It did not feel safe to talk about private shit with anyone else. Except . . .

I let my hand fall to my side, keeping the same manageable pace, and wondered why I actually did kind of want to vent to Jet.

It's not him. It's just that I want to vent, period. He just happens to be here, I told myself.

It was a load of crap. Turner stood right by the reception desk, and I knew and trusted him way more than this virtual stranger. But it had been a weird evening, and I found myself leaning into the instinct to talk to Jet.

"My dad is dead, my mom is the definition of flighty, and this new guy she's dating just won't go away," I blurted, severely simplifying all the shit pissing me off.

"Is this boyfriend hurting you? Or her?" Jet's voice was serious and low, and he looked right at me for the first time since we got on the treadmills. The sudden intensity took me a little aback.

"What? No. He's just around all the fucking time, and my mom expects me to play house with them all of a sudden when she hasn't been anything resembling a mother for years."

"Right." He stayed silent for a few moments, but I could feel him holding back whatever he wanted to say.

"Anyway, she lost her shit at me tonight because I refuse to play the good little daughter. Then the boyfriend tried to step in and talk to me like a father figure." I rolled my eyes so hard I nearly lost my balance on the treadmill. "I just had to get out of there for a while."

"Sounds frustrating."

"It is."

After another stretch of silence, he glanced at me again. "I'm sorry about your dad. Did he pass recently?"

"No, it was six years ago. Thanks." And that was about when I hit my limit for talking about my feelings. *Ugh*! I definitely wasn't getting into my dead daddy issues in the gym with some new guy I knew nothing about. "Anyway, I'm fine now. And you owe me some answers."

"I do?" He chuckled, but he was smart enough not to push me.

"Yep. I just spilled some really personal shit. I think it's only fair that you tell me about yourself too."

"I mean, I did pull you out of your funk, so I think we're even." A teasing smile pulled at his lips.

"I don't know what you're talking about. I had a momentary lapse of sanity and said things to you I hardly even talk to my friends about. Now it's your turn. I need something to hold over you so you won't go around telling people I have emotions and shit."

"I won't tell anyone what we talked about, Amaya. No mutually assured destruction necessary." He had that serious tone in his voice again, and I didn't like it. It made me feel awkward and kind of itchy.

"What's your deal, Jethro?" I forged on with the lighter topics—or at least ones not focused on me. "Why'd you transfer to Fulton so late in the year?"

"I got a scholarship." He shrugged. That explained the living situation but not the late admission.

"They hand out scholarships with barely two months left in the year? *Senior* year, no less?"

"I think we both know Fulton Academy doesn't hand out much of anything," he grumbled.

"True. So what's your deal then?"

"I had to move. They agreed to let me start now."

"Your parents got a new job or something? Why'd you have to move?" And why Devilbend North of all the shitty neighborhoods in the country?

"No, my parents are . . . they're not in the picture."

Oh, now this was getting interesting. "Siblings?"

"Only child."

"Same. So you're staying with a relative or something?" Did his parents both die suddenly? He had that look in his eyes—that look that people got when they'd seen some shit. I hoped I wasn't bringing up something painful.

"Nope." Despite the short answer, he didn't seem offended by my questions. Could be just a defense mechanism . . .

"Look, I'm sorry if I hit on a touchy subject. If your parents are—"

He cut me off with a loud laugh. "My parents aren't dead. They're just . . . not currently parenting."

"Yikes. Yeah, OK, say no more. I get it." My one remaining parent hadn't been parenting for some time. I guessed it was even tougher when you didn't have the kind of money we had. Mom may not have been around much, but the fridge was always full and the house was always clean.

"Are we done with the interrogation?" he teased. "Because I got shit to do."

"No, actually." I grabbed on to the safety bar and jumped to the sides of the treadmill so I could look at him properly without risking a face-plant. "Now that I know I'm not being a bitch by making you talk about your dead parents, I'd like an answer to my original question."

He grinned without looking at me, still maintaining a steady jog. I forced my eyes to stay trained on the side of his head instead of wandering down all that sculpted muscle and sweaty skin.

"If you must know"—he was actually starting to sound a

little winded after all that exercise—"I was supposed to finish my senior year last year. But, ya know, life got in the way and that never happened. So then I tried a few times to get my shit together this year but . . . yeah, life. To cut a long story short, I managed to get myself a scholarship at Fulton—for next year. But because I'm eighteen, I've aged out of the system, so to keep receiving benefits, I have to be in school. Fulton agreed to let me start now so I wouldn't end up homeless." He powered down the treadmill and stepped off, turning to face me. "You seem to be back to your demanding, abrupt self, so I'm going to get on with my evening now. See you tomorrow."

With one last dimpled grin, he turned and walked into the men's locker room, grabbing his stuff on the way.

I stared after him, slightly stunned, my treadmill still whirring under me. I didn't know jack shit about the system and benefits and homelessness, but I felt as if I knew a bit more about the real Jethro Collins now. He hadn't been dealt an easy life, yet he still walked around with a smile and a positive attitude every day. He still took the time to make me feel better when his problems made mine pale in comparison.

I admired him. And he probably thought I was a spoiled rich girl who had no idea how good she had it.

The next day at school, he sat with us at lunch again. He just waltzed up, and my friends made room for him as if he'd been a permanent fixture of the group for years. It irritated me, and I buried my face in the book I was reading. But it also made me feel . . . some kind of way to have him close by. I worried he'd tell people about the personal shit I'd shared with him at the gym, but I also wanted to go sit closer to him at the same time—I craved more of that calming, grounding energy he seemed to have.

It confused me and I didn't like it. He never even mentioned seeing me at the gym though. He kept my confidence. The few times I glanced up from my phone, he caught my eye, and for a split second, everything around me slowed to a crawl. It was as if he held me in his calm, steady gaze, telling me with nothing more than a glance that he remembered, that he cared, that he had me.

It was weird feeling like I could actually trust this relative stranger with my feelings. It was weird I even wanted to. I wanted to tell him about how my mom pretended nothing had happened when I got home. I wanted to tell him how Cal still being there made me want to punch a wall. I even wanted to tell him about my dad. Listening to Drew and Nicola and the others gossip about people at school, and even their parents, I wanted to pull him aside and tell him which parts were true and which were just sensational gossip. I wanted to ask him things too—to know him. More intrusive questions hovered on the tip of my tongue, but I held them in.

Because they were also talking about the gossip surrounding Jet and his apparently very active dating life. He'd taken half a dozen girls out on dates since he started at Fulton. They all had nothing but nice things to say about him, but not a single one had scored a second date.

He was a player—even though that didn't exactly fit with the parts of him I'd gotten to know so far—and I was not interested in that mess. I refused to follow in my mother's footsteps and choose shitty men. Not that I thought Jet was a shitty man, but he wasn't denying going on all those dates either. Nothing made fucking sense.

I left lunch early, over not being able to focus on my book because I couldn't stop obsessing over a guy. How cliché!

But there was no avoiding him now—not when he felt like a puzzle to solve.

That weekend, the sisters and I went to the diner where Mena worked, to get burgers and keep her company during her break. Jet was there in a booth at the back, bent over some notebooks and his phone. He waved to us but didn't come over. I kept my butt planted on the cheap vinyl seat, fighting the urge to go over there and snoop.

When I went to the mall to pick up shampoo, I spotted him in the food court with some guys from the lacrosse team.

He was even in my yoga class on Sunday morning! And he was surprisingly flexible for someone who could do that many pull-ups with ease. I lost my balance several times, while out of the corner of my eye, I could see him holding a perfect tree pose without so much as a wobble.

I rushed out at the end of the class, avoiding him as I had been since that night at the gym. This had to stop. If I couldn't figure out why he had me off-kilter every time I saw him, I'd just have to fuck him out of my system and be done with it.

The upcoming spring break trip couldn't come soon enough. I needed a break from him so I could *think*.

CHAPTER FOUR

I saw the car pull up from my bedroom window and grinned. My friends jumped out before the driver could come around to open the door for them.

It was not normal to be this excited before eight in the morning, but here we were. I'd been packed and ready for half an hour already, waiting for my ride to the airport. My bags lay at the bottom of the stairs, my shoes were on, and I'd been sitting in the window scrolling social media to kill time. I put my cigarette out half-smoked and closed the window, did one last scan of my room to make sure I hadn't forgotten anything, then rushed down the stairs and opened the door.

"Heeey!" Donna, Harlow, and Mena all singsonged at once, throwing their arms out. They were in shorts and T-shirts and had their sunglasses on. It was going to be a glorious Cali day, not a cloud in the sky. The view from the plane would be spectacular.

I whooped and put on my own shades. "Let's get this show on the road!"

I waved the driver through, and he carried my bags to the

car while I hugged my besties. Mena was literally bouncing with excitement.

"Amaya? What's all this racket so early in the morning?"

My mother's voice knocked the smile clean off my face, and I glanced at the sky. It was just as bright and cloudless as it had been a moment ago. Apparently the gloom was all in my head.

"Good morning, Mrs. Ellis," Harlow and Donna said in perfectly polite synchronicity.

". . . Mrs. Ellis." Mena was only a beat behind.

"Oh, hello, girls! How lovely to see you!"

I turned to watch Vivian walk down the stairs and nearly fell onto my ass from shock. She was actually dressed, her hair brushed and makeup done. She didn't even look hungover.

The gloom darkened when Cal appeared behind her, coming down the stairs as he adjusted his tie.

"What fun things are you up to today?" Mom asked my friends. "Shopping trip to the city? Maybe I'll join you!"

Oh god, no!

"We're going on a trip, Mom," I rushed out. "It's spring break."

"I wasn't aware of any trip," she said while giving my friends air kisses. "Isn't the school supposed to notify the parents of these things?"

"The school does. You're just never around to see it," I gritted out. "This isn't a school trip. It's spring break. A bunch of us just organized to go together."

"Where?" Mom smoothed a hand down my hair, and I flinched out of her reach with a huff.

"We're flying to the Bahamas," Donna interjected, picking up on my rising irritation.

"On a private jet!" Mena added, eyes so wide I worried they might fall right out of her head. Her excitement was infectious, and I couldn't help the small smile that quirked my lips. It died just as fast when my mother turned a stern look at me.

"Amaya Ann, you can't just leave the country whenever you feel like it without even telling me," she chided as if she cared.

"Why? You do. All the fucking time." I folded my arms.

Cal placed his hands on my mother's shoulders, and whatever bullshit she was about to spit at me died on her lips.

"Take three deep breaths, love," he whispered in her ear. "Just like we talked about."

I resisted the urge to gag as she did exactly as he'd ordered, but I saw my opening. "OK, bye!" I called, shuffling the girls out and following after them.

"Amaya!" Mom snapped and grabbed my wrist. I spun around and wrenched it out of her grip.

"You don't get to ghost me for my entire childhood, then decide to have an opinion on what I do with my life!" I shouted, surprising everyone with my outburst.

Mom's wide eyes narrowed as the shock quickly gave way to anger. Cal squeezed her shoulders, and she pressed her lips together so hard they went white.

"Amaya is a smart, responsible young woman," Cal said, and I gave him a WTF look. "I'm sure she's going to be perfectly safe with her smart, responsible friends."

I mean, one of them did have a secret double life for a while, another frequently did illegal shit online, and the third once joined her boyfriend in a confrontation with the man who killed his mother, but . . . yeah, I was totally safe with them. I trusted my Devilbend Dynasty girls with my life.

"Perhaps if you could give your mother the details of where you're staying and check in when you get there, it would give her peace of mind. We can discuss anything else after." The last part was directed more at Mom, and I didn't know what this "we" was. I had no intention of discussing anything with her—I sure as shit wasn't going to discuss it with *him*. But I was over this whole conversation and wanted to get the fuck out of there already.

"Sure. Whatever. I'll text you the details from the car. We have to go now," I said.

Donna stepped forward and held out a card. "This is the resort we're staying at, and my number is on the back too—just in case."

Her type-A shit was irritating sometimes, but I loved her for it anyway. Because of moments like these. Getting what she wanted (or had been convinced she wanted) totally defused my mom's anger.

"Thank you, Donna." She gave my bestie a warm smile. "You girls be safe and have fun."

I was walking away before she even finished the sentence, and I reached the car before the others.

"I love you, Amaya!" she called after me.

I ignored her, climbing into the car and bouncing my knee. The girls piled in behind me, and I didn't relax until we were through my front gates and on the road toward the airport.

Mena took my hand and gave it a gentle squeeze. "Are you OK?"

My friends were all wearing concerned expressions.

"Yeah, I'm fine." I squeezed Mena's hand back and then released it. "Just another day with Vivian Ellis as my mother. Let's talk about something else."

I really didn't want parental bullshit ruining our trip before it had even begun.

There was a tense moment of silence, and I could tell they wanted to push the issue, talk it out and sync periods or some shit. But I was not in the mood.

"So"—Harlow kicked off her sneakers and crossed her legs up on the seat—"Mena, how's your butthole doing?"

We all burst out laughing, and the tension of the past fifteen minutes started to leave my body. Trust Harlow to take the conversation in a completely unexpected direction.

"Seriously? What the fuck kind of question is that?" Donna smacked her sister on the arm, even as she laughed along.

"What?" Harlow swatted her back between giggles. "She's the one who wanted advice on anal. I'm just checking in."

"Oh god!" Mena dropped her red face into her hands. "Do you seriously want an update, because we did actually buy some toys, and, uh . . ." She peeked at us from between her fingers.

"Yes!" all three of us yelled at once.

Harlow's phone vibrated in her hand, and a rare serious expression washed over her face, cutting off Mena's butt-sex story before it even started.

"Hello?" She answered it immediately, then listened to whatever the person on the other end said.

"What? How?" She gave us a wide-eyed look, and my stomach bottomed out.

The call barely lasted five minutes, but it had those of us not clued in to the other side of it on the edge of our seats. All we caught from Harlow's end was the occasional, agitated "OK" and "what?" and "why?"

"Yes, yes, I promise to behave, Detective Hopkins." Harlow rolled her eyes, said goodbye, and hung up. "Well, shit." She sighed, then looked up at us. "Irene is dead."

"What?" Donna gasped.

"Oh my god." Mena flopped back against her seat.

I just gritted my teeth, waiting for the rest of the bad news.

"Apparently, she killed herself in her cell last night."

"Apparently?" I prompted.

"Yeah, that's what Hopkins said, but come on." She scoffed. "She has enough eye-witness evidence and digital proof to take down several high-profile members of BestLyf, if not the entire organization, and just as the authorities start building their case and questioning her, she offs herself? Please."

The implication sat heavy between us. No one needed to voice it. We all knew what this meant. BestLyf had managed to murder Irene in prison and make it look like a suicide to protect themselves.

"What did Hopkins want?" Donna always asked the practical questions. "I know he has to notify you because you're a victim of the crimes she's charged with, but what else did he have to say?"

"He was basically telling me to heel." Harlow shrugged.

"What do you mean?" Mena asked, her eyes still wide.

"He did this whole spiel about how there was so much happening behind the scenes that I was unaware of, that I needed to keep my hacker nose out of official police business, blah blah blah."

"Maybe you should," I said.

"What?" Harlow looked at me as if I'd just kicked her kitten.

"All I'm saying is, there's a reason they kept Irene's arrest and her involvement with BestLyf hush-hush. Whatever they're doing—"

"Whatever they're doing isn't fucking working." She cut me off.

"And what? You think you're gonna get your hacker crew together and solve this for them? Come on, Harlow. Look how that ended last time—Easton got fucking shot."

"I know Easton got fucking shot!" she yelled. "I was there,

Amaya! And it's not like I decided to start digging around for shits and giggles. I was being blackmailed!"

"I know that!" I forced myself to take a deep breath and speak in a calmer tone. "I know that. I'm not saying any of it was your fault, but you were in some deep shit. I just . . . I can't lose you. Any of you."

Mena's eyes were watery, and Donna pursed her lips. She'd stayed uncharacteristically quiet during our argument.

"No one's losing anyone," she declared as if calling an end to a board meeting. "And we're not going to let this evil corporation keep ruining people's lives. We've all been affected by it."

Harlow threw me a smug smile, but it turned into an eye roll as Donna kept speaking.

"But Amaya has a point. We need to be careful. Safe. We just got this information about Irene, and realistically, we can't do much about it until we have more details—if we can do anything at all. So for this trip, let's just . . . fuck, let's just *chill*. I need a break from all this life-or-death bullshit. Senior year is stressful enough."

"Agreed." I nodded and gave Harlow a nudge with my shoulder. "Love you."

"Love you too," she mumbled.

"I need a drink," Mena declared, releasing a breath. "With a little umbrella in it. Do you think they'll let us drink at the resort?"

The conversation turned to lighter topics, and I wondered if the driver would notice if I cracked a window and lit a cigarette. But we were turning into the gates of the airport and driving over the tarmac before I could dig the packet out of my bag.

The car drove right up to the side of the small jet, and the driver came around to open the door for us.

"Fashionably late, as always!" Nicola called from the

bottom of the stairs leading up to the plane, but she was grinning.

"You know us, darling! We like to make an entrance," Donna joked. I jammed my sunglasses on to hide my eye roll. Sure, that was why we were late. Not because my psycho mother delayed us with her tantrum.

Our friends—about twenty of us—were all mingling around the bottom of the stairs, greeting each other and chatting while our luggage was loaded. I took my cigarettes out but was thwarted yet again by a stern man in a neon orange vest. There was strictly no smoking on the tarmac. Fair enough, I supposed—all that jet-fuel . . .

We boarded the plane, and almost every seat on the small jet ended up occupied. I settled into my seat and closed my eyes, resting my head back and listening to the sounds of seat belts clicking and my friends chatting excitedly.

This vacation was exactly what I needed. A break from studying stress. A break from Mom's bullshit. A break from the insanity of having a cult in our hometown. A break from everything.

The engines started up, but when I opened my eyes, the door was still open. Nicola stood next to it, speaking with a woman in a smart uniform and a nametag.

What now? I frowned. If this trip got canceled, I was marching my ass to the commercial terminal and buying a ticket on the next flight out of here. I didn't even care where to—I was leaving.

Footsteps sounded on the metal stairs, and the reason for the delay entered the plane to a chorus of cheers and applause.

Jet held his arms up over his head, hands in fists in a kind of victory pose, grinning at all my friends. Then he hugged Nic, and they both went to find seats as the flight attendant closed the door.

Dammit! Too late to get off the plane.

I turned my face to the window as he passed my seat, but not before I caught the little wink he sent my way.

This was supposed to be a trip to escape all the stress of my life for a while—literal escapism. Yet here was this guy who seemed able to see right through me, coming along to make sure I couldn't enjoy it.

Fucking perfect.

CHAPTER FIVE

He was stealing my damn friends! I glared at Jet over the top of my phone—where the screen was stuck on the same page I'd been rereading for the past half hour.

Jet was a few rows down, sitting with Hendrix and Drew. Donna sat perched on Hendrix's lap, and Mena had wandered over to them too. I couldn't blame her. I'd whipped my phone out to read before we even took off, and Harlow was engrossed in something on her computer screen, her bright pink headphones firmly in place. I really hoped she wasn't doing exactly what we'd agreed not to do in the car, but no one could really tell Harlow what to do.

". . . flew through the air, and landed right in my lap!" Jet's voice rose over the hum of the engines as he finished telling some story. Apparently, it was hilarious, because my friends all lost it.

I wanted to stuff something into his mouth so he'd shut up. But I also really wanted to hear the funny story. I thought about just getting up and joining them, but then I realized I was staring at Jet's crotch. He'd gestured to his lap as he delivered the punch line, and my eyes had gone straight to the area.

I shot my gaze back up and caught him glancing at me as he listened to something Mena said. The moment our eyes met, he gave me a knowing smirk and adjusted his position in his seat, making sure to thrust his pelvis up as he did so.

That smug, infuriating jerk!

"Ugh!" I slammed my phone down on the seat next to me and got to my feet. Harlow looked up and frowned at me, but I waved her off and made my way to the bathroom.

I didn't really need to go, but I needed some space and privacy to get my shit together. I knew he wasn't really stealing my friends—my girls and I were solid. Chicks before dicks and all that. Jet's presence still felt like an intrusion though.

The whole point of the trip was to get away from our responsibilities and worries, and I couldn't do that with him around. He made me want to ask him questions, to get to know him more (*ugh!*), and to tell him things about myself. Like in the gym that night. It had been so easy to talk to him about real shit, shit I hardly talked to anyone about. It was disconcerting to feel so out of control with another person— to feel so seen by someone I hardly knew.

How was I supposed to relax on the beach and forget all my worries when I had to be vigilant around that asshole?

I leaned on the little sink and stared myself down in the mirror.

"You are not letting one arrogant, admittedly hot guy with a frustratingly good ass ruin your spring break," I told myself with a firm look. "You're better than that, Amaya."

I refused to be this affected by a guy. I'd just avoid him as much as possible. It was a big resort and there were a lot of us. How hard could it be to keep my distance?

But we weren't on a tropical island resort yet. We were in

a very expensive tin can speeding through the air, and when I stepped out of the bathroom, Jet was right there in front of me.

"You've been in there for a while. You all right?" he asked in a low voice. He kept his posture casual, but he was so close in the tight space next to the bathroom door I could smell him. A fresh smell, unfussy and masculine—just soap and aftershave that hinted at bergamot but crisp. I could feel the heat of his chest, inches from mine.

The urge to scowl and tell him to fuck off was strong, but I gave him a tight smile instead.

"Fine." I hoped the one-word response came off as dismissive as I'd intended. I moved to squeeze past. And because the universe hated me, we hit some turbulence at that exact moment.

The plane lurched to one side, making me stumble back against the wall. Jet stumbled too but managed to avoid crushing me by throwing a hand out against the wall next to my head. His other hand went to my arm, gripping firmly.

"Shit. You all right?" he asked, eyes slightly wide.

"Would you stop asking me that?" I shook his hand off. The plane lurched again, this time in the other direction. Jet's back hit the opposite wall, and I tumbled right against his chest. His hands went to my waist, and I was thankful for the contact this time. With his feet set wide, he stayed steady through the turbulence and kept me on my feet too.

As the shaking eased up, he licked his lips and looked down at me. I bit down on my tongue to keep it in my mouth, stop it from mirroring his.

"Are you—"

"Nope!" I clapped a hand over his mouth. "Do not ask me if I'm all right again."

The seat belt sign came on with a ding, and the captain

made a quick announcement that we were moving through an uneven patch but it was nothing serious.

Jet smiled under my hand, and his dark eyes sparkled with mischief. For a second I thought it was better that I couldn't see his lips. But it was so much worse. I could *feel* them. They were soft and warm under my palm, and I could feel them move as he smiled. I could feel them as they parted slightly and the tip of his tongue darted out to lick my palm.

The simple yet unexpected sensation shot up my arm and made the back of my head feel tingly.

I removed my hand and pushed myself upright. His hands stayed on my waist.

"Gross," I whispered and mentally slapped myself. Why was I whispering as if we were sharing a moment? This was like a meet-cute from one of my romance novels.

"We'd better get buckled in," Jet said, but his hands stayed on my waist, and neither of us moved.

The plane jostled under our feet again, literally shaking us out of our cliché staring moment. We stumbled to the nearest empty seats, which just so happened to be next to each other.

What the hell was wrong with me? If this was how I was acting before the plane even landed, how was I going to avoid him for the whole trip? At least the bathroom was at the back of the plane and no one had seen my moment of temporary insanity.

Harlow lifted herself as high as the seat belt would allow and looked over the back of the seat. When she spotted me, she mouthed *OK?* I gave her a reassuring nod and smiled back. She turned to face the front again just as the plane dipped, making everyone shout in surprise or laugh nervously.

I tightened my seat belt a little and wished I hadn't left my phone in the other seat. I'd been through worse turbulence—what bothered me more was that I didn't have anything to distract me from the guy sitting beside me. I did my best to ignore him, but it was next to impossible. He was inches away, his elbow brushing mine with every tremor, his hand gripping the armrest between us.

He had nice hands—strong and thick and . . . his knuckles were white, and his nails dug into the leather of the armrest.

Was carefree, cocky, cool-as-a-cuke Jet scared of a little turbulence?

A wicked smile pulled at my lips. I was going to have fun teasing him. But when I looked up at his face, my stupid conscience kicked in. His eyes were closed, his head back against the seat, his whole body so tense it looked as if he were in an electric chair rather than a soft seat in a private jet.

Instead of having my teasing fun, I placed my hand gently over his. His eyes flew open, and he gave me a deer-in-head-lights look.

"You're going to punch a hole in the leather if you don't ease up." I squeezed his hand a little. It flexed under mine, then relaxed, but still held on to the armrest.

"Thanks. I definitely can't afford to pay Nicola to have it repaired." His attempt at a smile looked more like a grimace.

"She wouldn't care." I waved it off. "Are you seriously this scared of flying?"

"Not flying, no. It's the turbulence. I haven't taken many flights, and this is the first time I've experienced turbulence. It's . . . unnerving. Like, it just really makes you aware of the fact that you're hurtling through the sky in a metal tube."

"You seemed fine before, when it first started." I clasped his hand a little tighter, wordlessly reminding him to ease up on the leather once more. Every time we lurched, his grip would tighten up again.

"Yeah, well, I was distracted," he said as he finally let go of the armrest completely—only to turn his hand and grip mine instead.

Now I was the one distracted.

"Do you want to hear a secret?" I blurted out.

"I love secrets." He turned his head in my direction, and I angled to face him more.

"Nicola's mom is having an affair with her driver." I kept my voice low, even though no one could've heard me over the sound of the engines.

Jet blinked, and one corner of his mouth quirked up. "That . . . was not what I was expecting."

We both chuckled, then he asked, "Are you going to tell her?"

"Oh, she already knows. She doesn't like her mom's third husband, so she doesn't give a shit, but it would cause a massive scandal if it got out."

"Right, because she's a movie star and all that."

"Yep. And the husband is a producer. Very high-profile divorce if it comes to that."

"Yeah, I can see that." He nodded sagely, then bugged his eyes out. "Scandalous."

"I know, right?" I rolled my eyes.

"I thought you were about to tell me one of *your* secrets." He stared at me with those eyes that made me feel naked— and not in a good way.

I leaned back slightly. "I don't give up my secrets so easily, but I can tell you one about Luke."

The turbulence only lasted another ten minutes, but Jet relaxed way before that as I chatted about Devilbend gossip. His eyes lost that panicked quality, and his hand no longer gripped mine as if it were the only thing keeping him from plummeting to his death. In fact, his thumb started to rub circles on the back of my hand while we talked. And I let him. It felt good.

The conversation naturally shifted to other topics, and I stayed sitting next to Jet long after the seat belt sign turned off. Once again, he'd lulled me into a sense of security. Maybe he was using some kind of magic to make me keep talking.

I just couldn't figure him out, and that bugged me.

At a lull in the conversation, I studied his profile. The deep set of his eyes made them look even darker, and his jawline was sharper from the side, dulling that baby face he had front-on.

"I don't get you," I said before I'd even decided to say anything.

"What is there to get?" He shrugged and flashed me a smile.

"That's just it, I don't know. You know all our secrets . . ."

"Because you just spilled them all!"

". . . but we hardly know anything about you."

"What do you want to know?" He looked like an open book, with his expression calm if a bit amused, his body relaxed and angled toward me.

I had a feeling he really would honestly answer any question I asked in that moment.

"What's with all the dates?" *That* was the question my stupid brain decided to throw out first? I mentally dragged a hand down my face.

Jet looked as if he was fighting a smile. "You want me to explain the concept of dating? Surely you've been on a date before?"

"Shut up, smartass!" I whacked him in the shoulder—his very solid, sculpted shoulder. "You know what I mean. Why are you taking all these girls out but then never on a second date? They all gush about how wonderful you are." I pretended to faint. "How you're a perfect gentleman, and so attentive, yet none of them seem to be mad about not getting a second date. You're obviously not just trying to get laid—the whole school would know you were a man-whore by now if you were. So what's your deal? What's the agenda?"

"Agenda?"

"Everyone has an agenda."

He frowned slightly, not liking or maybe not agreeing with what I'd said. "Maybe I'm just looking for a girlfriend. That's what dates are for."

I narrowed my eyes at him. "Maybe. But I don't think so."

He stared me down for a while, and I held his gaze. I'd never backed down from anyone, and I wasn't going to now.

"Smart and beautiful," he murmured. "You're dangerous, Amaya Ann."

I was taken aback, not expecting the sudden compliment. And what exactly had he meant by "dangerous"?

"Hey, you two!" Nicola appeared, leaning her elbows on the backs of the seats in front of us. "That turbulence was crazy!"

"Yeah, I nearly fell on my ass!" I laughed.

"I caught her though," Jet added. "Saved that ass."

"Of course you did!" She winked at him.

"Don't wink at him when he's saying things about my ass!" I pointed a finger at her, but she just laughed.

The last few hours of the flight were pretty chill. Everyone moved about the plane, changing seats and chatting, but most people congregated around the middle, which was set up like a living room with two long rows of couchlike seats facing each other. I tried to go back to my spot next to Harlow and read, but I couldn't concentrate, so I drifted over to the main group.

Nicola and a few of the others started talking about Best-Lyf, and not in the way the girls and I talked about it. They were all part of this youth program and raved about how much they were getting out of it, the people they got to work with, and some bullshit about elevating the different realms of their beings into perfect alignment so they could float above everyone else in their smug superiority. OK, maybe I added that last bit myself, but they sounded pretentious as fuck while having no idea how brainwashed they were becoming.

The last thing I wanted was to think about that mess, so I joined another conversation. I didn't really care about the specifics of what they were saying, but Jet definitely seemed to. He looked genuinely interested as he asked them questions about the program and the people involved and the kinds of things they did there.

I hoped he wasn't looking to join. He'd be sorely disappointed when he was knocked back—not because he wasn't intelligent or talented enough but because he wasn't rich or influential enough. Oh, yeah! Plus, the fact that it was a fucking cult.

I wanted to drag him away from them and tell him to stay clear of it, protect him from all the crap BestLyf had put us through. Looking out the window at the crystal blue water below, I added that to my growing list of bullshit to deal with after the trip.

CHAPTER SIX

THE SUN FELT WONDERFUL ON MY SKIN, AND THE GENTLE sound of waves crashing on the beach was almost enough to lull me to sleep. I didn't even know what time it was—long enough after breakfast to feel settled on the beach, but not close enough to lunch to really feel hungry. I didn't care. We were about halfway through the trip, and time had ceased to have any meaning.

We spent the nights partying or just chilling by the pool, and we spent the days island hopping, snorkeling, and just chilling on the beach. There was a lot of chilling. Exactly what we all needed.

"Do you think they're having sex out there?" Mena cocked her head and lowered her sunglasses a fraction. She was on the lounger to my left.

"Gross!" Harlow gagged on the lounger to my right. There was an empty one next to her. Donna and Hendrix had gone for a swim in the crystal-clear water some time ago. We could see them way out in the distance. They'd been . . . *hugging* in the same spot for a while.

"Yeah, they're definitely having sex out there." I chuckled.

Harlow gagged again. "Can you stop! I want to go for a dip soon and now I can't."

"Sure you can. They're miles away," Mena argued.

"No, I can't! They're in the same body of water. I don't want to be swimming in their juices!"

"Whose juices are we swimming in?" Drew leaned on the back of my lounger and grinned before exaggeratedly licking his lips. "I fucking love juice."

I tipped my head back and gave him a sweet smile. "Hendrix's."

The girls burst out laughing as Drew's face fell. Then he raised his eyebrows and tilted his head as though actually considering it.

The three of them started cracking dirty jokes and teasing each other until Drew picked Mena up off her lounger and ran for the water, Harlow chasing after them.

I reached for the packet of smokes on the little table next to me and lit one, watching my friends frolic in the water. The long drag I took made me feel lightheaded for a moment. I'd been smoking way less since we arrived, and this was my first one for the day. I guessed the stress-free environment was good from my health or some shit.

A wave of melancholy washed over me, tinged with loneliness. It was an odd feeling to have in paradise, surrounded by my closest friends. Irrational. I knew I could get to my feet, walk down to the water, and be welcomed with open arms. I knew my girls had my back no matter what, but . . . sometimes I felt as though I didn't matter. As if I could get up from this lounger and walk off into the sunset and no one would notice.

OK, that was dramatic. Of course my friends would notice if I just disappeared, but they'd get over it eventually. No one in my life would be so devastated that they'd struggle to go on without me.

I hadn't bothered checking in with Mom when we landed. She'd probably forgotten where I was as soon as the car had turned out of our driveway. I hadn't heard anything from her, no missed calls or messages demanding to know I was OK.

My friends were the closest thing I had to family. But Donna and Harlow were sisters and Mena was their cousin. They actually were family. I'd always be the extra. I knew they didn't see me like that, not really, but I couldn't help wishing I was tied to them by blood too. I wanted that irrefutable connection they had to each other.

I took another drag of my cigarette. I didn't want to be thinking about this shit. Didn't want to be feeling . . . *things*.

I grabbed my phone, put the cigarette out after one last puff, and snapped a photo of the paradise before me, making sure to position my legs just so and get them into the shot. Ignoring the countless notifications, I posted it. My followers loved the vacay posts, probably because of all the bikini shots. Two separate swimwear companies had already reached out to me, offering to pay me to wear their stuff. I couldn't be bothered dealing with any of it until we got home. Instead, I opened my reading app and lost myself in an epic romantic fantasy.

It did the trick getting my mind off everything, and an hour flew past before I realized. My friends had been in and out of the water, chatting and messing around while I was absorbed in my book. Now most of the girls were lined up on the sand tanning, and some of the guys were in the shallow water throwing a ball around.

I got to my feet, pulled my bikini wedgie out of my ass, and wandered down to the water. I was sweaty and over-heated from sitting in the sun for so long, but the ocean in the Bahamas always felt perfect. The softest sand ever squished between my toes as I stepped into the refreshing waves.

I'd waded up to my thighs when one of the guys threw the ball too wide and it landed with a splat right next to me. In the next moment, Luke and Jet both leaped for it, jostling and flailing all over the place, splashing the shit out of me.

I squealed, the shock of the water enough to startle me despite its mild temperature.

Luke and Jet turned wide eyes to me, the ball bobbing between them. Then they both burst out laughing.

"Fucking hell, Amaya! I thought you were dying!" Luke said through chuckles.

I huffed and leaned back into the water. "You startled me!"

Jet smacked Luke in the junk. "What he means is, we didn't mean to get in your way. Sorry."

I'd managed to avoid Jet on the trip so far . . . sort of. We spent most of our time as a group, so it wasn't too difficult to keep at least three people between us at all times. We hadn't had any "alone time," and I'd hardly had to speak to him directly at all.

His presence was still distracting though. I was constantly aware of him—talking to all my friends, roughhousing with the guys, having long conversations with the girls, going for runs on the beach while most of us were still in bed. And he was goddamn shirtless most of the time! All that toned muscle and tanned skin constantly in my face. He seemed to always be around whenever I got to a spicy part in my book. Which frustrated me in a whole other way.

I wasn't so stubborn that I couldn't admit the dude was insanely hot. But I was my mother's daughter and determined not to make her mistakes. I refused to chase men. Especially ones that dated so much and always managed to avoid sharing anything about themselves in any detail.

But I couldn't avoid noticing him—especially in this setting.

Most of the time his eyes looked so dark I'd thought they were black. But in the bright sunshine and the turquoise water all around him, I could see streaks of warm, rich brown. It was kind of mesmerizing.

I tipped my head back to wet my hair (and avoid licking him with my hungry eyes).

"Whatever." I waved them off as I got to my feet. "I'm all wet now anyway."

Jet cleared his throat and looked to the side, his lips pressed tightly together. Luke's shoulders shook and his face went red with the effort to hold back his own laughter.

I rolled my eyes. "Grow up."

They both lost it, the laughs busting out.

"Are we playing ball?" Drew called from behind them. "Or are you two just going to stand around and listen to Amaya talk about how wet she is?"

Trust Drew to take a double entendre and ride it even harder—pun totally intended. I flipped him off as Luke scooped the ball up and turned back toward the guys.

"Second option!" Jet called and threw me a heated look. "Every damn time."

Before I could process or respond, his eyes widened as if he hadn't meant to say that out loud—or at all. He turned and splashed past Luke in an awkward water run. Was he flirting? Or running away from me?

I raced after them and jumped onto Luke's back. With the element of surprise on my side, I wrestled the ball out of his grip but also managed to send us both splashing into the water.

I joined the guys for a while, trying to keep up with them. They tossed me around almost as much as the ball and lifted me into the air to make catches when someone threw it extra high. It was good exercise—and a good distraction from Jet and his perplexing behavior.

My mood had significantly lifted by evening. The melancholy I'd been feeling earlier completely vanished, chased away by the sun, sand, and splashing around with my friends. I wasn't even bothered by hanging around Jet all day.

A smug little voice in the back of my head suggested it was probably *because* I'd been hanging around Jet that my mood had lifted. That it was because he'd shared his fries with me at lunch, because he'd made me laugh when he cracked a joke about Nicola and Donnie looking as if they were on the verge of another breakup. That it was because he'd picked me up and thrown me around in the water more than any of the others—and I liked it. I'd stayed in the sun without reapplying sunscreen way longer than I would've at any other time. I liked his hands on me. A little too much.

"You ready?" Harlow asked, dropping her headphones on the bed before slipping her flip-flops on. She couldn't exactly have brought her ex-teacher boyfriend on our spring break trip. Turner didn't really know the rest of our group, so he hadn't joined Mena. And I was single, so the three of us were sharing a room. We were having a barbecue and a bonfire on the beach tonight. Mena had already headed down there.

"You go ahead," I called over my shoulder. "I'll catch up."

I put my focus back on getting my winged liner to match on both sides.

Harlow's grinning face appeared above mine in the mirror. "Why are you putting makeup on?"

I'd hardly worn any since we arrived. It was too hot and humid and messy with all the sand and constant layers of sunscreen.

"I just feel like it." I shrugged but narrowed my eyes at her.

She hummed, tapping her chin and squinting at me suspiciously.

"What?"

"I don't suppose you might be making an extra effort for a certain someone who you spent half the day splashing around with? Maybe someone named after an extremely fast aircraft?"

I burst out laughing at her dig at Jet's name but still waved her off. "As if. I'm not going to change any part of myself for any guy. I wear makeup because I want to."

"Naturally." Harlow dropped her hands on my shoulders. "I'm just saying—it would be OK if you wanted him to notice you. You deserve to be happy, Amaya. With or without a man."

I blinked at my friend in the mirror, the eyeliner hovering in front of my face.

Had I really felt as though I didn't belong with my girls? I swallowed around the lump in my throat and forced the emotion down. I didn't want to ruin my makeup. I also was really shit at talking about emotional crap. I blamed my two absent parents.

But of course, Harlow knew that.

"I'll see you out there." She gave my shoulders a squeeze and kissed me on the top of my head. "Love you."

"Love you," I whispered into the mirror, but she was already out the door.

I pushed the tricky thoughts and feelings away and finished my makeup. Halfway to the door, I caught a glimpse of myself in the mirror and decided I looked hot. My long, straight black hair was half up, my simple white slip dress fit me perfectly, and the eyeliner was precisely even on both sides. I could count on one hand the number of times I'd managed that feat on the first try.

I meandered up the path from our room, taking my time and enjoying the moment of peace in the dusk. All the rooms were set among lush, tropical gardens, connected to the communal parts of the resort by artfully manicured walkways. Cicadas sang loudly as rich colors shifted in the sky above.

My phone vibrated in the little crochet bag crossed over my body. A treacherous part of me immediately thought it might be Mom remembering she had a daughter that needed to be checked on, and my stupid excited hand reached for it immediately.

Of course, it wasn't her. My heart sank a little at the realization, but I opened the DMs responsible for the notification anyway.

I replied to a few messages, reported and deleted a dick pic, and scanned through the comments of my latest post as I walked. Habit made me turn left at the end of the path, toward the resort restaurants. I was halfway to our usual dinner spot before I remembered we were all meeting at the beach for the barbecue. Tucking my phone away, I decided to cut through past another row of rooms rather than go all the way around.

A distinctly male voice mingled with the ever-present buzz of the cicadas just before I rounded the bend in the path. It definitely sounded like Jet, but I couldn't make out exactly what he was saying over the noise of the insects.

I slowed my steps and peeked around a palm tree. He stood in front of the door to one of the rooms, his phone held to his ear. He was facing away from me, so I moseyed a little closer. It wasn't my fault he wasn't paying attention. I just happened to be coming past here, and if he wanted to keep his conversation private, he should've taken the call inside.

Not that I could hear much anyway.

". . . that's enough yet," he said, sounding more serious than I'd ever heard him. He listened to whatever the other person was saying for a few seconds. "Yes, if I can find a way to access the . . ."

The stupid cicadas got louder, and I missed the end of what he said. What was enough? What was he trying to find access to?

I was barely a few feet away from him when he hung up and tucked the phone into his pocket. He leaned sideways, planting one foot in the garden bed. He looked as if he was inspecting the window. Had he locked himself out of his room?

I glanced at the number on the door—308—and frowned. I could've sworn he was bunking with Drew in 312.

Stopping next to him, I crossed my arms. "What the fuck are you doing?"

CHAPTER SEVEN

HE LOOKED OVER HIS SHOULDER, NOT AT ALL STARTLED BY my presence, and held his finger to his lips. I raised a brow as he hunched over and reached for the window.

Was this guy seriously trying to break into someone's room? And who the fuck did he think he was, shushing me?

Before I could tell him off, he straightened and stepped out of the garden bed, his hands cupped in front of himself as if he was holding water.

"Check it out!" He grinned, stepping closer.

I leaned forward and rolled my eyes. "Seriously? Jet, those things are everywhere."

A little gecko rested in his hands. He stared at it as if it were some mystical creature no one had ever laid eyes on.

"Yeah, I know." He shrugged. "This is my first time out of the country, if you don't count that unfortunate trip to Mexico. I've never seen one up close. I've been trying to catch one since we got here."

Well, shit. Now I felt like a privileged bitch, and a judgmental one at that. I shouldn't have assumed he was being shifty, trying to break into someone's room.

I shuffled closer, and our arms brushed as we gazed at the little lizard darting around on Jet's palms.

"Cute little guy," I said softly.

Jet lifted his gaze to mine, and I realized how close we were. The cicadas continued to trill, and the last rays of sunlight disappeared as we stood there, staring into each other's eyes. Subconsciously, I licked my lips, and Jet's gaze shot to my mouth. I started to lean in and—

The gecko leaped out of Jet's hands, the sudden movement startling us both. He stepped away as the little creature scuttled into the garden and disappeared under the foliage.

Jet cleared his throat. "Shall we? I'm starving."

He started walking before I could reply. I fell into step with him, willing my heart to stop hammering as we walked the rest of the way to the beach in silence.

Thankfully, the staff started serving food just as we arrived, and I grabbed a seat among my friends while everyone was distracted. The last thing I needed was for Harlow to tease me about showing up with Jet. Especially since my heart was still beating that little bit harder after our near-kiss.

"Holy shit, this is amazing!" Hendrix announced between heaping mouthfuls of barbecued lobster and conch. A chorus of agreement went up from everyone at the long table that had been set up in the sand for us. It was piled high with fresh seafood and sides of all kinds, while a bartender mixed tropical cocktails at a makeshift bar off to the side. The legal drinking age in the Bahamas was eighteen, but no one gave a shit that some of us hadn't had that birthday yet.

The jovial mood only continued to get more fun as the night wore on. Jet was seated at the other end of the table with Drew and some of the other boys, and I irritatingly couldn't stop glancing in that direction through dinner.

"Damn, you got it bad," Harlow said, keeping her voice

low. I shot her a warning look and glanced around to make sure no one had heard.

Donna leaned across the table. "I don't think I've ever seen you this into someone. Ever."

I took another glance up and down the table, but the only other person listening in was Mena. She had her chin propped on her hand as she stared at me with love-heart eyes and an excited grin.

"You bitches better drop this right now," I said in a low, even tone as I lifted my mojito to my lips. "I have a reputation to uphold."

That got some laughs out of them, but they dropped it, thankfully. I forced myself to keep my eyes away from the guy at the end of the table while I finished off my drink.

Everyone was half-drunk by the time they brought out dessert and cheese platters, and the roaring bonfire gave everything a warm glow. Someone turned the volume up on the music, and a few of the girls started dancing around the fire.

The night was still, the sky clear, the stars shining bright beyond the tall flames licking up at the sky. The sound of waves softly lapping at the sand was only just audible under the music. There was something electric in the air.

When the staff had cleared the tables and left us to our own devices, leaving only the bartender, Nicola announced she had enough molly to get us all fucked up three times over. I knew we'd flown in a private plane, but bringing that amount of drugs internationally was still ballsy as fuck.

At least half the group decided to partake. Hendrix and Donna, who'd been making out on the cushions by the fire for a good half hour, declined and left—probably to go have kinky sex in their room. To my surprise, Mena decided to try some.

"I've never done drugs." She shrugged, but I could see the

nervousness in her eyes. "Seems like as good a night to try as any."

"You don't have to if you don't want to." I lit a cigarette and leaned back in the sand. "I'm not having any. Because I don't feel like it. Don't let these assholes peer-pressure you."

She gave me a kiss on the cheek. "They're not. I'm curious."

"All right." Harlow sighed and got to her feet, holding her hands out for Mena. "Let's get you high. I'll take care of you."

Mena giggled, and they headed for Nicola hand in hand.

I stuck with mojitos and danced a bit with the others, keeping an eye on Mena. She was totally fine though, marveling at the sand and the water with the most wonderous smile I'd ever seen on anyone's face. And Harlow followed her around like the good friend she was.

I'd managed to stay distracted enough not to look for Jet the whole night, only catching glimpses of him here and there. And he was staying away from me. Was that on purpose? Did I intimidate him? Or maybe I was the one who was intimidated. Because the girls were right—no guy had ever had this effect on me before.

With the fire dying and everyone either gone back to their rooms or enjoying the tail end of their trip by staring at the stars, I decided to go for a stroll before bed.

Leaving my shoes and bag behind, I made my way down to the ocean. The warm water lapped at my feet as my toes dug into the wet sand. A bright waning gibbous moon reflected off the waves and, away from the fire's glow, cast everything around me in silvery, shadowy grays.

It was beautiful, and kind of soothing.

I'd nearly reached the end of the beach, some rocks creating a natural end point with what must've been staff quarters beyond, when I realized I wasn't alone. There was someone sitting in the sand, looking out over the water.

The strong shoulders and closely cropped hair told me it was probably a man, and I paused. If it was one of the staff, I didn't want to bother them during their time off. And regardless, alarm bells went off in the back of my mind just from being in a dark, secluded place with a male I didn't know.

Just as I was about to turn around and walk a little faster back to my room, the man on the beach tilted his face up to the sky. The moonlight illuminated Jet's features, and the tension in my body seeped out of me.

He didn't look in my direction, but surely he knew I was there. Even as I moved forward—my feet carrying me to him without me really making the decision—he still remained staring at the moon as if it had all the answers.

I wished I knew what the questions were.

It wasn't until I'd sat down next to him that I wondered if maybe he wanted to be alone. Why else wander out here in the middle of the night?

"Are you stalking me, princess?" he asked, his voice low, his gaze still refusing to meet mine.

"Not this shit again." I sighed dramatically. He quirked his lips in a barely there smile, the dimple making a brief appearance before it was gone.

We fell into silence for a while, nothing but the light of the moon and the sound of gentle waves between us.

"Did you have any of Nicola's treats?" I asked. Maybe that explained why he was so mesmerized by the sky.

He chuckled. "Nah. Not really my jam."

I nodded, secretly satisfied I'd chosen not to partake tonight. I didn't want him to judge me, or think less of me.

"You?" he asked, flicking me the first look since I'd joined him.

I shook my head no, and he nodded.

The several cocktails I'd had were quickly draining out of

my system, so I wasn't so drunk I'd make reckless choices—just buzzed enough to do something a bit out of character. I'd never made the first move with a guy, but the liquid courage made me feel as if maybe I should. Maybe this time. Maybe this guy.

"Jet?" I had no idea why I whispered, but he heard me just fine.

I tucked one leg under me and turned to face him. He leaned back on one hand, angling his body a bit more toward mine. He looked at me with an open expression, waiting patiently.

"Earlier." I licked my lips and forced myself to at least appear confident, even if I didn't feel it one bit on the inside. "Before the barbecue. We had a moment, right? I didn't imagine that."

His eyes softened slightly, but he held very still before answering. "Yeah, we had a moment."

"I think I'd like to have another moment, with you. One that doesn't get interrupted." My heart beat so fast I was sure the sound of it was drowning out the waves. Nervous but exhilarated, I slowly leaned forward.

Jet's lips parted on an exhale, and his gaze flicked down to my mouth. He leaned in too. Our lips were barely an inch apart, my eyes were drifting closed, my skin tingled with anticipation, and—

He pulled away.

With a sigh, Jet turned his head to the side and leaned back. His hand gripped my upper arm, as if he had to physically hold me back from trying to jump him.

"W-what . . . ," I stammered, genuinely confused. He was into me; we had a connection. I could see in his eyes that he wanted to kiss me just as badly.

"We . . . I . . . I can't . . ." He seemed to be struggling as much as I was to form a complete sentence. He removed his hand from my arm as if I'd burned him and flashed me a wide-eyed look.

"Fuck," he muttered as he scrambled to his feet. Dragging a hand down his face, he walked away from me.

I was confused, hurt, embarrassed—all the emotions. And that asshole had scampered away before the anger set in and gave me back my words.

I wanted to storm after him, give him a piece of my mind. But I stayed put. No point making my humiliation even worse by causing a scene in the middle of the night. At least this way, Jet and I would be the only ones who knew what a fool I'd made of myself.

Angry tears tracked down my face as I sat there in the sand and my own misery. There was a reason I hadn't had a proper relationship, never made the first move. There was a reason everyone thought I was a cold, heartless bitch. Because when you cracked your chest open and let someone take a peek at your heart, they'd just reach in and crush it the first chance they got.

They'd leave the vulnerable organ bleeding silver in the moonlight and run away as if you didn't matter.

The angry tears turned into sad, miserable, self-pity tears. Thank God this had happened in such a secluded part of the island.

I stayed in that spot until my tears dried up. I stayed there until the light of the moon gave way to the brilliant colors of the sunrise.

It all still looked gray to me though.

CHAPTER EIGHT

THE WEATHER MATCHED MY MOOD WHEN WE LANDED IN San Francisco: rainy and miserable. I wasn't the only subdued one as we filed off the private plane. The shitty weather and the post-vacay blues had set in for the whole group.

Maybe my bad attitude was rubbing off on them too, although I'd kept mostly to myself for the last few days of the trip. I'd let myself get drawn in by a piece-of-shit man and I'd gotten hurt. I had only myself to blame. Which was why I was reluctant to talk to anyone about it, or let my misery ruin everyone else's good time.

My girls had noticed my shift in mood right away, but when I made it clear I didn't want to discuss it, they'd dropped it. I knew it wasn't over, that they were worried and would likely bring it up again after giving me some space, but I wasn't ready to admit my humiliation just yet. It was still too raw.

The rest of our group didn't notice anything until probably the last day. I couldn't blame them—we were all there to have fun, and there were plenty of activities and distractions. But by the time we left, Nicola and Drew had both pulled me aside to ask if I was all right, and the others threw me looks the entire flight. They'd picked up on the tension, and it probably hadn't escaped anyone's notice that I refused to speak to Jet. I left every room/conversation/activity as soon as he appeared and didn't make any excuses.

They could all speculate as much as they wanted. I didn't give a fuck.

"Ugh! Can't believe I have to be at work tomorrow morning." Mena groaned. She'd gotten a great tan.

Sometimes I wished I could just give her some of my money, but I knew that would be patronizing. I really admired her. She'd been through a lot of shit.

"School on Monday," Hendrix added to the list of things we had to look forward to. I'd never seen him so miserable. Even when he thought he'd lost Donna.

"Not for me!" Harlow was the only one with pep in her step. She was about to start her new job with some tech company, and she probably couldn't wait to see her boyfriend —and screw his brains out.

The limo pulled up then, and the boys helped the driver with our luggage as we all piled in.

By the time we reached Devilbend, the sun had come out. Unfortunately, it did nothing to chase away the dark and stormy clouds in my own head.

The Mead sisters were the only ones left in the car when we reached my place. Everyone else had been dropped off on our way. As the driver started getting my luggage out, I found myself still sitting in the limo, staring at my front door. Despite how miserable and angry I'd been for the last few days of the trip, it still seemed preferable to going home. Would Mom even be there? Would she notice I was back? She seemed to have forgotten I'd ever left. Or existed at all.

Donna squeezed my knee, snapping me out of my staring contest with my house.

"Come over if you want," she said, her voice sympathetic. "I'm just going to watch movies and do a face mask."

"Thanks, D." I mustered up a smile for her. The girls knew all about what a nightmare of a mother I had. "I'll see what the situation is inside."

"Love you." Harlow pulled me into a tight hug, and Donna piled on too. I held them firmly for a long moment, then extracted myself with a sigh.

The driver carried my bags inside, I waved the girls off as he drove away, and then I was alone.

The house was empty. It had that stillness I'd become all too accustomed to. I wasn't sure if I was relieved or disappointed. Probably a bit of both.

Putting an audiobook on, I decided to distract myself with some self-care and spent the rest of the day taking a bath, putting a hair mask in my hair, exfoliating and soaking and moisturizing. I booked a nail appointment too, as my nails were looking a bit ratty after all that frolicking in the sand.

I headed downstairs in the evening, wondering if my empty stomach had the patience to wait for takeout to be delivered.

"Come on, fridge, do me a solid," I mumbled to myself as I opened the refrigerator. To my utter astonishment, it was stocked—and not just with the basics. This was next level. There were half a dozen bottles of coconut water lined up neatly on the top shelf, cold cuts, fresh vegetables in the crisper, at least four different types of cheese, and containers of what looked like leftovers.

I lifted the lids on a few of the tubs. "Don't suppose any of you contain mac and cheese?"

"Nope, but I'd be happy to make you some," a male voice answered.

I literally jumped. The contents of the fridge door rattled with how hard I slammed it shut.

"Jesus! Fuck!" I pressed a hand to my chest, willing my heart to stop trying to bust out of my rib cage as I glared at Cal. "You scared the crap out of me!"

"Sorry, sorry!" He held his hands out and winced, backing up a step. "I didn't mean to, I swear."

"What the fuck are you doing here? Where's my mom?"

"She's in a meeting that's running late." He frowned slightly as he moved into the kitchen, grabbed a pot and macaroni from the pantry, and dug around in the fridge.

I watched him, noting how comfortable he was in my kitchen, how he knew where everything was.

"You're persistent, I'll give you that," I said as I perched on a stool, putting the island between us.

"What do you mean?" He stayed focused on the cheese he was grating.

"No man has hung around this long. Either Mom gets bored with them, or they decide her bullshit isn't worth the money she comes with. No one has lasted longer than two weeks."

He leveled a disapproving look at me, but I was only stating the truth. Not my fault if he couldn't handle it.

"That's probably because none of them bothered to get to know her. Not really. Your mother is—"

"Save it." I cut him off. "Don't waste your time trying to convince me that you think she's the greatest thing since sliced bread. Vivian doesn't put much stock in my opinion on anything, let alone the men she's fucking. She hardly even remembers she has a daughter most of the time."

He was at the stove with his back to me, but I saw how his shoulders slumped with his sigh. He didn't speak as he served me up a steaming bowl of fresh, homemade mac and cheese.

"I understand why you're wary, Amaya." He slid a fork across the island to me. "I get why you might feel like you need to scare me off, or maybe you're testing me. I don't know."

"You don't know shit, Bob." I flashed him a saccharine smile, deliberately getting his name wrong, before scooping some cheesy pasta into my mouth. Dammit! It was actually really good—creamy and rich, with a slight biteyness from the aged cheddar he'd added.

He ignored my bratty retort. "But I love your mother. Trust me when I say that neither of us expected this, but we genuinely care for each other. I have my own money, so I'm not after hers. I have no ulterior motives. I just want to make her happy." He shrugged. "And I want to get to know you. You're important to her, so you're important to me."

"She's got a funny way of showing it," I grumbled. I didn't know how to take what he was saying. He seemed genuine, but I didn't have much experience with genuine, so maybe he was totally bullshitting me. Lacking the energy to try to puzzle it out, I made my way over to the pantry to distract myself. The mac and cheese tasted amazing, but it was missing something—some other element from when I used to have it as a kid.

I found turmeric and chili powder and sprinkled some into the bowl just as the click of heels on marble announced my mother's arrival. She breezed into the room with a bright smile, then froze when she spotted me.

I stirred the spices into my meal and took a tentative bite. Close, but something was still missing. Maybe it needed more turmeric. I reached for the small jar of the yellow stuff, but suddenly Mom was there, moving it out of my reach.

I frowned up at her, but she'd already turned her back to me as she poked around in the pantry. She emerged a second later, came to my side of the island, and added some cumin to my bowl.

"Turmeric, cumin, and chili," she said as she stirred it in and held a forkful up to my mouth. Confused as fuck, I took the bite.

Holy shit! That's it! I bugged my eyes out at my mom as I chewed and slumped in my seat. She gave me a warm smile and ran her hand through my hair. The look on her face, the affection—it felt real.

The attention from my mom and the flavor on my tongue made me feel like a little girl again.

"Sri Lankan mac and cheese," she murmured, her smile turning melancholy. "It was your favorite when you were little. It was your dad's favorite too. He used to make it all the time."

I'd gotten through half the bowl, but the last bite caught against a lump in my throat.

Memories came flooding back. My dad in the kitchen, turmeric stains on the counters, his eyes shining with so much love. She hadn't so much as mentioned him since . . . I couldn't even remember when. I could hardly believe she'd brought him up at all.

I took a shuddering breath, my vision turning blurry.

"I'm such a terrible cook." Mom chuckled, wiping some moisture from under her own eyes. "I always was. But now that Cal is moving in, he can make it for you whenever you want."

Too much.

It was too much.

The memories of my dad. The first real connection my mom and I had shared in years. Cal was moving in? What the fuck was happening?

I shot to my feet, the stool scraping on the floor, and shoved the bowl away. It slid all the way across the island, and

Cal caught it before it fell off. He was looking at me with something resembling sympathy. Or maybe it was pity.

It was all *too much*.

Swiping at my tears angrily, I rushed up the stairs.

"Amaya!" Mom called after me, the usual angry, disapproving tone missing from her voice. Another thing to be confused and overwhelmed with.

I locked myself in my room before she could catch up with me.

CHAPTER NINE

FOR THE NEXT TWO WEEKS I WENT INTO FULL DENIAL mode. I was practically Cleopatra—that's how well acquainted I became with that particular river in Egypt.

I went to the gym in the mornings, when Jet wasn't there, and even started taking my yoga classes in the mornings too. It had the added bonus of getting me out of the house early enough to avoid my mom and Cal.

Fucking Cal. He was around all the damn time. At least Jet was easy enough to avoid at school, seeing as how he worked just as hard to stay away from me. If I walked into the cafeteria to find him sitting with our friends, I went off campus to eat. If he walked in last, he'd sit with someone else. He was friends with half the school anyway.

Our friends had noticed the tension between us and how determinedly we were avoiding each other, but neither of us was saying shit about it, so the rumor mill had gone into a frenzy.

I knew I could talk to the girls about the Jet thing and about the shit at home, but then I'd have to acknowledge all the shit I was dealing with and . . . yeah, Cleopatra. So I avoided them a bit too, only hanging out in bigger groups. I buried myself in my books, my social media following, and my exercise. I even studied more than usual, which was probably a good thing considering our exams were fast approaching.

It was a Friday afternoon when it all came crashing down around me.

I'd been making sure to come home late enough that Mom and Cal were in the living room at the back of the house and unable to corner me before I could make it to my room. There'd been no more mac and cheese, but a plate of something homemade waited for me on the stove every day. Without fail. Even if they weren't home when I got in, the food would be there.

More often than not, I'd eat it, scowling at the delicious food the entire time, resenting the person who'd prepared it and the person who'd brought him into my life. Mom must've been telling Cal what my fave dishes were, because he was making them all. Spicy noodle soup, baked rice with chicken, sloppy joes (don't judge me! It was another childhood fave). I was honestly impressed she even remembered.

She'd tried to talk to me several times. Sometimes through the door of my room, sometimes trying to catch me as I passed through the house. She'd even called and texted me. She hadn't yelled or raged or done any of her usual bull-shit at all. I brushed her off every time. All I'd wanted since Dad died was my mother's attention, and she'd chosen to shower it on me when I wanted it least.

That Friday, I drove straight home from school—rather than spend the afternoon doing literally anything else, as usual. I pulled up outside our house, parking crookedly.

There was a moving van in the driveway and two dudes carrying boxes into my home.

"What the fuck is happening?" I demanded, bursting through the open front door.

Mom and Cal stood side by side at the kitchen island, chopping, matching glasses of wine in front of them. My mother was in the kitchen. *Chopping.*

"Amaya." She blinked, clearly surprised to see me, then gave me a small nervous smile. "You're home."

"What the fuck is happening?" I repeated, enunciating each word.

Mom frowned, probably at the cursing, and it was Cal who answered.

"I'm moving in. I sold all my furniture, so it's mostly just clothes and personal items, a few sentimental pieces. Nothing much will change. I know this is your home, and I want to—"

"You didn't think to ask me if I was OK with some random dude moving into my house?" I cut him off deliberately, practically shaking with rage.

"I told you two weeks ago Calvin would be moving in. I admit, I could've done that more tactfully, but—"

"It's like I don't even exist to you!" I screeched at her. "You clearly wish I wasn't around, cramping your style, so why didn't you just move in with him? It's not like you've been here half the time anyway. This is *my* home!"

A brief flash of hurt passed over Mom's face, but it quickly disappeared as she ground her teeth.

"I've been trying to talk to you for two damn weeks, Amaya Ann. What am I supposed to do? The world doesn't revolve around you, you know!" Her tone had gone screechy too. I knew she'd been waiting in there somewhere—my self-ish, quick-to-anger mother.

I scoffed and shook my head as I backed out of the kitchen. Upstairs, I grabbed my gym bag and a change of clothes, then stormed right back out the front door, past the pile of boxes in the foyer and the stunned moving guys.

The tires squealed as I tore out of there, speeding all the way to the gym.

I found a spot in the back lot and grabbed my bag. As I got out of my car, the back door of the gym opened and Jet came out. His head was down as he held his cell phone to his ear and walked a few paces.

Great. Fucking fantastic. Just what I needed now on top of everything else.

I didn't even entertain the idea of getting back in the car and leaving. He was not going to keep me from my exercise. I chose to ignore the little feeling deep in my gut that told me I was staying not out of stubbornness but because I was secretly happy to see him.

Shoulders back, I marched across the lot, doing my best not to glance in his direction.

It was a bit irritating he hadn't noticed me yet, but the person on the other end of that call was not sharing happy news.

Jet looked . . . well, not as pissed off as I felt, but I'd never seen him look even remotely angry. I couldn't help peeking over as I got closer, fascinated with the way his brows furrowed in a deep frown, the way his jaw worked as he listened, how the tension in his shoulders made them look even harder and more defined than usual. And he hadn't even had his workout yet—his tank was completely dry.

"Yes, of course I understand that." He pinched the bridge of his nose. "You try not getting emotionally—"

He cut himself off as soon as he spotted me. I gave him a flat look and opened the door to the gym. I badly wanted to eavesdrop and try to figure out who he was talking to and what about. But I wouldn't hear anything interesting now that he knew he had an audience.

"I have to go," I heard him mutter as the door started to swing shut behind me. "Yes, sir."

He stopped the door before it slammed shut and jogged to catch up to me.

"Amaya, hey," he called, and I turned to face him just before I reached the locker rooms.

"Hey," I said, voice emotionless. "Listen, can we not do this today?"

He frowned, concern entering his gaze as he scanned me. I resisted the urge to fidget with the hem of my T-shirt. I was still in my Fulton uniform and really wanted to just get into my gym gear.

"What's wrong?" he asked and moved closer.

I stepped to the side, avoiding what I knew would be a comforting touch on my arm. He stuffed his hands into his pockets.

"This is exactly what I'm talking about. I've had a really shitty day, and you . . ." I huffed. "You just seem to always find some way to get me to talk about it, and I really, really don't want to today. So please, let's not."

He took a few steps back and leaned against the opposite wall, then watched me in silence for a beat. He was giving me physical space, and I had a feeling he was trying to give me emotional space too.

A sweaty middle-aged man came past clutching a towel and a water bottle, interrupting our eye contact for a split second before disappearing into the men's locker room.

"Do you ever just . . . wish you could be someone else?" Jet asked.

I cocked my head to the side. I'd been expecting him to push me to talk, or to drag me to the treadmills like last time. I hadn't expected this random question, and I found myself actually thinking about it.

Did I wish I could be someone who wasn't constantly fighting with her mother and hadn't lost her father when she was eleven? Did I wish I could have normal teenage worries—like homework and boys and whether I was pretty enough—instead of having those worries *and* the insanity of a cult in my town and best friends whose lives were periodically in danger?

"I mean, yeah, sometimes. Doesn't everyone?" I shrugged.

He smiled, but it lacked his usual enthusiastic positivity. "No, I don't think everyone does."

"Do you?" I threw the question back at him.

He nodded slowly and sighed. Then he pushed off the wall, some of that signature energy returning. "Let's do it."

"What?"

"Let's go be someone else," he said, as if it were obvious and I was the slow one in this conversation.

"Jet, what the fuck are you talking about?" I groaned.

"Just for the afternoon." He took my hands and leaned in, looking me right in the eye. "Let's go somewhere that's not here and pretend to be people we're not. Say yes!"

It was sad how tempting that sounded. I looked down one side of the hallway, then the other. Was I actually considering this?

"Fuck it, OK, whatever." I rolled my eyes, but something like excitement started to stir in my belly. "But if you turn out to be some psycho axe murderer, I'm going to kill you. Slowly."

"You're so violent." He chuckled before ducking into the locker room to get his bag. He reappeared before I could change my mind, grabbed me by the wrist, and pulled me out the door. I let him. I was pretending to be someone else, after all.

"Your ride or mine?" he asked as the door swung closed behind us. "Or should we really lean into this 'being other people' thing and take public transport?"

"Ew!" I scrunched my face up. "Let's not take this too far. Where are we even going?"

"Wherever the road takes us."

"Fine, you can drive then, since this whole ridiculous idea was yours."

Without answering me, he changed directions, and we stopped next to his bike near the entrance to the parking lot.

"Ugh! I forgot about the crotch rocket," I said.

He threw his head back and laughed, pulling a helmet out of his bag and another one out of the compartment under the seat. He held one out to me, and I stared at it without taking it.

"Never mind. I'll drive." I started to turn, but Jet always knew what to say to make me pause.

"Don't tell me you're scared." He laughed. "Have you never been on a motorbike before?"

"No, I haven't, and no, I'm not scared." I crossed my arms. I was kind of scared, to be honest.

Jet dropped the teasing smile and held the helmet out to me again. "I'll keep you safe, Amaya, I promise."

Despite my better judgment, I quickly braided my hair and took the helmet. I was someone else today—not some girl afraid of getting on a bike with a boy.

Jet stuffed our bags into the compartment, put his own helmet on, then helped me with mine. It was heavy and tight on my head, but he assured me it was meant to feel like that. Once he'd finished fiddling with the strap under my chin, he smacked the top of my helmet and swung his leg over the seat.

Without thinking about it too hard, I got on behind him.

"Hold on tight." He pulled my arms around his waist, forcing my body flush with his. "If you need me to stop, tap my shoulder."

I couldn't force my throat to spit out a response. In the next second, he started the engine with a roar, and I couldn't have been heard over it anyway.

We took off, Jet navigating the streets of downtown

Devilbend, the traffic forcing us to go slow. After a few minutes, I started to feel more comfortable. This wasn't so bad. There was no reason for me to be hugging him so tightly, really. I tried to put some distance between us, sitting up a bit straighter and peeling my legs away from his.

But then we finally got out of the city and onto a highway, and Jet *took off*.

The engine roared beneath us, and the wind whipped past as I released a high-pitched sound of surprise and fear. He probably hadn't heard me over the noise, but I didn't really care. I was too focused on holding on for dear life.

Any semblance of distance I'd tried to put between us vanished—left behind at the start of the highway, alongside my stomach. My front was flush with his back, my arms locked around his waist, my legs plastered to his. I could feel every shift of his thigh muscles, every flex and release of his back and abs. His body heat and the firmness of his frame against mine were comforting.

As my breathing started to settle and my stomach caught up with the rest of my body, I realized I had my eyes closed. I forced them open and gasped at how quickly the trees were flying past. We were going at an obscene speed! Or did it just feel faster without the illusion of safety provided by car doors and seats and a roof?

I didn't dare turn enough to look behind, but we weren't gaining on the car ahead of us, so I figured Jet was sticking to the speed limit.

Eventually, fear gave way to exhilaration, and I started to really enjoy the ride. The noise made conversation impossible, but there was something calming about that. We were moving in the same direction, together, just occupying the same space without filling it with awkward words. Between that and the wind tugging at our clothes, the trees occasionally giving way to a view of the valley below, I found myself feeling profoundly . . . free.

I even loosened my death grip on Jet—not to force distance between us but simply because my body relaxed into the rhythm of the ride. I even let myself acknowledge and enjoy the way his body felt against mine.

Between the feelings of freedom and the feelings stirring between my legs, I wasn't paying any attention to where we were going. We could've been riding for twenty minutes or two hours. I had no idea. All I knew was the feel of him pressed against me, the shift of his body as he controlled the bike, the lashing of the wind and roaring of the engine.

Everything else fell away, and for a little while, I didn't have a care in the world.

And then we pulled onto a quieter street, somewhere totally unfamiliar. Jet took a few turns and parked at the edge of a strip mall.

"Where are we?" I asked once he killed the engine. The shopfronts didn't give any clues.

I struggled to get the helmet off as much as I'd struggled to get it on, so we got off the bike and Jet helped me with it.

"Does it matter?" He gave me a dimpled smile as he put my helmet away.

"It does if you're about to murder me and bury my body behind that Wendy's." I nodded toward the first store on the strip. The signage was faded, the door rusted in the bottom corner.

"That sounds like a very Amaya thing to say." Jet shook his head in disappointment.

"Right. Forgot we were playing this stupid game." I put on a plastic smile. "Oh my gosh, Jethro! I can't wait to see what you have planned!"

He chuckled and took my hand, pulling me along. I followed willingly, matching his pace up the sidewalk.

Unfortunately it wasn't a long walk. In the middle of the strip mall, the biggest storefront belonged to a thrift store. We paused at the entrance to let an elderly man with a cane exit, and then Jet dragged me inside.

It smelled musty—like a closet full of clothes that hadn't been worn in a decade. I supposed it was exactly that. Racks and racks of clothing that hadn't been worn in years. At the back of the store was a section with some furniture and housewares, sad-looking toys, and faded paperbacks.

I raised an eyebrow at Jet. He was already looking at me, trying to stifle a laugh.

"This is a thrift store." He leaned in and spoke low. "All the items in here—"

"I know what a thrift store is, asshole." I cut him off with a smack to his stomach. The back of my hand stung for a second—it felt as if I'd whacked a brick wall.

I'd been to plenty of thrift stores—usually in the city. It was amazing the kind of things people threw out. You could find some real fashion treasures if you were willing to dig through the literal mountains of polyester trash.

"Let me guess." I turned to face him. "You're going to find the ugliest outfit you can for me, and I'm going to find the ugliest outfit I can for you, and then—"

"Nope!" He gave me a self-satisfied grin. "I'd never try to tell you who you should be or how you should dress. This is about being whoever the fuck we want to be. Pick your own outfit, beautiful. Just make sure it's one *Amaya* wouldn't go for."

With that, he walked off, strolling down an aisle packed with men's pants.

For lack of anything better to do, and secretly excited to get into this weird little exercise, I headed for the ladies' section.

Before I knew it, a half hour had passed, and I had about a

dozen items slung over my arm—half of them quirky, fun finds I could actually work into my wardrobe. I even had a whole series of posts planned for Instagram. One of my finds was a vintage nineties Diesel denim skirt. There was no label on it, and it was creased in all the wrong places, but I knew Diesel when I saw it.

The other half of the items were things I'd never wear in my regular life.

I flicked hangers from one side to the other swiftly, going through the last rack of dresses. Most of them were hideous.

"I swear it wasn't me." Jet popped up on the other side of the rack, startling me. He was wearing a golf hat that had seen better days, and his own pile of clothing hung over his arm.

"What?" I snapped, pressing my hand to my chest in a vain effort to get my heart to stop hammering. That seemed to be a losing battle whenever Jethro Collins was around.

"The look on your face." He pulled his lips into an almost snarl—apparently an imitation of my expression. "You look like you've just walked into a fart cloud. Just saying it wasn't me."

I forced my features into a blank mask, embarrassed he'd caught me letting my thoughts show.

Jet's teasing smile faltered. "Hey, no, don't do that," he said softly, leaning his forearms on the rack between us. "I thought you knew by now you can't hide from me."

Yeah, that's what I was afraid of.

"I was offended by the horrendous scraps of fabric that pass for clothing in this place," I said, ignoring his statement.

He chose to ignore mine too. "I like it when you let your emotions show on your face, Amaya. It's beautiful."

The words hung between us among the musty second-hand clothing as we shared a loaded look. A look almost as intense as the one we'd shared on the beach that night—when

I'd been convinced he felt the same way. When I went in for a kiss and he rejected me.

I forced myself to look away and started flicking hangers again, not really seeing any of the dresses whipping past.

Jet ducked down, shoved the clothing apart, and crouched through it so he was on my side of the rack. I couldn't help the chuckle that bubbled up.

"Are you ready to go try our new personalities on?" He flashed me an easy grin, dimples popping, eyes sparkling.

I shrugged, grateful for the switch in mood. "Sure. Let's do it."

He moved past me toward the changing rooms.

As I passed the end of the rack, a swath of floral print caught my eye. I grabbed the dress without even looking at it properly and rushed to catch up with Jet.

We spent the next half hour trying on increasingly ridiculous combinations of the clothes we'd picked out, making sure to step out at the same time. We laughed and teased each other and made way too much noise for the two elderly ladies manning the register.

The best moment was when we both emerged dressed as old people, matching without even trying. I had a calf-length wool skirt on, paired with a crocheted cardigan, pearls, and a bag with a snap closure. Jet shuffled out from behind the curtain wearing pants three sizes too big and cinched so high with a belt they practically reached his armpits. He'd paired them with a tweed coat and fedora and came out leaning heavily on a cane.

When we saw each other, we collapsed into uncontrollable laughter before standing in the mirror side by side to admire our matching looks. He talked about his time in 'Nam. I offered to make sandwiches before we went to church. We linked arms like an old married couple and

pretended to worry about our sixteen grandchildren and the
state of youth these days.

We kept it light and fun, but just before we went back to
change again, I caught his eye in the mirror and wondered if
he was thinking the same thing—how easy and natural this
felt. I hoped I'd find someone to grow old with one day.
Someone who made me laugh and forget my worries as well as
Jet did.

In the dressing room, I put my final item on—the dress
I'd grabbed at the last second. It was a strappy sundress with
big flowers all over it in shades of pink. It hit the floor even
with my shoes on but fit OK otherwise. There was nothing
particularly outrageous about it—just a floral-print dress. I
wore dresses all the time. I wore pink too. But the particular
style, the fact it was some no-name brand, the general vibe of
it just wasn't me. Did I wish it was me? I didn't know, but I
liked pretending I was the kind of girl who would wear this
dress. The kind of girl who didn't care about labels and felt as
loose and free as the skirt swinging around my feet.

I took my hair out of the braid, letting it hang loose down
my back, and stepped out.

Jet stepped out a moment later, and we silently took each
other in. He'd chosen a preppy outfit—pleated shorts, a polo
shirt, even a sweater over his shoulders with the arms looped
together on his chest. The pastel blue of the shirt contrasted
with his near-black eyes. It gave him a dark edge, despite the
baby face. The look suited him. I could totally picture him on
a sailboat with a Rolex on his wrist. But then, Jet looked good
in everything.

"I love it when you let your hair out," he said, stepping
closer. He stuffed one hand into his pocket and grabbed a
strand of my hair with the other, fiddling with it gently.

"Oh, thanks, I . . ." I was about to tell him it needed a
wash and was all frizzy from the braid and helmet, that I

usually wouldn't be caught dead with my hair looking like this. But then I remembered the game we were playing and forced all that down. The girl who wore no-name-brand floral dresses with sneakers didn't care that deeply about her hair. "Thank you."

I left it at that and ducked my head to hide my smile. Apparently floral dress girl was also fucking coy.

"You look great too." I smoothed out the collar of his shirt. "The old-money, Ivy League look suits you."

He shrugged, letting go of my hair. "I'm not going to be in your world very long, but when in Rome and all that . . ."

With a grin, he spun on the spot, leaving one hand in his pocket. Of course his ass looked good in a smelly pair of secondhand shorts.

We kept the outfits on as we went to the counter and paid for them. As I laid out the handful of other items I'd decided to buy, I wondered about Jet's choice of words, his choice of outfit. He wasn't going to be in my world for very long. He was on scholarship and would only be at Fulton for one more year, but did he *want* to be in my world? Was he referring to the bubble of privilege I'd grown up in, or was he talking about being in *my* bubble specifically?

"You hungry?" He pulled me out of my thoughts as we exited the store, an ugly plastic bag stuffed with clothes hanging over my arm. "There's a pizza place at the end of the strip mall there. Or we can drive to someplace else?"

"Pizza sounds good." I took off up the street, not quite ready to be so close to him on the bike after the confusing thoughts I'd just been thinking.

We got a giant slice and a soda each and took them to a picnic table in a grassy area behind the row of stores. We ate in comfortable silence, then joked about some of the more horrible clothes we'd tried on. The hum of traffic in the background mingled with birdsong, and the air was warm.

Summer was just around the corner, and I leaned back on my hands, enjoying the easy moment.

It didn't last long. Jet's attempts at distraction were valiant, but I couldn't force the complicated thoughts from my mind in every in-between moment of stillness. I could feel him watching me, but he stayed true to his word and didn't try to make me talk.

For the first time since we'd met, I offered up the information. "My mom's new boyfriend is moving into my house. I came home from school to a van in the driveway and moving boxes everywhere."

Jet rested his elbows on his knees, his legs propped up on the bench seat. "You don't like him? Do you not feel safe with him around?"

"It's not that." I shook my head. "He doesn't give me the creeps at all, actually, unlike most of Mom's previous men. Not like that anyway."

"Abuse can look like a lot of different things."

"I'm not being abused," I rushed out, a little irritated. "Unless you count the years of neglect from my mother."

"I do," he responded immediately, but I ignored him.

"It's just that they didn't even give me a chance to say no. I mean, shouldn't I get a say in who lives in my fucking house?"

"Of course you should."

"I just don't understand what the hell is happening, you know? Like, Mom's suddenly around all the damn time, and it's kind of suffocating, even though I don't really feel like she's there for me. Like, I don't really have a mother back because *he's* around all the fucking time too. And I'll straight-up murder you if you repeat this to anyone, but I actually think he might be a decent guy. Like, he's good for her or something. But . . . I don't know. It feels like everything is changing around me and I don't have anything solid to hold on to, ya know? Like nothing is certain, and that's fucking terrifying."

I took a deep breath and dug my nails into the dirty wood of the table.

"Yeah, I know how that feels. Change can be scary."

"Oh god." I sat up and ran my hands through my messy, frizzy hair. "You must think I'm such a drama queen. You don't have either of your parents, and you live in a shitty apartment on your own, and here I am complaining about my mom being around more and feeling like my literal mansion is not big enough to give me space from her boyfriend."

"Did you say my apartment was shitty?" Jet chuckled. "You've never seen it. How'd you know it was shitty?"

I looked up at him with wide eyes, mortified. "Oh crap, I'm so sorry. It was just . . . I was just trying to say . . ."

He cut me off by getting to his feet and coming to stand in front of me. "Amaya, it's OK. I'm just teasing. I know you didn't mean it like that. I don't think you're a drama queen. And I can totally see why your situation at home has you upset. Please don't pile guilt on top of it all. Just because other people have problems that may seem bigger than yours doesn't make your problems any easier to deal with, or any less valid."

I looked up at him, tears stinging the backs of my eyes, everything from the past few weeks spilling over. Last time, I'd made myself hold the tears back until he was gone. This time, they tracked down my face as he stood close enough to taste them.

That time I'd been crying over him; this time I was crying for a whole bunch of other reasons. That was how I justified it to myself.

Something cracked in his expression, and he looked pained at the evidence of my own pain. He gently cupped my face with both hands, wiping the salty moisture off my cheeks with his thumbs. The tenderness in his touch, the broken expression on his face, made me cry harder.

He pulled me into his chest. One arm banded around my waist, and the other gripped the back of my neck, his fingers tangling with my hair. I held on to him so tightly my hands ached, and I let go completely in his warm embrace. Just for a few indulgent moments. His strong arms, his firm chest—he made me feel safe.

Even though he'd been the one who made me cry last time. How fucked up was that?

The thought was sobering, making it easier to stem the flow of tears and lean back. I still struggled to fully pull away from him though, and my fingers clung to the front of his new, old shirt.

"Why . . ." I started to ask what I'd been dying to know for weeks. Why had he not kissed me? Why was no one good enough for him? Why was *I* not good enough?

But I stopped myself before the rest of the words tumbled past my trembling lips. I forced a deep breath into my lungs and made myself release my grip on his shirt.

"Why what?" He tilted his head to the side, trying to catch my gaze.

I couldn't help it; I looked into his eyes.

He saw it right away. As if the image of that beach at night, of our lips nearly crashing together like the waves on the sand, was reflected in the depths of my irises. His expression hardened, something like regret flashing across his features before he took a tiny step back.

I wrapped my arms around my middle. I couldn't take another blow to my softest parts.

"Take me home, Jet." I was so fucking tired.

CHAPTER TEN

FRESHMEN SCURRIED OUT OF MY WAY AS I MARCHED through Fulton Academy after the end-of-day bell. They always scurried, but I was in a particularly shitty mood, so they scurried particularly well.

I didn't let any of it show on my face as I headed for the library, forcing my shoulders back and striding as if I owned the place. Which, to be fair, most of these freshmen would tell you I did.

The library doors were in sight ahead when the one asshole who never scurried from me came around the corner.

"Hey, Amaya." Jet walked directly toward me.

"Jethro." I barely spared him a glance as I walked past—or tried to. He stepped sideways and blocked me, forcing me to come to a stop a few feet away from the library.

"Amaya, can we please talk?" He leaned in and kept his voice lowered.

"About what?" It had been three days since our impromptu thrift shop adventure. I'd ignored just about everyone for the weekend, but come Monday, he'd spent all day trying to talk to me. I'd managed to dodge him so far, but he had that determined look on his face. As if he was ready to throw me over his shoulder and tie me up until I agreed to speak to him.

"About the other day. I feel like we left things unfinished. You wanted to go home, and I wasn't going to keep you somewhere you didn't want to be, but I don't think our conversation is quite over."

"It's over. Trust me."

"I just . . . I've been worried about you." He swallowed hard, his Adam's apple bobbing. For the first time since we'd met, he looked uncertain—maybe even nervous.

"Look, I appreciate you getting my mind off shit on Friday, but I shouldn't have unloaded on you like that." He shook his head, but I forged on. "You're not interested in me. I get it. But I'm not interested in being just your friend, so we have nothing to talk about anymore. You don't get to be worried. I have my girlfriends to be there for me, to worry about me, to talk to. You're off the hook, OK?"

He stared at me with an indecipherable look on his face. I could tell he wanted to say something, a lot of things, but he couldn't seem to find the words.

"Speaking of friends, I'm meeting mine in the library to study, and I'm late." I gave him a firm look. After a long moment, his shoulders dropped in defeat, and he stepped aside.

"See ya, Amaya." He sounded sad, and as I passed, his fingers brushed against mine. I forced my hand to grip the strap of my bag so it wouldn't grab on to him and never let go.

"Goodbye, Jet." I said it softly, more for myself than him, but I had a feeling he heard it anyway.

I found the girls and Hendrix at a table in the back of the library. They'd set up right next to a window, away from all the shelves. Weaving through the desks in the study area—

half of which were full with other seniors studying for exams —I made my way over.

They all gave me halfhearted waves of acknowledgment, already buried in books and flash cards. Donna was methodically crosschecking some English notes against the relevant reading. Mena had that deer-in-the-headlights look as she switched between her math and political science notes every few seconds. Hendrix's head was in his hands as he stared at a blank page on the table before him.

If I was going to be miserable, at least I'd be in good company. Dropping my bag, I flopped into the last free chair. I reached down to grab my books, but I just slumped against the back of the chair instead.

Exams were fast approaching and I'd come here fully prepared to study. But . . . *ugh*! This was all Jet's fault.

Mena's hand covered mine on the table, and I looked up to find she'd abandoned her frantic attempts at study to instead study me. Across from us, Donna sat up and looked at me too. Hendrix was still stuck in whatever depth of despair that blank sheet of paper had him trapped in.

"What?" I frowned.

"You look sad," Mena said, sounding sad herself.

Hendrix looked up from his existential crisis, and then all three of them were watching me with worried expressions. Mena didn't resist when I pulled my hand out from under hers, but Donna never let anyone get away with shit.

"A, you've been off for weeks and you won't talk to us. We're seriously getting worried here. Please . . ." I could count on one hand the number of times I'd seen Donna Mead lost for words.

"We just love you and we want to be here for you. That's all," Mena practically pleaded.

"Others are starting to notice too," Hendrix added. Damn him! He knew I hated having people up in my business, that it would bother me more than anything to know they were talking shit about me.

I opened my mouth to . . . say something, and I just made a weird strangled sound before closing it again.

Shit. Fuck! I could feel all the pent-up emotions building up, literally choking me to the point I couldn't speak. In school, with half our year sitting all around us, dammit! I glanced around the library and then at my friends.

I must've looked like a caged animal. I wanted to talk to them, I did, but there was so much shit to let out it was clogging the way.

But my friends knew me—like, *really* knew me. Donna and Mena packed their books up right away. Hendrix frowned and hesitantly started grabbing his stuff too.

Donna placed a hand on his shoulder. "We need some girl time. You need to stay here and actually study."

"Harlow will meet us downtown," Mena announced, tucking her phone away and zipping up her bag.

Looking disappointed, Hendrix slouched back into his seat and took out a book with actual words on it.

"Whatever it is, Amaya, we got your back," he said, and I gave him a genuine smile. Then Donna gave him a big, sloppy, totally-inappropriate-for-the-school-library kiss, and we turned to leave.

"How the fuck am I supposed to focus on equations with a raging boner?" Hendrix grumbled as we left, making us and a few others nearby laugh.

Twenty minutes later, we were settled in the courtyard of our favorite smoothie place in Devilbend, four large cups with straws sitting on the table between me and my very attentive friends.

They all had expectant looks on their faces. It was a little unnerving being stared at, and I found myself leaning back in my chair.

Harlow grabbed her drink and slurped the chocolate-peanut-butter smoothie while narrowing her eyes at me.

"Bitch. Start talking." Donna was done handling me with kid gloves and was back to her straightforward, demanding self.

Weirdly, it made me feel better. It was comforting in that way familiar things were.

"My mom's latest man-thing is moving into my house, and the strange thing is they both seem actually serious about it and are acting vaguely like adults, and it's bringing up all kinds of feelings." I gagged. "Like, about my dad, and about my mom too, and for some infuriating reason, I find it really easy to talk about all this shit to Jethro fucking Collins, and I think I really fucking like him, which is super inconvenient because he clearly does not like me back, because we had a moment on spring break and we nearly kissed, but he practically recoiled from me and ran away, and then the other day when I was upset about the douchebag invading my home, he went out of his way to cheer me up—like, boyfriend level of effort—and that's two times now that I felt things for him but it didn't go anywhere, and I'm fucking humiliated and pissed off, because I still fucking like him."

I sucked in a deep breath, then released it with a huff before reaching for my green goddess smoothie. I took big gulps while looking between my friends, waiting for their reactions to the pile of emotional shit I'd just dumped on them.

All three wore matching wide-eyed looks.

Harlow was the first to speak, giving me a smug little smile. "I knew you had a thing for him."

I flipped her off.

"You guys nearly kissed?" Mena looked as though she wanted to smile at the romance of it all, but the rest of the heavy crap was weighing it down.

"Your mom is in a stable relationship?" Donna sounded as if she wanted proof that would stand up in a court of law. I didn't blame her. I wouldn't have believed it either if I hadn't seen it with my own eyes.

"Yep." I didn't know which of them I was responding to. "So, yeah. The past few weeks have been . . ."

"Overwhelming?" Mena suggested.

"A clusterfuck?" Harlow added.

"Bullshit." Donna frowned.

"All of the above." I nodded.

"Why didn't you tell us any of this?" Mena asked.

I shrugged and fidgeted with my straw. "The thing with Jet happened on our vacation, and I didn't want to bring the mood down. And also I was embarrassed. Then after, I was determined to just ignore him until he went away since nothing is ever going to happen between us. And the shit with my mom . . . I honestly didn't even know where to start. I still don't really know how I feel about it all."

For the next hour, we sat around that little table in the quirky courtyard of a juice place, and I poured it all out for my friends. They listened and asked questions and offered unwavering support as I worked through my feelings.

I had the best friends. They didn't judge me or rush me, but they called me out on my crap too. It was exactly what I needed, and I felt so much better after letting it all out.

Yes, the situation at home was still upsetting and overwhelming. And yes, I was still confused and embarrassed about the crap with Jet. But at least I didn't have to deal with it all on my own.

The girls made me realize I needed to talk to my mom. Properly talk to her, without getting into a fight, and tell her how I felt about everything. I also probably needed to talk to a therapist, maybe with my mom there too. I wasn't quite ready for either of those things, but I promised my girls I'd keep thinking about it, and I'd at least try to talk to my mom soon in a mature way.

When it came to Jet, the unanimous decision was that he was dead to us.

"Want me to look into him?" Harlow asked, glancing around the busy courtyard. She meant by using less-than-legal hacking ways. "I might find something we can use."

I wasn't sure I wanted to hurt or embarrass Jet. I just wanted him to stop doing the same to me.

"Nah." I shook my head. "I don't want to waste any more energy on him."

"Good." Mena nodded and crossed her arms. "As a very good friend of mine once wisely told me—he should be ride-or-die. He didn't ride, so he should die. Literally."

"I believe I said figuratively." I chuckled. "And this is a completely different situation."

"Yeah, well, I mean *literally*."

"OK, murder fairy. Let's tone down the violent tendencies, shall we?" I patted her on the arm.

"He's going to regret ever coming to Fulton Academy. There might only be a few weeks left in the year, but that's plenty of time to make his life hell." Donna slurped the last dregs of her smoothie aggressively, probably already plotting Jet's demise in detail.

"Donna, stand down." I gave her a firm look, then threw the same look at the other two. "Everyone stand down. Please. It's not like we were together and he cheated or something. He never made me any promises. We haven't even fucking kissed. He just doesn't like me. It might hurt, but it's not a crime."

"It should be. You're fucking fabulous," Mena grumbled.

"Fine. No absolute destruction. But only because you asked," Donna conceded.

"All right, I gotta get some more work done before I head

to Easton's for dinner." Harlow got to her feet, and we followed suit. It didn't escape my notice that she hadn't agreed not to look into Jet on the dark web or whatever, but there was no arguing with her when she got a digital mission in her head.

We chatted about her new job on the way out. She was really enjoying the flexible hours and doing something she was genuinely good at. After years of feeling like a failure at school and life, she seemed happy, and that made me happy.

"Let's take a photo!" Mena whipped her phone out, and the three of them shoved me into the middle and hugged the breath out of me. "Everyone say, 'Amaya is a bad bitch'!"

"Amaya is a bad bitch!" the three of them chanted as I laughed and Mena snapped multiple pictures. She posted one with the same caption and #besties. She'd caught me mid-laugh with my friends' love surrounding me, and I made a mental note to get it printed and framed.

When I got home, the house was empty. Not for the first time, I didn't know whether to be relieved or disappointed.

I headed to the fridge for a snack and paused with my hand on the handle. There was a thick piece of paper with silver embellishments stuck to the door with a magnet. The word *BestLyf* caught my attention, and I forgot all about the snack as I snatched the paper off the fridge.

In raised cursive script, the invitation was addressed to my mom. Raine Clayton was throwing a fundraiser, sponsored by BestLyf, at her private residence. I didn't even read what cause they were raising funds for or any of the other details on the invite. As soon as I saw my mom's name in the same vicinity as Raine Clayton's, I started to hyperventilate.

CHAPTER ELEVEN

I DIDN'T WANT MY MOTHER ANYWHERE NEAR RAINE fucking Clayton or anything remotely related to BestLyf. Why was she even invited to this party? What was the point of it?

I tried calling her several times, but she didn't answer. It wasn't unusual for her, but it was extra irritating when I actually wanted to talk to her.

The worst thing was I *knew* this would turn into a fight. I'd just vowed to try to talk to my mom calmly and rationally, like an adult, but there was no way that "hey, don't go to this party, because I can't tell you why, but you have to promise not to go" wouldn't turn into a screaming match.

After pacing the kitchen for a good twenty minutes, I decided to go for a run. Hopefully she'd be home by the time I got back and I'd be calmer from the endorphins.

I changed into running gear, put my earbuds in, and jogged up our ridiculous driveway. Barely half a mile in, I started to get cramps. I ran all the time, I was fit, and these were definitely not the kind of cramps one got from too much cardio.

Stopping with my hands on my hips, I glared at my uterus. "Really? Now?"

As if she were answering me with attitude, I felt that tell-tale sensation of the first bit of blood leaking out and stiffened, squeezing my thighs together.

Muttering under my breath, I made my way home. Even after I showered, took a couple of Advil, and accepted that the universe hated me for some reason, Mom was still not home.

I tried her phone one more time, then grudgingly gave in and called Cal. Mom had put his number in my phone weeks ago before I could snatch it back, for "emergencies."

He picked up on the second ring. "Hello?"

"Cal, it's Amaya. Is Mom with you? Do you know when she'll be home?"

"Not right this second. Is everything OK?"

"Yeah, fine. Do you know where she is?"

"We're both in the city. She's having drinks with friends while I take care of some work matters. We were planning to spend the night here. Do you need us to come home?"

I hesitated. "No, that's OK. I'll talk to her when you get back."

"Are you sure?"

"Yeah, it's fine." The party wasn't for a few weeks yet. I had time to talk her out of it.

I hung up after quickly thanking him.

It annoyed me that he'd been so . . . accommodating. I had a feeling he would've actually found Mom and come home if I'd said I wanted them to, and that bothered me. I didn't want to like him. I didn't want to admit he was good for her.

I hated him for being the one to convince her to get her shit together. Why couldn't she have done it for me?

Suddenly, the house I'd wanted all to myself felt too empty. Without any plan, I grabbed my keys and headed out.

My first instinct was to head to the Meads' place, but I needed to get out of this neighborhood. I thought about going to my lookout, but I was in a state and didn't want to navigate those tight turns in the dark.

Frustration steadily rising, I decided to head downtown and get some dinner, but somehow I found myself at Mena's apartment building instead. Yes. Fine. Good. I'd go up and hang with her for a while, maybe see if she wanted to go get ice cream with me or something.

But a few steps from Mena's entrance to the building, my feet turned and marched over to the next entrance instead. Jet's address was in the secret spreadsheet the girls and I kept. It contained the names, occupations, and addresses of people we knew, along with any other information we had. Knowledge was power, and information was currency. Next thing I knew, I was in the elevator, smacking the button for Jet's floor. The doors opened before I had time to come to my senses, and I rushed to his apartment and banged on the door.

When it didn't immediately open, I banged on it harder, even adding a kick for good measure.

Then it dawned on me that I had no idea if he lived alone or if someone was sleeping.

"Fuck!" I whisper-shouted, feeling like a total fool. I'd already turned to get out of there when the door opened with a squeak that echoed in the hallway.

"Amaya?" Jet frowned at me through the gap. He slammed the door closed, making me jump, then a metal chain jiggled against the wood, and he opened the door fully. "What are you doing here? You all right?"

"No, I'm not fucking all right! I—ugh!" I huffed. "Never mind. I shouldn't have come here."

He grabbed my wrist before I had a chance to run away. He was shirtless and barefoot, wearing only that pair of beach shorts I'd seen him wear repeatedly in the Bahamas. I hated that I knew how good his ass looked in those shorts, even as I fought the urge to tell him to turn around so I could have a look.

Was I panting before I realized he was half-naked? Probably. I'd practically run here I'd been working myself up so much in the car.

"What happened?" he asked, his thumb caressing my wrist.

"Nothing happened." I half-heartedly tried to twist out of his grip. "I'm just over everything. I feel like I'm drowning half the time, and just as I manage to catch a breath, some other bullshit comes up to push my head under the water. Between Mom and school and this BestLyf —" I cut myself off. Better not to go into detail about all that.

"What about BestLyf?" He frowned. I didn't blame him for being confused. I was a total rambling mess.

"Never mind. I'm sorry for just showing up like this." I glanced behind him, mortified that someone may have overheard all that.

Jet chuckled. "There's no one else here."

I clung onto the change in topic. "Where is . . . uh, who lives here with you?"

"Nobody." He shrugged. "I live by myself."

"What?" I blinked, not following. "How? Is that even allowed?"

"I'm not a minor and . . ." He sighed. "It's a long story."

"Tell me? I need the distraction." I slid my wrist out of his grip enough to take his hand with mine.

"Maybe someday." He smiled sadly and looked away.

"Are you embarrassed? I would never judge you." I seemed

like a total bitch to most people, but I thought Jet knew me well enough to know who I was underneath it.

"No, I'm not embarrassed. I just can't . . . it'll change things and I . . . can't talk about it yet."

"OK," I said softly. I knew what it felt like to not want to open all your deepest wounds. Vulnerability was fucking scary.

"You wanna grab something to eat and tell me what's brought you here all worked up?" He gave me that dimpled smile, paired with that deep look in his eyes. He was clearly deflecting, but I was stubborn. If he wasn't going to open up, I wasn't either. And anyway, wasn't I mad at him? There was a reason I'd refused to speak to him for days.

I dropped his hand, irritation flaring up inside me again. God, my fuse was short tonight.

I'd started paying more attention to our surroundings as we spoke, and my brain finally registered what I was seeing in the apartment behind him.

"Jet, what the fuck is that?" I pointed at the coffee table.

He glanced over his shoulder, then turned back with a completely neutral look on his face. "A gun," he said matter-of-factly.

A dirty rag was spread out on the surface of the table. A handgun, along with a few other metal things I had no names for, sat on it.

"What are you doing with a gun?" I hissed.

"Cleaning it."

"Why do you even have that thing?" Didn't he know how often the police came looking for someone in this part of town, how quickly Fulton Academy would cancel his scholarship and dump his ass if he was caught doing anything remotely illegal?

"I have my reasons." He leaned on the door frame, blocking my view of the weapon.

I opened my mouth to argue but snapped it closed. I had enough shit to worry about. I'd reached my threshold.

"You know what? Whatever." I held my hands up and took a step back. "I shouldn't have come here in the first place. I'm gonna go."

"No, Amaya, wait. Let's head out and talk somewhere else. Just let me put a shirt on."

"Why? So you can drag more of the most personal things in my life out of me while not telling me shit about yourself?" My voice rose along with my ire. "So I can feel close to you and then you can reject me again? I am so sick of this shit, Jet!" OK, I was pretty much shouting, and I needed to get the fuck out of there before people started coming out of their apartments—or before the tears pushing at the backs of my eyes spilled over.

"Amaya." He said my name softly, pleadingly. My heart tugged against my chest, wanting me to fall into his arms. But no. I took another step back and shook my head.

"No, Jet. I hate that I came here. I hate that you always have a way to make me feel better about my fucked-up life. And I hate that I keep letting you hurt me. Do not follow me."

I turned on my heel and rushed toward the elevators as the tears trickled down my cheeks.

I heard Jet curse behind me before his door slammed shut.

Part of me had been hoping he would chase after me, pull me into his arms, and make it all better. I hated that part as much as I hated that he'd slammed his door on me instead.

I turned the corner and bashed the elevator call button repeatedly. It didn't sound like the thing was moving, so either someone was holding it up on another floor or it had broken down like the one in Mena's part of the building often did.

With a growl of frustration, I pushed the door to the stairs open and started heading down, desperate to get to my car and far away from here.

I was so wrapped up in my own emotional mess I didn't even hear the group of people climbing up until we were practically on top of each other. A loud laugh followed by indistinct chatter clued me in moments before we crossed paths on a landing.

Three men in their midtwenties stumbled toward me, eyes glassy and limbs loose. The one in front spotted me first and slapped at the other two until I had the full attention of all three of them. I tried to rush past, but they stood practically shoulder to shoulder, blocking the stairs.

"You're pretty when you cry," the one in front said. "You must be an absolute knockout when you're happy."

"Yeah, come on, sweetheart," one of the others slurred. "Give us a pretty smile."

"I dunno," the third one chimed in, "I kind of like it when their makeup is all messed up and running down their cheeks."

He leered at me as the others laughed.

"Excuse me, I'm running late." I tried to push past again, my tears drying up as a chill of fear skittered down my spine.

They didn't budge, and the one in front grabbed my arm.

"Hey, we're trying to have a conversation here," he snapped.

"And I'm not interested." I set my shoulders and fixed him with a hard look. "Now take your dirty fucking hand off me before I scream so loud half the building comes running."

They all stared at me for a beat, then burst out laughing.

"Folks know to mind their own damn business in this neighborhood, princess," Douchebag 2 said. "Scream all you want. No one's coming to save you."

Adrenaline pumped through my veins at the implication.

Flight wasn't an option—they were blocking the stairs—and I was not a freeze kind of girl, so I guessed I'd go down fighting. Because they would have to kill me before I let myself get raped.

I brought my knee up, aiming for Douchebag 1's balls, but he dropped his grip on my arm and twisted out of the way. I shoved him, hoping he'd break his neck on the stairs. Then I turned to run up the way I'd come. They were drunk and I ran nearly every day. Maybe I could outrun them long enough to make it back to Jet's door.

Douchebag 1 stumbled and nearly met the fate I'd hoped for, but his buddies caught him. Douchebag 3 was tall and threw out a long arm, catching my hoodie over the railing and thwarting my escape attempt.

Panic shot through me, and I did scream—a piercing sound that echoed off the concrete walls. I thrashed and kicked, shouting profanities at them between banshee screeches.

Only seconds passed between me shoving the first guy and the three of them crowding me into the corner.

A clanging sound of metal on metal made us all look up. There was Jet, standing a few steps above us, leaning casually on the railing. I'd never been so happy to see someone in my entire life.

"Boys." He flashed them his easy, dimpled grin. "You're keeping half the building up with all this noise. Is there a problem?"

"Nothing that's any of your business, kid. Get lost." Douchebag 2 turned to face Jet and pulled a knife out.

My panic tripled at the sight of the weapon.

Jet sighed and raised his right hand, the one gripping a gleaming gun. He rested it on his left forearm, still leaning on the handrail.

"Yeah, see, the thing is, she is my business." He nodded at

me. "And if you don't get your hands off her immediately, I'm going to get really fucking pissed off." He dropped the easy smile and stared them down.

"Bullshit she is," Douchebag 1 spat but released his hold on me anyway.

Jet took the safety off slowly, deliberately, his expression not cracking. It was unnerving how calm he was—how comfortable he was pointing that gun at people.

The Douchebags must've come to the same conclusion, because they tucked away their silly knife and their stupid attitudes and backed away. Jet waited until they were out of sight before he moved toward me.

"Joke's on them for bringing a knife to a gun fight," I quipped, but there was no humor in it, and to my horror, my chuckles turned into sobs.

Next thing I knew, my face was pressed to Jet's chest—covered in a T-shirt now—and his arm wrapped around my back to keep me from sliding to the dirty floor. I held on to him, fighting to get my shit together as the adrenaline exited my body as violently as it had invaded it.

After a while, the sobs stopped and the tears dried up, but I couldn't seem to pull away from his comforting embrace. His hand on my back rubbed soothing circles, while his other hand still gripped the gun by his side.

I lifted my head as a horrible thought struck me. "What if they come back? With more people and guns and stuff?"

Jet wiped a stray tear off my cheek, his eyes scanning me. "They won't come back. I'll keep you safe," he declared. I believed him. "Did they hurt you?"

I shook my head, perversely pleased at the way his jaw had ticked and his eyes had flashed with menace when he voiced his concern.

"Good." He took a small step back. "Let's get out of here. It smells like piss."

I managed a laugh that didn't collapse into sobs again. It really did smell awful, and my skin was starting to crawl— especially on my back where I'd been leaning against the wall.

He took my hand as we descended the stairs, and I held on to it tightly.

"Did you put your gun back together before coming after me?" I asked, the barrier between my brain and my mouth severely compromised. I immediately felt like an idiot for even assuming he'd been coming after me at all. Maybe he'd just decided to go out.

"No. This is a different gun," he said softly, managing to keep his voice from echoing off the walls.

I gave him a wide-eyed look. "How many guns do you have?"

"A few." He smirked, refusing to meet my eyes.

By the time we reached the ground floor and exited the building, I felt more like myself. Meaning I was pissed off at the audacity of those jerks for trying to attack me like that, and I was back to being frustrated and confused by Jet.

The parking lot was empty, but I didn't miss the way Jet scanned it repeatedly before tucking the gun into the waist-band of his shorts and hiding it under his T-shirt.

"Want me to drive you home?" he asked as we reached my car. "Or somewhere else? I don't want you driving in this state."

"What state?" I crossed my arms and gave him a chal-lenging look.

"There she is." He grinned at me.

"Who?" I cocked an eyebrow.

"The strong, beautiful, infuriating woman I've come to . . . know."

Was that really how he saw me? That wasn't a casual kind of thing to say about someone—*to their face*. If he thought so highly of me, why did he keep me at arm's length?

Ugh! I did not have the emotional bandwidth to go down that track again.

A familiar figure caught my attention, and I frowned as two men came around the corner of the building. Jet followed my gaze, and we just stood there watching for a few moments.

"What is it?" he asked.

"I know that guy. That's Shady . . . er . . . I don't know his last name. Actually, I don't think that's his first name either." There was no missing the red tracksuit the man always wore. For someone who ran a criminal empire, and probably needed to stay under the radar, he sure did wear a lot of bright clothing.

"Shady, eh? How do you know him?" There was an edge to Jet's question, and his jaw tightened, but I didn't have time to worry about that, because I realized I knew the other guy too.

"Actually, I know both of them. The other one, in the suit with the neat brown hair—that's my mom's boyfriend." What the fuck was he doing talking to Shady? What the fuck was he doing in Devilbend North when he'd just told me on the phone half an hour ago that he was in San Francisco with my mom?

"That's the guy who's moved into your place?" Again Jet sounded a little intense. Was he being protective? He'd certainly protected me tonight.

Shady made his way to a dark SUV that took off right away. Cal walked off in the opposite direction and disappeared around the corner. I returned my attention to my protector.

"Would you really have shot them if they didn't leave?" I was morbidly curious. His bluff had worked like a charm, but how much of a bluff was it? "Is that thing even loaded?"

He watched me intently for a beat, some kind of inner

conflict clear in his eyes. Then he slowly pulled the gun out and held it between us. Releasing the clip, he showed me it was fully loaded before tucking it away.

"I would've blown every one of their brains out over those piss-stained stairs and not given it another thought." He looked me right in the eye as he said it, his gaze full of calm conviction.

CHAPTER TWELVE

I WAS THE BABY OF MY FRIEND GROUP. THE LAST ONE TO turn eighteen. And I used it as an excuse to throw the most epic party of the year.

The girls and I arrived in a limo about an hour after it started. I liked to make an entrance, and I was indulging all my whims on this glorious Saturday night. The weather was warm, my makeup flawless, my friends in a good mood, and in a few short hours, I'd officially be an adult. Nothing could ruin this night for me.

"To Amaya!" Harlow held up her champagne flute and we toasted, finishing off the last of the bottle we'd shared on the drive over. The driver opened the door for us, and we made our way up to my party.

The elevator opened on the rooftop of the tallest building in Devilbend, and as we stepped out, everyone cheered. I flipped my sleek ponytail over my shoulder and smiled widely before moving into the crowd to say hi to everyone.

During the day, the roof was reserved for residents of the high-rise's top few floors, but at night it became a venue for hire. A pool hung over the edge of the building, and there was a covered bar, a dance floor, and seating areas. Pearl- and champagne-colored balloon arches and cascading balloon installations decorated the whole area, along with carefully placed lighting. It looked as if the rooftop was dripping in giant glowing bubbles, and it was filled with a hundred of my closest friends.

"Happy birthday, sexy!" Drew darted up to scoop me off the floor in a massive hug.

I laughed and swatted him as he set me down. "Watch the Prada!" I chided, smoothing the green silk and making sure it still looked good on my ass. The minidress had a plunging neckline that made my small boobs look great. "Thank you, Drew."

"Let's get you a drink." He looped my hand through his arm and started leading me toward the bar, but I pulled out of his grip.

"I have a few more people to say hi to. Can you get me a champagne?"

"Anything for the birthday girl!"

I made my way through the crowd until I found my besties again. They were standing near the railing with their men, the stunning view of Devilbend behind them. They looked amazing. All of them. They looked happy.

I was happy for them, but a pang of something else stabbed at me too. It wasn't jealousy exactly. I didn't begrudge my friends their happiness—they deserved it after everything we'd been through. It was just . . . well, didn't I deserve it too? I wanted what they had.

The girls had gotten ready with me at the Meads' place, but I hadn't seen the guys yet. Hendrix came up first to give me a hug and a happy birthday. Turner was right behind him with a warm hug and warmer wishes.

Harlow's boyfriend, Easton, looked awkward as he stepped forward next. He gave me a chaste kiss on the cheek, then quickly backed off with a murmured birthday wish. Harlow took his hand and squeezed it, beaming up at him.

Was it weird to have my former English teacher at my birthday party? A little, but it helped that he wasn't in one of his uptight suits, instead sporting a more casual shirt with the sleeves rolled up to expose his tattoos.

"How's it feel being at a party with your students, Easton?" Turner asked. He was the most casual with Easton, as he went to another school and had only ever met him as Harlow's boyfriend.

"Well, my eye is twitching a little at all the underage drinking." He chuckled. "But it's not too bad. They're not my students anymore."

"Got you a GlenDronach." Easton's brother, Ford, joined us and handed him a glass with amber liquid in it. His own drink was some kind of orange fruity cocktail with a pineapple garnish and an umbrella. "Hey, birthday girl!"

He dashed forward as soon as he spotted me, and the hug he gave lasted longer than any hug with a guy you weren't even really friends with should last. He pressed his whole body flush with mine and whispered "happy birthday" into my ear.

"Thanks, Ford." I gave him a smile as I pulled away. Reluctantly, he let me go.

"Save me a dance?" He flashed me that flirtatious smile before wrapping his lips around the colorful paper straw in his drink. It wasn't the first time Ford had flirted with me. I'd only met him a few times, and he'd managed to come onto me during most of them.

My initial knee-jerk reaction was to turn my nose up and tell him "you wish"—like I had all the other times. But I wondered if maybe I should dance with him, let him flirt, flirt a little back.

Because the person I actually wanted to do all those things with wasn't here.

Jet had ghosted me after that frightening incident at his apartment building.

His violent words, on reflection, had been a bit disturbing. But the neglected, abandoned, sad girl inside me perversely reveled in how fiercely he'd been ready to protect me.

A week had passed since then, and he'd almost dropped off the face of the earth. He'd been at school on Monday and Tuesday—I'd seen him rushing through the halls—but he hadn't been at lunch, and I could've sworn he was avoiding me. Then he didn't even show up at school for the rest of the week. Nicola told me he was out sick, but I didn't believe that for one second.

I still texted him to say I'd heard he was sick and hoped he was OK. Then I texted him to say thank you for stepping in with those creeps again. Then I invited him to my birthday party. He ignored all my messages, but I knew he was talking to Drew (he'd mentioned as much at lunch on Friday), so I wasn't worried about him. I was pissed.

By the end of the day on Friday, I sent him one last text, telling him he was *un*invited from my party and from my life in general.

"You know what? I'm in a good mood, so sure, I'll dance with you." I gave Ford an easy smile, and he winked at me. Winked! This guy . . .

The girls gave me knowing looks but didn't say anything. They were determined to make this night fun and carefree for me, but they knew everything. Since that day at the juice bar when I'd told them what a mess my life was, I'd been keeping them updated.

They were appropriately reproachful when I told them I'd gone to his apartment, totally horrified when I told them about being attacked, then grudgingly forgiving when I told them Jet had come to my rescue. Plus, Harlow had dug further into him, even though I'd told her to leave it, because of course she had. She'd decided he was a walking red flag because he had barely any online presence. His school records were sparse, and even her shadiest contacts couldn't dig up anything about his parents or his life before coming to Devilbend.

It was a little odd, but whatever. I was never speaking to him again anyway. I'd flirt with Ford, maybe hook up with him for a bit of birthday fun, and forget all about *Jethro*.

"You better not be giving away dances to any of these inferior peasants!" Drew appeared and handed me my champagne before slinging an arm around my neck. "Your ass is mine tonight, A."

"I belong to no man. Especially not tonight." I cocked an eyebrow at him and took a delicate sip of my drink.

Maybe I could hook up with Drew. He was always up for some fun. Plus, he was a genuinely good friend and wouldn't hurt me. Maybe I could talk Drew and Ford into some group fun. It was my birthday, after all.

"Come on, let's dance!" Donna pulled me out of my dirty fantasies just before I let my mind acknowledge that I'd rather have one night with Jet than multiple nights with any number of dudes I didn't feel as strongly about.

We made our way to the dance floor area near the pool, where I greeted some more friends and let the music chase my thoughts away. For the next several hours, I danced, drank expensive champagne, ate the best hors d'oeuvres money could buy, talked to my friends, and forgot about all my worries.

Donna made a speech with assistance from Harlow and

even Mena—though her cheeks went so red it was visible under her makeup. They almost made me cry. Then a giant cake was brought out. Donna demanded no one sing "Happy Birthday" until the clock struck midnight, since it was technically my actual birthday tomorrow. She was going to make us do a countdown as if it were New Year's Eve. It was ridiculously over the top, and I loved it!

The cake was cut up and distributed, and we got back to dancing. They were playing all my favorite songs.

"I believe I was promised a dance," a deep, teasing voice said behind me, and I turned to find a smiling Ford. He lifted his eyebrows and held his hands out in something between an invitation and a request.

With a carefree laugh, I stepped into him and draped one arm over his shoulder. He gripped my hips, and we started swaying to the music. Between the alcohol, the attention from all my friends, and the thumping bass, I was riding an almost euphoric high.

Ford's body moved incrementally closer to mine, and I leaned into him until we were chest to chest. One of his hands went to my lower back just as the music changed to some nasty song that was impossible not to grind your hips to. He was a surprisingly good dancer and we moved in sync, our hips rolling.

He held my gaze as he started to lean in for a kiss.

Jet's stupid face flashed in my mind, and for a split second I wished it was him about to kiss me. But I shoved the errant thought away and forced myself to focus on my cute, *interested* dance partner.

His nose brushed mine, but before our lips met, another body appeared at my back. I gasped and giggled—I was definitely getting drunk if I was giggling. Ford lifted his head and threw a crooked grin over my shoulder, not put out at all by the interruption.

I looked back to see who was holding my waist and crowding me in.

Drew's eyes were a bit glazed over but still glinted with his signature mischief.

"Birthday girl sandwich!" he called out, and as if they'd been friends for years, the two guys high-fived.

"Am I the meat in this sandwich?" I asked.

"Wait, I don't wanna be bread," Ford complained. "Bread is boring."

"I've got all the meat you need, birthday girl." Drew plastered his chest to my back, and we all laughed as we somehow managed to find the beat again. Our hips swayed in rhythm, and I started to get that heavy, pressured feeling low in my belly.

Maybe some three-way fun was actually in the cards for tonight. If one guy couldn't drive Jet from my mind, surely two would.

I don't know what made me glance in the direction of the elevators, but it was as if my thoughts had summoned him. Jethro Collins stepped out onto the rooftop in blue slacks and a white shirt right when I'd devised a multi-penis plan to forget him. His eyes scanned the crowd for barely a second before they found mine.

Instead of holding his gaze, I rested my head on Drew's shoulder and raked my fingers through Ford's hair. If I said I wasn't putting on a show to make Jet jealous, I'd be lying.

Drew drifted off and started dancing with others after a short time, but Ford got that intense look in his eyes as soon as we were alone again. When I glanced back toward the elevator, Jet was gone.

I really, really wanted to crane my neck to find where he was, if he was still looking my way, if he appeared jealous. But I forced myself to keep dancing—even though I was hardly aware of Ford and his roaming hands anymore.

As it turned out, Jet was like the devil. I'd thought of him and he appeared, right by my side.

"Hey, can I cut in?" Jet's jaw was hard, his brilliant eyes narrowed.

CHAPTER THIRTEEN

FORD, COCKY BASTARD THAT HE WAS, LOOKED JET UP AND down and held me even closer. His hand splayed over my belly possessively.

"No. Fuck off," he said with a little smirk, his gaze glued to mine.

"Wasn't asking you," Jet said, his voice deceptively calm. He had that look in his eyes—the one he'd had when he confronted those douchebags in his building, the one that promised violence. Was he jealous?

"No. Fuck off." I lifted my chin haughtily as I repeated Ford's words. Where did he get off acting all jealous and entitled when he'd rejected me more times than my ego cared to admit?

"Amaya." Jet sighed. "Can we just—"

"She said no, dude." Ford twisted a little, putting himself between us. "Back off."

I stumbled but caught myself on Ford's shoulder.

"I don't know who you *think* you are, but trust me, you don't want to mess with me." Jet cracked his neck with a sharp cant of his head, his mouth pulling up into a mocking grin.

I was inclined to agree. Everyone thought Jet was this fun, friendly, nice guy, but I'd seen another side of him. He was dangerous.

We'd started to draw a crowd. I mean, it was a party, so there was already a crowd, but we were drawing all their attention. A few people even had their cell phones out, hoping to capture some drama on video.

"Oh, you wanna go?" Ford threw his head back and laughed. "Let's go, pretty boy."

He dropped his grip on me as the two of them faced off.

They were acting like Neanderthals. At my fucking birthday party. The audacity of these testosterone-fueled muscle bags.

Neither of them was even looking at me. Did they even remember why they'd started this bullshit in the first place?

I caught Donna's eye from across the crowd. The others were nowhere to be seen, but she was saying something to Easton while keeping her focus on me. Ford's brother pinched the bridge of his nose.

I gave Donna a smirk and an eye roll. *Men.*

She returned my smirk, amusement in her gaze. *Can't wait to see you put them in their place.*

The two idiots were still bickering, chests puffed, really in each other's faces.

I moved to stand at their sides and folded my hands behind me. When I leaned forward, bringing my face close to theirs, they both stopped what they were doing and gave me frowns. As though I was the one acting weird.

"Is this the part where you kiss?" I asked, looking between them. A couple people chuckled.

Ford leaned back and grinned. "I'm up for it, if that's what you're into."

Jet's expression was the complete opposite—all serious and intense—his full focus on me. "I'm only interested in kissing one person here."

What? "What?" I huffed. "Seriously? It's my fucking birthday, Jet. I refuse to deal with your bullshit on my damn birthday!"

More people looked our way, ironically because of me and my raised voice. As usual, this asshole was getting under my skin.

"Can we please go somewhere quiet and talk?" he asked, voice low, as he stepped in close.

I moved back to regain my distance and folded my arms over my chest.

"No. Fuck you!" I didn't bother to keep my voice down. "I'm not leaving my birthday party to have you—I'm not doing this, Jet. I'm having a fun night, and that's the end of that."

A cheer went up from my friends and acquaintances, and a few people I'd never seen in my life, backing me in my quest for a fun time.

"You." I pointed at Ford. "Go get me a drink." My buzz was wearing off.

"And you." I pointed at Jet. "Go away."

Ford headed toward the bar, laughing as he went, but Jet was not as good at taking directions.

"I'm not leaving until I give the birthday girl a kiss," Jet said, his expression no longer so serious but still kind of intense. Those damn dimples came out as he stepped closer again. This time, I didn't move away.

I pursed my lips as I tipped my head back. I'd had more than a few people cower under my bitch-face. It made me feel strong, and I refused to be anything other than the badass bitch I wanted to be in this moment. Jet had made me feel like shit one too many times. He'd rejected me and humiliated me one too many times. I refused to let him make me think he wanted me before he inevitably changed his mind at the last possible second. Not in front of all these people. Not on my fucking birthday.

"If you insist." I gave him a mocking smile. "You can kiss my foot."

He could either do exactly that or turn around and leave. I was fine with either option.

He narrowed his eyes at me, but his smile didn't seem forced—he looked amused. Keeping his gaze locked on mine, he took a step back. A pang of disappointment shot through my chest, but I didn't let it show. I wanted him to leave, and he was leaving. What did I expect?

To my utter surprise, he didn't turn on his heel and bail. He lowered himself to one knee and leaned forward to wrap a hand around my calf.

His warm hand on my bare leg steadied me when I felt ready to fall on my face from shock. Still, I kept my bitchy look firmly in place. I wasn't paying attention to anyone else. All the people and the music and everything else faded into the background as my focus zeroed in on his touch. He tightened his grip and nudged my leg gently, and I let him guide my heeled foot to rest on his knee.

He kept his eyes on mine as long as he could as he placed a kiss on the top of my foot. I couldn't hold back a small gasp as his pillow-soft lips connected with my skin. He'd actually fucking done it. His lips lingered on my foot for a brief moment before he looked back up at me. His thumb caressed my calf, sending tingles up my leg.

"I'll happily kiss any part of your body if you'll let me, Amaya," he said, his words only for me. Still, everyone heard, and I became aware of all the people around us, watching and making all kinds of amused sounds.

I sighed dramatically and rolled my eyes. "Don't push your

luck." My foot dropped back to the floor, and I waved my arm dismissively in his general direction. "I suppose you can stay."

He caught my hand and kissed the back of it as he got to his feet. A massive grin split his face. "Thank you."

"I don't know why you look so damn happy. I'm still mad at you."

"I know."

The grin didn't even falter as he stepped in closer. A crowd favorite came on, and someone turned the volume up.

"Well, now that I've successfully cut in, dance with me?" He held his hand out like a gentleman and everything.

"Bold of you to even ask, to be honest." I raised a brow.

He shrugged. "I'm feelin' plucky."

I knew I probably shouldn't, not after the way he'd treated me, but it was my birthday and I really wanted to dance with Jet.

He flashed a grin, those dimples popping, when he saw the acquiescence in my expression. Before I'd even said anything, he placed his hands on my waist, and I slowly reached up to rest mine on his shoulders.

"I never stood a chance, did I?"

I turned to find Ford watching us with my champagne in his hand.

I opened my mouth and closed it, like a moron. I didn't know what to say. Jet's grip on my waist tightened slightly, but he was smart enough to keep his mouth shut.

Ford sighed dramatically and downed half of my champagne before giving me a confident smile. "It's all good. Gimme a call when it doesn't work out and you're ready to level up from high school boys."

Sipping more champagne, he stepped back and disappeared into the crowd. He didn't seem all that hurt, and his cocky attitude made me feel not so bad after all.

"Amaya." Jet drew my body closer, holding me tighter as the music changed to something with a more sultry, sexy tempo. "About this past week—"

"No." I covered his mouth with my hand. "I don't want to hear it. I really don't even want to think about it tonight, Jet. You've been a colossal jerk to me, but for some fucked-up reason, I'm still glad you're here. So I'm going to let myself enjoy this for tonight. But come tomorrow, I'm done. You don't want me? Fine. I don't want to play these games. So just stay away from me for the last few weeks of school, and we never have to see each other again."

We turned slowly around the dance floor, our bodies in sync with each other and the music. I liked the feeling of his strong shoulders under my touch, and I ran my hands over the muscle there.

Jet flattened his palm on my lower back, making me reflexively arch into him. With his free hand, he gripped my wrist and removed my hand from his mouth. He planted a gentle kiss on my palm, then placed my hand over his heart and held it there.

"I don't want to never see you again. I don't want to play games either. I like you, Amaya. A lot."

"You've got a funny way of showing it," I muttered.

"I know. I'm sorry. You don't want to get into any of that stuff tonight, and that's fair. I'm going to respect your wishes, but I am sorry."

I watched him for a few moments as we swayed, mulling over the sincerity in his gaze, acutely aware of every spot our bodies touched.

Was it a little convenient that he wanted to honor my wishes by not getting into explaining himself? Maybe. But he was openly telling me he liked me, pulling me closer instead of pushing me away. He'd literally gotten on his knees and kissed my feet in front of everyone.

Whatever. I'd overthink it all tomorrow when it wasn't my birthday party and I wasn't half-drunk.

"You're sorry, huh?" I threaded my fingers together behind his neck and took the lead in our dance.

"Absolutely." He nodded.

"So you've had a change of heart?"

"For sure."

"And you don't care if everyone sees that you're into me?"

"Nope." His eyes sparkled with amusement. He was enjoying this.

"So, if I tried to kiss you this time . . ." I leaned in, my murmured words just for him. "You'd let me?"

"I'd get on my knees again and beg if it would get me another chance to kiss you, and do it right this time."

Aww! That was kind of sweet. I almost felt bad for what I was about to do. But I'd already made up my mind, and I could be stubborn like that sometimes.

"Good to know." I spoke the words millimeters from his mouth, my lips barely brushing his. His eyes started to close, and I made my move.

I took a quick, sure step backward, planted my hands on his chest, and in one swift move shoved him right into the pool.

He hadn't even noticed me maneuvering us toward the edge as we danced, and the shocked look on his face as he went sailing backward toward the water was priceless. Totally worth another missed opportunity to finally kiss him.

I laughed out loud. I laughed with my whole body, throwing my head back and not giving a shit what I would look like if someone happened to snap a picture. Everyone around us laughed and cheered too as Jet emerged from the water half glaring and half chuckling. Those who hadn't seen what happened moved closer, drawn by the sudden sound of splashing water and whooping people.

When Jet stood, I realized my mistake. The water of the pool reached to just below his chest, and if he looked hot in a dress shirt, he was positively irresistible with it soaking wet and plastered to his body. Droplets of water trickled down his face and neck. It was like a scene from one of my romance novels, and I was so here for it.

Suddenly the music cut off, and my girls came rushing toward me through the tight crowd. For a second, I panicked, wondering what the hell was wrong, but then I realized they looked excited and happy. Donna raised a microphone as they reached my side.

"Everyone, shut up," she demanded, her voice amplified. "Only fifteen seconds to go until my girl is eighteen!"

She checked the phone that Mena held up for her, then started the countdown from ten. Everyone joined in, and a rooftop full of drunk, happy people rang in my birthday like it was 1999.

Jet joined in, grinning up at me as he swiped the water off his face and waded to the edge of the pool. Everyone was still cheering like crazy when the DJ started up the music again with a banger.

The atmosphere was electric!

Electricity and water didn't mix, but Jet looked too good to resist, all wet for me as he was.

I kicked my shoes off, dropped my purse next to them, and launched myself into the pool yelling, "Happy birthday to meeeee!"

I didn't even care about the designer dress or my makeup getting ruined as I let myself sink to the bottom. Kicking up to the surface, I laughed as I brushed water out of my face.

Others joined in, shucking pieces of clothing or jumping in fully dressed. And then half my friends were in the pool, and suddenly it was a pool party.

The warm water felt wonderful against my skin—

refreshing after all the dancing and drinking—and it sobered me up quite a bit too. So I can't blame what happened next on the alcohol. It was all me. Well, me and Jet.

I lost track of him with everyone jumping into the pool, but he found me. A strong arm wrapped around my middle from behind, and I turned to face him.

"There's no getting away from me now, unless you plan on throwing me off the building," he joked, pulling me in closer.

"Just shut up and kiss me before I change my mind." I draped my arms around his neck but waited for him to lean in. I'd done enough chasing with this guy. If he wanted me, he'd have to come and get me.

And he did. Confidently, he captured my lips with his, and I could've sworn a round of fireworks went off. The party, the music, all the people splashing around us faded away. There was just Jethro's lips on mine, Jethro's arms holding me close, Jethro's tongue swiping at my mouth, pleading and demanding more all at once.

I opened for him, and our tongues danced. Everything seemed heightened, my skin hyperaware of everywhere we touched, of how the water itself seemed to flow around us as though trying to push us closer. My legs circled his waist, and he gripped my thighs as we kissed for what felt like hours and barely a few seconds at the same time.

This was the best birthday ever!

CHAPTER FOURTEEN

THIS WAS THE WORST BIRTHDAY EVER.

I rolled over and groaned. My stomach seemed to keep rolling long after the rest of my body was still. I pulled the covers over my head to hide from the light, but I had to tug them back off immediately when I started to gag from the smell of my own breath.

After Jet and I finished making out in the pool, I got very drunk. To be fair, I wasn't the only one, and it was my birthday, but I had only vague memories of Hendrix and Jet trying to wrangle us girls into a waiting car. I had no idea where the other boys had ended up, nor how we'd managed to get out of the car and into my house.

Did I puke at some point? Was that why my breath was so horrible? Come to think of it, we all might have puked, other than Donna. She had the alcohol tolerance of a large middle-aged man who'd been working a physical job and drinking a six-pack every day for two decades.

I cracked an eye open and saw my bestie in the bed next to me, her short blonde hair fanning out over her face as she snored.

Someone farted—loudly. A snort-laugh came from the direction of the daybed in the opposite corner of my room, and I lifted my head to find Mena propped up on some pillows, scrolling through her phone.

"Morning," I croaked, my voice sounding as horrible as my breath smelled.

"Morning, birthday girl." She smiled at me, then burped and looked as if she might follow through for a moment.

When I was sure she wasn't going to hurl again, I asked, "Where's Harlow?"

The younger Mead sister had passed out on the other side of me, but it was definitely just me and Donna in the bed now.

Mena pointed to the corner between my desk and a window. I rolled over, and there she was—rolled up into a ball, tucked in among my oversized cushions, sleeping in my reading nook as she drooled on my throw blanket.

"Ugh! I feel like shit." I groaned as I flopped back against the pillows. The bounce woke Donna, and she made one, loud snore as she jerked up in bed.

"I'm up!" She rubbed her eyes, then frowned. "What?"

Mena chuckled again. I smiled, scared that laughing would cause too much movement in my gut.

"We should get something greasy into our stomachs." I yawned.

Donna reached for her phone to check the time. "Breakfast burritos will be here in twenty."

"How?" I gaped at her.

"I ordered them last night and scheduled delivery."

"I love you."

"Of course you do. I'm fucking fabulous."

She really was fucking fabulous—even with her mascara smeared down one cheek and her hair so messy I wasn't sure it could be saved. But, hey, if anyone could rock a shaved head, it was Donna Mead.

Twenty minutes later, the four of us stumbled down the stairs, our faces clean and our teeth brushed but our insides still feeling like sewage. The doorbell rang, our breakfast arriving at just the right time.

Harlow had yet to communicate with anything more than a grunt, but she rushed to the door before the rest of us and yanked the paper bag out of the delivery driver's hands. I gave the stunned guy a tip and closed the door before following the girls into the living room.

"There you are, sleepy head!" Mom came bouncing in from the patio in activewear and a light sheen of sweat. Was she exercising? On a Sunday? Before . . . I checked my phone. To be fair, it was half past eleven, but time meant nothing to this woman.

"Morning." My voice sounded marginally better.

Honestly, it surprised me more that she was actually home on my birthday. She'd missed the last two. I'd woken up to an empty house on my sixteenth and seventeenth birthdays and had received over-the-top gifts several weeks later—out of guilt that she'd forgotten.

"Oh, hey, girls!" She smiled brightly at my friends as she grabbed a water out of the fridge. "I was just thinking about going up to wake you."

The girls all greeted her as politely as their hangovers would allow, and we settled into the couches in the adjoining living room. Harlow's breakfast burrito was nearly half gone by the time the rest of us unwrapped ours.

Mom meandered into the living room and perched on the arm of the couch next to me. Cal walked into the kitchen, talking on his phone as he rummaged in the cupboard. He was in shorts and a T-shirt, barefoot and comfortable—as if he lived here. Because he fucking did.

I ignored him. It was easy to do since I felt pleasantly surprised my mom was actually here. She really did seem to be changing her life. I mean, she was exercising and drinking water! I had to admit there were a lot of positive signs. So I let myself hope she'd remembered her only child was eighteen today, that maybe she'd already gotten me a gift and had wanted to wake me up to give it to me.

"So, what's on the agenda for today?" Mom asked the room.

I shrugged. "Nothing. We're all pretty—" I stopped myself from saying *hungover*, not in the mood for a fight. "Tired. It was a late night."

"Mm-hmm. Tired. Right." Mom glared at us each in turn but with a teasing smile on her face. The woman could write a book on hangovers, so it was probably naive to think she wouldn't know. We all chuckled a little, Mom included. I was relieved she wasn't mad about it, that I could actually have a moment of lightness with my mother.

"So, what did you girls get up to last night that's got you so tired?" she asked.

"Uh, there was a party," Mena answered while I had a mouthful of burrito. Harlow had finished hers and fallen right back to sleep on the other end of the couch.

"Ooh, a party! I hope it was worth the hangover. What was the occasion?"

No one answered on my behalf that time, shooting me subtle looks as they busied their mouths with breakfast. I swallowed my bite with some difficulty. My throat was suddenly tight, and all the food in my stomach felt heavy.

"Mom." I set the remainder of my burrito down and faced her, forcing myself to be calm. There was no way she'd forgotten. Again. *No way*. "It was my party. I threw it."

"You did?" Her brows furrowed slightly, but she still

smiled at me in curiosity. "Where? Why not do it here? There's plenty of room."

"Why were you coming to wake me up? Or asking what I was up to today?" Un-fucking-believable.

She shrugged. "Just have nothing much on today. Cal and I are planning to go to lunch, so I was going to ask if you wanted to join us. Maybe we could do some shopping after."

"What day is it?" I got to my feet even though I was exhausted—spent right down to my bones. I just couldn't be sitting when she admitted it. I needed to be standing.

"Uh . . . Sunday? What's gotten into you?" She looked very confused now, and she got to her feet too, crossing her arms over her chest.

"What is today?" I gritted out, digging my nails into the palms of my hands. "The date."

The volume of my voice startled Harlow awake, but I was hardly aware of my friends—awkwardly watching this shit show with front-row seats.

"I don't know, Amaya. What . . ." She huffed. "Like, May . . ."

"May eleventh." Cal appeared next to her, inserting himself into the situation, as usual. Apparently he'd finished with his call.

"Right. May eleventh." Mom nodded and leaned into him. It was almost comical seeing her expression change as the lightbulb went off in her brain. Her shoulders stiffened, and she looked at me, horrified. At least she had the courtesy to feel embarrassed.

"And why might this date be important to me?" I asked with sarcastic pleasantness, grinding my molars.

"Oh, Amaya." Mom's eyes got watery. "It's . . . your . . ."

"It's my fucking birthday!" I yelled into her face, perversely satisfied when she flinched. "I am your only child. You are my only parent. And you've forgotten my birthday for the third year in a row. What the fuck kind of mother are you?"

"I'm sorry. My sweet girl, I am so—"

"Oh, shut up!" I cut her off. "I don't believe you."

Cal rubbed her back soothingly, but they both looked remorseful, or something like it.

"I'm sorry too," he said. "I didn't know it was today, but I should've made an effort. We'll do something special—"

"Fuck off, Cal!" I cut him off too. "No one asked you. You're not my father and you never will be. Because he's gone. The only good parent I ever had is fucking dead, and I'm stuck with *you*." I pointed at my mother with a scowl. "I wish it was you who'd died and not him."

My mother gasped and her tears spilled over. Cal looked shocked.

I didn't care. I turned away from them all and rushed up to my room, locked the door, and dived back under the covers. Maybe if I just slept some more, I'd wake up and realize this had all been some horrible nightmare.

Donna had the only other key to my room. She must've walked home to get it, because it was some time—and several rounds of knocking and calling through the door from both my friends and my mother—before I heard the door open.

My girls climbed into bed with me and just held me while I cried.

Worst birthday ever.

CHAPTER FIFTEEN

THE FULTON ACADEMY PARKING LOT WAS EMPTY, THE HOT afternoon sun baking the concrete under our feet. Trevor, the security guard, had been happy to take the three neatly folded hundred-dollar bills to let us in on a Saturday. He hovered around the front doors, making sure we stayed in the parking lot as agreed, but other than that, Jet and I were alone.

"Oh my god, it's so heavy." I tensed all my muscles, trying to stay upright. My hands ached from how hard I gripped the handlebars.

"It's OK, just find your balance. I got you, beautiful," Jet encouraged me.

Once I was sure I wouldn't face-plant and take his motorbike with me, I nodded.

It had been a week since my birthday. A whole week of feeling hurt and avoiding my mother. I'd spent this morning studying with the girls, but then the sisters had some tennis thing to get to and Mena had a shift at the diner, so I'd called my . . . er . . . Jet. I'd called Jet.

We hadn't had that conversation yet, so I didn't feel right calling him my boyfriend. But neither of us was seeing other people, and he wasn't shy about holding my hand or kissing me at school, so whatever. Labels were so 2013.

Jet and I had lunch at Mena's diner, and then I managed to talk him into teaching me how to ride a motorbike. Which was how I now found myself at school on a Saturday afternoon with my butt on the bike and my toes touching the ground on either side, trying my hardest not to fall before we even started.

I squeezed everything in an attempt to stay upright as my right leg started to jiggle from the strain. Jet's hands were there, steadying me before I could even ask. Holding the handlebars and the back of the seat, he kept the massive thing under me stable, and I took a breath to release my tension.

"You good?" he asked, but I was too distracted by the muscles and veins popping out on his forearm, by all that tanned skin stretched over strong muscle. I wanted to feel his big hands gripping my thighs just like that.

"Amaya?" He leaned in close with a little smile. "You wanna learn how to do this or just keep eye-fucking my arms? Because you didn't need to waste all that money bribing Trevor for that—we could've just gone to the gym."

"Shut up." I chuckled. "I can do both."

"No, you can't. You need to focus."

"Yeah, yeah. OK, let me try the balance thing again." I flapped my hands at him to back up, but he leaned in instead. With one smooth move, he swung his leg over the back and settled himself behind me.

"Let's go over some basics first." He placed my hands firmly on the handles and pointed to things as he explained. I didn't know how he expected me to focus with his insanely hot body pressed up against mine and both his forearms doing their sexy dance right in front of my face.

Somehow, I managed though.

He ran through how to work the throttle, the brake, changing gears, and all the other knobs and levers—the basics of taking off and stopping. He had me repeat back to him all the functions of the controls, then he checked the helmet was on tightly, zipped his leather jacket up to my chin, and got off the back. I pressed my toes into the ground, making sure to keep the heavy machine upright.

"OK, start her up." Jet crossed his arms, making his chest and biceps bulge. I swear he was doing it on purpose at this stage. I turned the little key, and the engine under me rumbled to life. I grinned, feeling accomplished already, even though I hadn't even done anything yet.

"Now, you're going to powerwalk it first, like I showed you. Then lift your feet when you feel balanced, and you're going to go to the other end of the lot." He pointed to the far side, where the grass sloped down toward the tennis courts. "And then you're going to stop and plant your feet once more. Got it?"

"Got it." I fixed my gaze on my target. Without waiting for any more instructions, or giving myself time to freak out, I revved the engine and slowly released the clutch. The motorbike lurched forward, and I screamed and jammed the brake on.

Jet was there instantly, grabbing the handlebars, balancing me, and fighting a laugh. I smacked him, but he gave me a few more tips and I tried again. And again, and again.

An hour later I was drenched in sweat under the heavy leather jacket, but I could take off, drive to the other side of the lot, and come to a stop. I couldn't turn yet, but we decided to work on that some other time.

We sat in the shade of a tree and passed a bottle of water between us to cool down.

"You did great. I'm proud of you." Jet slung an arm around my neck and planted a kiss on my temple.

I shoved him back. "Don't! I'm all sweaty and gross!"

"I don't care!" With a laugh, he jostled me onto my back in the grass, then rubbed his cheeks all over my face and hairline while I squirmed and screamed and laughed all at once.

When he finally relented, we just stared up at the canopy of the tree, our fingers tangling between us as we caught our breath.

"Thanks for teaching me how to ride a crotch rocket," I said. "It was good to keep my mind occupied with something other than study."

"Anytime," he said. Then after a long pause: "Things still tense at your place? Have you spoken to your mom yet?"

"Yes, they are, and no, I haven't."

Mom had spent every day since my birthday trying to make up for forgetting my birthday. A new gift appeared in front of my door every morning, one of my favorite meals waited for me in the kitchen every night, and in between, she was pretty much love-bombing me. She called and texted all the time with apologies and compliments and declarations of love. All the gifts sat in the hallway outside my door unopened, all the meals went uneaten, and I hadn't replied to a single message.

She and Cal were constantly home now too. She was *always* there, trying to talk to me, trying to be a mother all of a sudden. I just pretended they didn't exist. I could see it getting to her, the frustration building behind the niceties. It was only a matter of time before she blew up at me, and then shit would go back to normal.

"How long are you planning to freeze her out?" Jet asked. His tone was casual, but I knew he wanted me to make up with my mom. I'd shut him down hard the first and only time he'd tried to argue I should talk to her, but he kept nudging me on it. He knew everything that had happened. I wasn't sure why he was so invested, but I had a feeling it had to do with his own absent parents.

"Well, *she* froze *me* out from the moment Dad died so . . . like, seven years, give or take." I shrugged and sat up.

He placed a gentle hand on my back. "I just hate seeing you hurting. That's the only reason I want you to talk to her."

I nodded but didn't reply.

After another long silence during which I locked all that emotion crap down, I turned to face him.

"Let's go for a drive. I have a spot I want to show you." I stood up and pulled on his arm, ready for another distraction.

We got back on the motorbike, Jet driving this time. I hugged him close and leaned into the bends in the road as we headed up the hill. I navigated by pointing. We flew past the concealed turnoff and had to double back, but then we rode up the bumpy dirt road to the lookout.

"Wow!" Jet took a deep breath as we walked closer to the edge of the cliff, hand in hand. It was the kind of lung-expanding, life-affirming breath you couldn't avoid taking when coming face-to-face with a spectacular view.

There wasn't a single cloud in the sky, and the blue stretched out before us infinitely, the California landscape and Devilbend baking in the sun below.

"Absolutely stunning." Jet wrapped an arm around my middle and pulled me close.

"If you crack a joke about how the view is all right too, I'm going to dick-punch you," I warned.

His shoulders shook as he laughed. "I thought you liked all that romantic stuff from your books."

"You know what's romantic? Finding a unique way to express your feelings that's specific to the person you're with. You know what's not romantic? Clichés."

"Personalize the compliments. Got it."

I turned to face him and wrapped my arms around his

neck. "Your eyes are practically sparkling. It's fucking enchanting, since they're so dark most of the time."

"Thanks?" He struggled to keep the mirth off his face, his dimples flashing.

I wanted to reply with something witty and flirty, but I was genuinely mesmerized by his eyes. The clear blue sky and the bright sunshine made them look amazing—as if I could dive into their sparkling depths and all my worries would be soothed away.

I lifted onto my tippy toes and kissed him instead. He held me a little tighter as we kissed languidly, getting lost in each other.

It didn't take long for a tingle to build between my legs, that warm, pressured feeling of arousal. I hadn't hooked up with anyone since before our spring break trip, probably longer, and I was horny AF. And despite my valiant efforts, Jet just wasn't getting into my pants.

To be fair, we hadn't had many opportunities to really make magic happen, but the few times we had been alone long enough, he'd stopped before things got to third base. He insisted he wanted to take things slow. I would've started to feel rejected all over again if I couldn't feel the rock-hard evidence of his arousal anytime I so much as brushed against him. He clearly wanted me, and he wasn't shy about showing me care and affection in a nonsexual way.

So I did my best to respect his boundaries and not pressure him, but man, I was starting to get serious blueballitis here. There were only so many nights in a row a girl could get off with her own hand before she needed someone else's touch.

Just the thought of Jet's touch between my legs kicked my arousal up another few notches. I moaned lightly into his mouth and rolled my hips against his. His hands tightened on my back and then dropped to my hips.

As predicted, he broke the kiss and pressed his forehead against mine, both of us breathing hard.

"We should slow down," he whispered.

"Why?" I breathed.

"Anyone could come up that road at any second."

"No one ever comes up here," I argued.

"Still . . ."

I shook my head a little to clear it and leaned back to look at him properly. "Do you . . . not want to?"

"Of course I want to," he declared with so much conviction it took me a little aback. "I want you so badly it's scary, Amaya."

I bit my lip and smiled. "OK, well, I want you too. So why do you keep pulling back? Are you scared? Have you never . . ."

"Hah!" He threw his head back and laughed. "It's not that. I'm . . ." He rubbed the back of his head, looking embarrassed for a moment. "I'm more experienced than I care to admit."

"OK . . ." I waited for him to elaborate. I didn't really care that he'd been with others before—so had I. Jealousy was such a pointless emotion.

"I just don't want to move too fast. I don't want you to feel pressured or . . . anything."

"Wait." I chuckled. "Do you think I'm a virgin?"

"I don't mean to assume anything but . . ."

Now it was my turn to throw my head back and laugh. "First of all, virginity is a bullshit, patriarchal social construct. Second, I'm plenty experienced too, so when I say I want you inside me, I mean it."

Jet watched me with a mixture of emotions on his face—surprise, amusement, admiration maybe? And something really tender I could've easily interpreted as love if I wanted to.

"Noted," he finally responded.

"Come on." I pulled him over to the motorbike, then gestured for him to get on.

"Where are we off to now, princess?" he asked as he swung his leg over.

In answer, I settled myself in front of him, facing him.

He caressed the exposed skin below the hem of my hiked-up skirt. "We're not having sex in a public place in broad daylight. I'm not comfortable with that."

"Noted," I parroted his own sentiment before leaning in for a kiss. I wanted to fuck him right on the back of the motorbike, but we could work up to that. That didn't mean we couldn't fool around a bit though.

I had my back to my favorite view in all of Devilbend, and I didn't even care. Because in front of me, between my legs, was something that interested me even more.

Jet didn't seem all that impressed with the sprawling landscape or the setting sun anymore either. He only had eyes for me. There was something really addicting about that.

He'd dated practically half the girls at school since he arrived, but none of them had held his interest long enough to even get a kiss. Then he went and practically claimed me in front of everyone and looked at me like *that*. Who wouldn't be intoxicated?

"What's going on in that complicated head of yours?" he asked, the dimples barely flashing with a soft smile.

"Just thinking about you," I said, then nearly reared back in surprise at my own honesty. I hadn't even hesitated. There were exactly three people I was ever that candid with. I guessed now it was four.

"Yeah?" The dimples deepened. "What about me?"

I pulled back slightly, but I didn't have much room, and his grip on my waist tightened. I didn't want to stroke his ego, but I also didn't want to close up completely. I kind of liked being more vulnerable with him. A little. Just dipping my toe in the vulnerability river. The water was nice.

"Those damn dimples, for one." I leaned in and licked the left one, making him chuckle. "And those eyes."

"What about my eyes?"

They see so much—even things I don't want others to see.

"They're pretty." I smirked, wanting to keep it light.

"Pretty." He raised his eyebrows.

"And your thighs." I ran my hands up the solid muscle to his hips. "I love the way they look, spread like this. It's so . . . masculine."

"Mm-hmm." He watched me intently, his thumbs dipping under my shirt to rub at the skin above my waistband.

"And your ass." I reached around to grab it. "You have a great ass. Especially when you're riding."

His hands dropped to my own butt, and with a sure squeeze, he yanked me closer. We ended up chest to chest, my core firmly against his rapidly growing erection. Reluctantly, I released his ass and wrapped my arms around his neck for balance.

"Keep going," he murmured against my lips.

"Talking time is over." My voice was breathy as I closed the minuscule distance and kissed him hard.

Our conversation earlier had cleared the air and apparently lifted some mental block for him. Because he wasn't holding back anymore. There was no hesitation in the way he kissed me—he was letting go, and I wanted all he had to give.

When I moaned into his mouth and ground myself against him this time, he didn't break the kiss or push me away—he drew me in closer. His fingers dug into the hair at the back of my scalp, and he used the leverage to tilt my head a little more, giving his mouth greater access to mine. He devoured me. His tongue, his lips, even his teeth. He was hands-down the best kisser I'd ever had.

His hips started to jerk under me, matching my movements and giving me more of the friction I craved. It was sweet torture. I was exactly where I wanted to be, but it wasn't enough. I didn't think I'd ever get enough of Jet.

My body became a ball of sensation, heat coursing through me. My pussy clenched around nothing as I shamelessly rubbed myself against him. I was definitely soaking through my underwear, probably making a mess on his jeans, and I didn't even care.

I could feel an orgasm building as we clawed at each other as though possessed, but I just couldn't get there. The pleasure was heady, every nerve in my body on the precipice, but I couldn't get over that edge.

I broke our kiss, panting, and groaned. The sound was something between sexy and frustrated.

"What's wrong?" Jet's husky voice, even deeper than usual, made me shiver. Or maybe it was his swollen mouth trailing kisses down my neck as his hand on my ass encouraged me to keep grinding against him.

"Nothing. Everything is very, very right." I swallowed and gasped as he found that sensitive spot at the curve of my neck and sucked. "It's just . . . uh . . ."

He pulled back to look at me, his eyes hooded with desire, his chest rising and falling with labored breaths.

"What is it, Amaya?" Some of the lust fog in his gaze cleared, and I hated it. I wanted to stay in this bubble of hormones and pheromones forever, drunk on each other.

"I just, uh, need more. To get there." I gave him a meaningful look, and he smirked, immediately catching on to what I was saying.

"I told you I'm not going to fuck you here," he said, and I couldn't stop my shoulders from slumping dramatically. I may have even stuck my bottom lip out in a full-on pout. "But I can make you feel good in a thousand different ways without even taking my pants off."

I stared at him, my mouth falling open as I trembled a little. Was the sun setting? It could've been rising on the next day for all I cared.

"Tell me what you need, beautiful." He swiped his thumb over my bottom lip, dragging it down slightly, and I reflexively darted my tongue out to lick it. I wanted to lick every inch of this guy. And I always got what I wanted.

But right now, I wanted to come. "Touch me. Make me come."

With my permission and my demand, Jet gripped my waist and kissed me savagely. He encouraged my hips to keep rolling against his hard length as he dipped his hands under my shirt. There was no hesitancy or uncertainty in his touch; he just went for it, cupping my tits and giving them a light squeeze.

For a split second, I was self-conscious about my meager B cups, wondering if he would be satisfied with them. But then he groaned into my mouth, his kisses became sloppier, and I realized he didn't care. Guys never cared about the size of your boobs, really. They were just happy to be touching boobs.

Moving one hand to my back, he quickly discovered the bralette I was wearing didn't have a clasp, so he just pulled the flimsy lace aside and started playing with my nipples. It was just the right amount of pain as he pinched lightly, then the perfect amount of pressure as he cupped them and massaged again.

It was driving me wild, but it still wasn't enough.

"Jet." I licked his lips, panting. "I need more. *Touch me.*" I gripped his wrist and guided his hand between my legs. "Touch me here."

He didn't respond. There were no more words between us

—just panting breaths and moans as he gave me what I needed.

His hand dipped under my skirt, his strong fingers caressing my thigh. Every pass of his touch moved higher until his thumb skimmed the edge of my underwear. Then he pressed that thumb right at my entrance and rubbed it up to my clit, making me gasp.

"Jesus . . ." He swallowed, then shuddered lightly. "So . . . fuck . . . wet . . ."

It wasn't anywhere near a complete sentence, but I knew what he was saying. He could feel that I'd soaked through my underwear, and he liked it. A lot.

He wriggled his thumb under the sodden fabric and repeated the same caress from my dripping entrance to my clit. With nothing between me and his touch, the sensation was a thousand times more intense. I could feel just how wet I was, his touch gliding over my engorged flesh. After all that buildup, I was so close, but he wasn't done teasing me, exploring me.

He grazed my opening, glided up and down my lips, and flicked my clit with light movements.

I cried out and bucked my hips, but the touch vanished just as suddenly as it had appeared. I whined and frowned at him, but he wasn't looking at me. His head was hanging, his gaze fixed on the spot where his hand disappeared up my skirt.

I reached down and yanked the hem back so we'd both have a better view.

He took my lead and extracted his other hand from under my shirt. As I leaned back slightly to give him more room, he shoved the gusset of my panties to the side. I was completely exposed to him and the warm breeze, which only served to ratchet up my excitement.

He started rubbing my clit more firmly and consistently, and that breathless, rising tide began to course through me.

Shifting slightly, he brought two fingers to my entrance, but the way he had to lean to get the angle right jostled the motorbike and made me feel as if I might topple off. I startled and grabbed on to his shoulders.

We shared an amused look, and he encouraged me to lean back again. I found a good grip on the handlebars behind me, and his thick, strong fingers got back to work.

His hands grasped my upper thighs as one thumb circled my clit and the other did the same at my entrance. My arousal was dripping down between my ass cheeks, probably making a mess on the leather seat, but I didn't give a shit.

I rolled my hips, wordlessly asking for more. The thumb working my most sensitive spot circled a little harder, while his other thumb pressed at my entrance in a kind of pulsing rhythm. It was a new sensation for me—like the pressure just before a cock or finger pushed inside. Torturous but addictive, and I fucking loved it.

I started making incoherent sounds, moans, and gasps. My hips rutted against his touch, seeking more, more, more. I grabbed his arm with one hand and braced myself with the other. His bicep was like stone, even as the muscles in his arms shifted under my touch with what he was doing to me.

The thumb at my clit had found the exact rhythm and pressure I liked best, and Jet didn't change a single, minuscule thing about it. But the other thumb, the one at my entrance, dipped inside. It was the tiniest intrusion, but after so much teasing, it made me throw my head back and moan.

He took the hint, pushing his finger in as far as it would go. He found a good, firm rhythm there too, his hands working in harmony and . . .

I shattered. Pleasure coursed through my body, spreading from my pulsating cunt in electric waves. I felt it at the tips of my toes, the ends of my fingers, the top of my head. The moan I released was long, almost keening, all the ecstasy pouring out of me in that one carnal sound.

Jet slowed his movements, helping me come down from the orgasm gently. When I tried to sit up and my legs and arms wobbled like jelly, he enfolded me in his arms and drew me up against his chest.

I wrapped my arms around his neck and nuzzled against him, feeling sated and safe.

CHAPTER SIXTEEN

MY HEAD WAS STILL IN THE CLOUDS WHEN JET PULLED INTO my driveway. I hadn't been able to wipe the smile off my face, and with the helmet hiding it, I didn't bother to try.

He kissed me long and hard after I got off the bike. It didn't even occur to me to worry about helmet hair. That was how wrapped up I was in him.

"Let me know when you have the house to yourself," he whispered against my mouth, then gave my bottom lip a teasing nip.

"It's a big house." I chuckled. "I'm sure we can find privacy if we really want it. You could come in now . . ."

I took half a step back, tugging on his collar. He may have made me come only an hour earlier, but I was ready for more already. And he hadn't allowed me to return the favor.

He groaned. "I can't. I have to go do some shit."

"What shit?" I pouted.

"Boring adult shit."

"You're an adult?" I bugged my eyes out.

"I'm over eighteen, aren't I?" He raised an eyebrow.

I gasped. "Oh my god! *I'm* an adult."

With one last kiss, I peeled myself away from him and watched his ass as he rode down the driveway and out of view.

I was still thinking about that ass as I let myself into the house. But then my bubble popped.

My mother was sitting on the stairs, hands clasped between her knees, as if she was waiting for me. She looked up at the sound of the door. I couldn't remember ever seeing such a calm, serious look on her face—a face free of makeup. She actually looked like an adult.

I had a thousand questions and snarky remarks on my tongue, but I honestly could not be bothered. I just wanted to go to my room and think about Jet until the light, warm feeling in my chest returned—even just a little.

I started up the stairs, pointedly ignoring her. The staircase could have easily fit four people standing shoulder to shoulder, so it was easy to keep my hand on the banister as I passed, my gaze forward.

"Your father used to ride a motorcycle," she said when I was a few stairs above her.

The mention of my dad made me halt, every fiber of my being unable to walk away from anything to do with the parent I missed most.

"Did you know that?" she went on. "He had it when we met in college. Used to take me on dates on the back of it. I felt like such a rebel, riding around with him, knowing very well my parents would disapprove."

I gripped the banister harder, my knuckles turning white as the metal warmed under my palm.

I looked over my shoulder and glared at her. "What are you doing?"

She was staring up at me, a million different emotions in her clear eyes. The one I could make out clearly was resolve. Whatever this was, my mother was on a mission.

It made me deeply uncomfortable.

I still couldn't walk away. When was the last time she'd even mentioned Dad, not in response to something I'd said—and sober?

She'd been sober for weeks, I realized. Obviously, I'd been avoiding her and what's-his-face like the plague, but every time I'd bumped into her in the house, she'd been sober.

"Something I should've done a long time ago. Something I should've been doing all along." She smiled sadly.

"What the fuck are you talking about, Vivian?" I crossed my arms but turned to face her despite myself.

"I'm making sure you know your father."

What? My breathing sped up as I glanced up the stairs. Half of me wanted to run away from whatever this bizarre conversation was, and the other half wanted to stay, hear more, ask a million questions.

As if she could sense my instinct to bolt, Mom kept talking. "When your dad died, it broke me. He was the love of my life, and I literally didn't know how to exist without him. But that's not an excuse for how horribly I've failed you as a mother. I have not been here—physically or any other way. I know that. And I am so very deeply sorry, Amaya."

I gaped at her, my brain struggling to process what I was hearing. In total shock, I flopped down on the stairs. She was actually admitting it? She was sorry? *What?*

Mom scooted her butt up two steps so she was sitting next to me. "You've grown into an amazing, capable, smart young woman, and I missed it. Parents say that all the time—blink and you'll miss them growing up—but I really did miss it all. And I can't tell you how much I regret that. I regret so many things, especially not talking about your father. I see a lot of him in you, and I should've kept his memory alive. I should've been here to talk about him and show you pictures and tell you stories. Instead, I . . ."

She trailed off, and I forced the lump in my throat down before speaking. "Instead, you were off self-medicating and pretending like it had never happened. Pretending you didn't have a daughter."

"You're right." She nodded, resigned. "You reminded me so much of him. You still do."

"And that makes it OK? How is that my fault?" I could feel the anger rising along with my tone. This was it—she'd yell at me, and we'd end up in a pointless fight like usual. At least it was familiar territory.

Except she didn't yell. She wiped at the moisture under her eyes and spoke in a calm, if strained, voice. "It's not. It's not. I'm just trying to be honest with you, Amaya. And to apologize. I'm sorry."

"You think that's going to fix everything?" I gripped the step on either side of my hips. "You can't just say 'oops! I fucked up for seven years straight. My bad!' and expect everything to be OK."

"Of course not." Once again, she didn't let her anger rise to meet mine. It stumped me—again. "I know an apology is not going to fix all the pain I've caused you, all the damage I've done to our relationship. Maybe nothing will, but as long as I'm breathing, I'm going to show you with my actions and my words that I'm serious. I want to repair our relationship, and I'm going to be here. I'm going to keep trying, keep showing you as long as I live. And I know those are just words too, that it's going to take time for you to start to believe me, but I'm going to prove it to you. I love you, Amaya, and I want to be in your life."

What the fuck was I supposed to do with that? How dare she spring this emotional clusterfuck on me when I was mad at her? Although I'd been mad at her for years now, so maybe that was neither here nor there.

I stared at the grain in the wooden step beneath my feet.

This was exactly what I'd wanted to hear from her since . . . I didn't even know when. It had been years. But I was too jaded—I couldn't trust her.

But I wanted this so badly. I hated to admit it, even to myself, but I wanted my mom.

"I can't pretend like none of it ever happened," I told the wood grain, my voice low. Out of the corner of my eye, I could see her nodding. "And I'm not ready to forgive you. I don't know if I'll ever be." More nodding and a stuttering inhale from my mom that made my own throat tighten. "But I've wanted to hear you say some of this stuff for a long time. I'm just not sure if I can trust you yet."

For a few long moments, we sat in silence.

I sighed. "I am sorry I said I wished you'd died instead of Dad though. That was harsh."

She chuckled—a watery, emotional release of tension—and I finally looked into her eyes.

"Way harsh," she agreed. "But I probably deserved it."

I shrugged, not disagreeing. Still, wishing death on someone was pretty fucked up, and if I was being honest, it had been playing on my mind.

"Can we have dinner together?" she asked tentatively. "If you don't have plans. We can just get takeout, nothing fancy. And I'll send Cal out for the night. I don't want to force him on you, and I'm sorry about how that situation has gone down too."

I rolled my eyes. "He can have greasy burgers with us if it's not below his high standards. It's fine."

"Great!" My mom beamed. I hadn't seen her look so happy since I was in elementary school.

"What's brought on this sudden change?" I had to ask. "You get a personality transplant or something?"

She laughed. "It may seem sudden to you, but I've been working hard to change things for months now. It's not an easy road, but I found something that helps to smooth it out. It's how I met Cal, actually. I know he seems like he came out of nowhere too, but we've actually known each other for over a year."

"OK." I was starting to feel drained from the heaviness of the conversation.

We stood at the same time.

"I'm going to take a shower." Before I could think about it too much, I leaned forward and gave my mom a quick hug. I ran up the stairs and into my room without looking at her. Without letting her see the tears on my own face.

CHAPTER SEVENTEEN

I LEANED FORWARD TO TAKE A SIP OF MY GREEN GODDESS smoothie, doing my best to keep my hands steady for the nail tech.

"What shape did you say you'd like?" She glanced up at me as she finished cleaning up my cuticles.

"Coffin, please." I gave her a smile, not even bothered that I'd had to repeat myself. I was in an unusually good mood, and nothing could ruin it.

I'd taken my last final exam the day before, prom was tomorrow night, and there had been no drama with Mom. I felt lighter than I had in ages.

Donna sat to my right, Mena on her other side, as we all got our nails done for prom. Harlow hated having any length on her nails and wasn't going to prom, but she didn't want to miss out, so she was hanging out in a spare chair between me and Donna.

"I can't believe you and Jet still haven't boned." Harlow shook her head, rehashing a conversation from last night.

I wanted to smack her, but my hands were otherwise

occupied, so I settled for glaring. "We've only been together for a few weeks."

"Never stopped you before," Donna added helpfully.

"True," I mumbled. "Honestly, between exams and my mother being an actual parent, we've hardly had any time together lately."

"I'm so happy I didn't have to do the exams." Harlow stretched her arms over her head with a blissful expression on her face. "Best decision I ever made, quitting school."

"So, things are still good with your mom?" Mena asked me.

"Yeah." I smiled to myself. "For now."

I'd told the girls about Mom's bombshell apology and how things had been progressing since then. They were as shocked but tentatively happy as I was. As good as things were now, it had only been a few weeks, and I couldn't let myself trust it completely yet. Still, the hope grew with every day. My mom and I had been having dinner together almost every night, we hadn't gotten into any fights, and she was asking me about everyday shit and listening as if she really cared. Cal was growing on me more and more too. He treated my mom well, and he had his own money, so I knew he wasn't using her.

"Hey, what did you guys put for question eight on the statistics paper?" Donna asked, chewing her bottom lip.

Harlow, Mena, and I all groaned. Donna hadn't been as unburdened by the end of exams as the rest of us. She couldn't seem to stop questioning her answers.

"Shut up, Donna," Harlow whined in that way only a sister could. "As if you won't have the best results of the entire graduating class."

"You shut up." Donna jerked her head to the side to glare at her sister, earning a disapproving look from her nail tech.

"I couldn't tell you a single thing that happened within the walls of Fulton Academy over the past four years, let

alone a specific question on an exam. I've blocked it all out,"
I declared.

"I'm sure you aced it, Donna." Mena gave her a sweet
smile. "You have nothing to stress about. I'll be happy to get
average grades. It's been a hell of a year."

We all nodded and fell into silence. Between the kidnapping, roofie-ing, blackmail, fight clubs, and shootings, it had
certainly been a doozie. Someone needed to write a book
about this batshit year we'd had. It would make a great
romantic suspense.

The conversation turned to lighter topics, and we went
out for lunch after. It ended up being a perfect day with my
#DevilbendDynasty girls, and I was walking on air when I
got home later that afternoon.

There didn't seem to be anyone around downstairs, but
when I headed up, I could hear faint music coming from
Mom's side of the house. I dumped my purse and a few shopping bags in my room and wandered over.

Briefly, I second-guessed the decision—what if they were
having an afternoon delight? Gross! But I glimpsed the wide-
open door to Mom's bedroom, and her voice floated down
the hall singing along to "Total Eclipse of the Heart," totally
off-key. Confident I wasn't about to get an eyeful of Cal's bare
ass—or worse—I walked into my mom's room.

I knocked softly on the doorframe and leaned on the wall.

Mom turned to face me, a dress on a hanger in each hand,
and beamed.

"Amaya! Thank God you're here. I need help deciding on
a gown. My boobs look great in this one." She held up a
sparkly red number, then switched to the other dress—a lacy
blue one. "But this one brings out the color in my eyes, I
think. But then, I was thinking . . ." She mumbled something
I couldn't hear as she skipped over to her bed. It was
covered in dresses every color of the rainbow, making it

impossible to see what the sheets even looked like underneath.

I shoved some of the dresses aside so I could sit. I used to hang out in my parents' bedroom all the time as a kid. I loved jumping on their big bed, or sitting in the middle and watching Mom get ready for some fancy event. She'd let me play dress-up sometimes, and Dad would come in wearing his tux and dance with me, my feet on the tops of his, before they went out. I hadn't been in this room in years. It was a little strange to think about—a room in my house I'd avoided for that long.

"What's this for?" I asked.

"A party tomorrow night. It's black tie."

"Not buying a new gown for it?" She usually did. Vivian was never seen in the same outfit twice.

She shrugged and dug around in the pile. "My wardrobe feels like a boutique anyway, so I figured I'd pick one I already have. But now I'm having so much trouble deciding . . ." She propped her hands on her hips. "Maybe I should just go out and get something new. Wanna go shopping?"

I laughed. "I'm sure we can find something."

We started going through the dresses together. I ended up in a vintage eighties number with massive shoulders while Mom tried on dress after dress. Some of them didn't fit anymore and some were too dated, but we found a few options that we had fun styling with the accessories she had.

A shimmery silver fabric near the corner of the bed caught my eye, and I dug it out.

"Oh, that one's too short for black tie." Mom waved it off.

I held it up, inspecting it. It was strapless with a corseted top and looked as if it would hit about mid-thigh. The fabric was stunning, the shape perfect for Mom's delicate shoulders. She was right though; it was too short for black tie.

"I have an idea." I jumped up and went to her wardrobe,

digging through her clothes until I found what I was looking for. I handed the silver dress and the other item I'd found to my mom and ordered her to put them on. She gave me a skeptical look but started to remove the dress she was currently in.

I ran to my room and grabbed a clutch I knew would be perfect.

By the time I came back, Mom had the silver dress on and was stepping into the midnight-blue tulle A-line skirt I'd pulled out. The skirt was knee-length.

"I don't think this works, baby." Mom frowned down at herself.

I held up a finger and went in search of the perfect shoes and accessories. With everything gathered, I turned Mom's back to the mirror and dropped to my knees. I pulled the skirt down and tucked it in under the hem of the dress, then gestured for Mom to try on a pair of silver heels. After she put in some earrings and I secured her necklace, I swiveled her to face the mirror.

She gasped and turned a shocked look at me. I grinned at her in the mirror, satisfied with myself.

With the midnight-blue skirt tucked underneath the silver dress, it suddenly looked like a fit-and-flare floor-length gown. The silver shoes with jeweled detail matched the silver of the dress and went great with the jeweled blue clutch I'd grabbed. A sapphire choker and earrings completed the look.

"I can sew the skirt onto the bottom of the dress," I explained as I gathered her hair up. "It won't take me long. But I think you should wear your hair—"

I lost my grip on her locks as she turned to pull me into a hug. "It's perfect!" She bounced on her toes for a moment, then held me out at arm's length and looked at me as if she'd just made some amazing discovery. She'd been doing that a lot lately—gaping at me as if she couldn't quite believe what

I'd turned into. "I'm so proud of you, Amaya. You're amazing."

"Thanks, Mom." I ducked my head and started tidying up some of the mess we'd made. Her affection still made me uncomfortable, but at least I wasn't running out of the room anymore. Progress, or whatever.

"Are you going to do fashion design at college? Or something else?" Mom asked, taking everything off and placing it in a neat pile.

I shrugged. "Not sure yet. I've applied to a bunch of colleges but . . ."

"What?" she prodded as she pulled on yoga pants and a T-shirt.

"I'm thinking about taking a gap year."

"Oh?" She started putting the dresses back on their hangers. We floated around each other, keeping our hands busy while I mustered up the courage to say what I wanted to say.

Fuck it. "I think I want to travel for a while first."

"That's a great idea!"

"I want to spend some time in Sri Lanka. Do you think Uncle Inesh and Aunt Ravima would want to see me?"

Mom paused with her back to me, her hands on the hanger she'd just returned to its spot on the rod.

After a moment, she took a breath and turned to face me with a brittle smile. "I think they'd be beyond ecstatic to see you, baby. They can show you where your dad grew up, tell you things about him that I don't know—his childhood and stuff."

"Yeah?" I didn't know what I'd expected, but relief flooded through me at her positive, if strained, response. I really wanted to get in touch with my Sri Lankan roots. My father's parents had passed away before I was born, we'd lost touch with his family after he died, and I had no idea about his culture. But something deep inside me craved to know more. I felt as if I could know him better through learning about his heritage.

"Of course. It's my fault you don't have a relationship with them. I'll reach out and talk to them."

"Thanks, Mom." I gave her a hug and let her hold on for a long time. I could tell it was hard for her to talk about this—about *him*—but she was making an effort for me, and I really appreciated it.

CHAPTER EIGHTEEN

I DIDN'T REALIZE UNTIL THE NEXT DAY WHAT I'D HELPED my mom prepare for. The girls and I had plans to get ready for prom together at Donna's place. We had someone coming to do our hair and makeup, and the boys would come pick us up in a limo.

I had all my things ready to go in a duffel, and I went to the fridge to grab a kombucha before leaving. Cold drink in hand, I shut the fridge door and came face-to-face with the invite to Raine Clayton's party.

"Fuck." I snatched the invite off the fridge and double-checked the date. It was definitely tonight. I tried to tell myself that maybe they were going to something else, that I shouldn't let my worry get out of hand, but I didn't want my mom anywhere near the culty weirdos of BestLyf. All previous experience pointed to the organization being seriously dangerous.

Kombucha forgotten on the counter, I headed back upstairs. I had to know.

"Mom!" I called as I took the stairs two at a time.

"In the sitting room," she called back, and I rushed past

her bedroom to the cozy lounge area. She and Cal sat in armchairs facing the massive window, cups of tea in hand. "Did you forget something?"

They both turned to face me. I'd already said goodbye and made plans for them to pop over to the Meads' on their way out so they could see us all ready for prom.

"Is this where you're going tonight?" I thrust the invite at them. Mom frowned down at it, and Cal took the thick piece of impending doom from my outstretched hand.

"Yeah. Why?" Mom leaned on the arm of the chair to face me more fully.

"Please don't." I could hear the desperation in my voice.

She took my hand. "I promise I won't forget to stop by the Meads' to take pictures, baby. We're planning to be late to the party."

I kneeled down next to her chair. "It's not that. I just . . . these are bad people. I'm worried. Please just skip this one."

Mom and Cal shared a look that I was too frazzled to decipher. Were they just concerned about my weird behavior? Or was it something more?

"Holy shit," I breathed out as I sat back on my heels. So very many things were clicking into place at the same time, and the weight of it all nearly crushed me.

She said she'd been working on herself for over a year. She'd been going to "meetings" even though she didn't work. Just yesterday she'd told me that was how she met Cal—through whatever this journey of self-improvement was.

"It's just a party, sweetheart. There's nothing to worry about." Mom tried to calm me down, but I could hear the concern in her voice. I was just as concerned about her, and I had better reason to be.

All the horrible shit that had been happening—all of it tied to BestLyf—flashed through my mind like a waking nightmare. And it jogged my memory of something else. It had been a traumatic night, and I'd forgotten about it, but I'd seen Cal talking to Shady in Devilbend North that night. Shady definitely had his finger in multiple BestLyf pies.

"You dragged her into this," I said, getting to my feet. I needed to be higher than him.

Cal remained seated, slowly placing his mug on the side table. "No, I didn't. We met through BestLyf, but only after Vivian had been attending the seminars for some time. I swear to you, I had nothing to do with recruiting her."

"I don't believe you." I didn't know what to believe.

"Amaya." Mom got to her feet and took my hands in hers. "One of my friends took me to my first BestLyf seminar. Not Calvin. I wouldn't have even gone if I wasn't wasted when she dragged me there. Now, I won't lie and say I wasn't sucked in —I was. They're very persuasive. I spent a lot of money on their seminars and courses, started to get a bit obsessed with passing up to the next level. But Cal helped me realize what was really important." She threw him a warm smile—a look that lingered—and I realized my mom was falling in love with this man. If she wasn't in love already.

That was a whole Pandora's box of mixed feelings I wasn't ready to open.

"We both came to realize that BestLyf is not for us," Cal agreed but didn't elaborate.

I looked between them. "What do you mean?"

"It's . . ." Mom sighed and glanced at Cal again. "Look, we can talk about it some other time, OK? You're going to be late for your hair and makeup."

"Fuck the hair and makeup, Mom! I don't want you involved with these people."

"I'm not." She squeezed my hands for emphasis. "I prom-ise. I'm glad I went, because it was helpful initially, and it led me to meeting Calvin, but I'm done with it."

"Then why are you going to Raine's party?"

"A lot of important people will be there. Raine is very well connected—even with people not part of BestLyf. Calvin and I are planning to start a business, and this party is a great opportunity to network."

"You're starting a business?" Maybe some of those meetings actually were business related. My mother was making my head spin with all these surprises. But I started to feel better about the whole situation. She didn't seem to be sucked into a cult. She was happier and healthier than I'd seen her since before Dad died. Maybe I was overreacting.

"Yes. I'll tell you all about it tomorrow. I promise. Now, go get ready for prom." She nudged me toward the door. I looked between her and Cal, chewing on my bottom lip.

"I won't let anything happen to your mom, Amaya," Cal said with a serious expression. I supposed he wanted to reassure me too, and he had been consistent so far.

"OK, fine," I relented. They would be in a room full of the most prominent members of Devilbend society. What was the worst that could happen? Still . . . "Can you please check in with me during the night? Just so I'm not worrying."

"If it'll get you to go and enjoy your prom, fine, I'll send you a few texts." Mom rolled her eyes.

"Every half hour," I demanded.

She pursed her lips. "Every hour."

"On the hour." I raised a brow.

"Deal."

"Deal."

Then she literally herded me out of the room, and I headed out with a smile on my face.

Mom would be fine. And I would have fun tonight. I fucking deserved it.

CHAPTER NINETEEN

WHILE MOST GIRLS LIKED TO MATCH THEIR DRESS TO THEIR date's tie, my girls and I picked our outfits to match one another. This plan had been in the works for months—well before Harlow dropped out—so she joined us in getting ready too. Even though she wasn't going to prom. Easton was taking her out on an elaborate date to some fine dining place so the outfit wouldn't go to waste.

She was in a mini dress with a sweetheart neckline and a sheer layer that fell to the ground, her hair in a high, sleek ponytail. The dress was a rich royal blue, and she wore hot pink heels and accessories with it. We'd all agreed on royal blue as our theme color. It matched all our complexions and was easy to individualize.

Donna wore a dramatic fit-and-flare with a black leather corseted top. She was leaning into her Dark Donna vibes with smoky eye makeup and killer heels.

Mena had gone full ballgown after saying, "Fuck it! How many opportunities are we going to get to wear a completely over-the-top princess dress?" It had a cream silk bodice and silk flowers around the bottom hem with layers and layers of tulle.

I'd gone for a solid royal-blue halter-neck gown with a slit and detailed white beading around the waist. I loved how well we matched while still expressing our individual flair.

We took a bunch of pictures on our phones, gushing about how amazing we all looked, before we headed downstairs.

The boys had arrived to pick us up, and my mom and Cal stood with the girls' parents, chatting and waiting for us to make our grand entrance. Even Easton was there to pick up Harlow. He stood at the complete opposite end of the foyer from her dad, looking constipated. But his eyes practically turned into hearts when he caught sight of Harlow leading the way down the curved staircase.

Hendrix looked Donna up and down as if studying the dress and figuring out the fastest way to get it off her. He was lucky all eyes were on us, multiple cameras going off.

Turner was the first to step forward, taking Mena's hand and placing a gentlemanly kiss on the back as she reached the bottom of the staircase. His thoughts were just as dirty as Hendrix's—he just hid it better.

Everything became background noise when I caught Jet's eyes. He looked ridiculously hot. I loved him in jeans and his leather jacket, could hardly keep my eyes off him in shorts at the gym, but I'd never seen him in formalwear. He was in a gray suit, his tie perfectly matched to the blue of my dress. All the guys had royal-blue ties on, indulging us girls and our matching-outfits vision.

"Wow," he mouthed as he watched me. His eyes practically sparkled, taking in all the details. If I was the kind of girl that blushed, my cheeks would've been red as a fire truck. I still couldn't hold back the little grin that tugged at the corners of my mouth.

The boys stepped forward with boxes that they opened to reveal three unique corsages. We'd all hated the idea of a traditional corsage—it would've completely clashed with the style of my dress—so we'd opted for ring corsages. Jet slid the delicate arrangement of little flowers onto my finger.

The parents all oohed and aahed, taking more photos.

Harlow and Easton used the distraction to have a chaste kiss.

"Can I meet the boy who has my daughter smiling so wide?" Mom gripped my elbow and looked between Jet and me with a smile.

"Sure! Mom, this is Jethro. Jet, my mom."

"It's a pleasure to meet you, Mrs. Ellis-Lahari." Jet took Mom's hand in a polite shake and turned on the charm. "I can see where Amaya gets her beauty from."

Mom threw her head back and laughed. "Yes, well, she gets her stubbornness from me too, so good luck with that." She didn't even bother to correct him on her last name. She was an Ellis, and I'd gotten both my parents' last names.

"She knows her mind. I love that about her." And just like that, he had my mom in his pocket and me falling a little harder for him.

"Mom, you look amazing." I took a step back to take her in. I'd sewn the skirt on the night before, and she had on the outfit I'd put together for her.

"Thanks to you." She beamed at me before taking a spin.

Mom introduced Cal, who shook Jet's hand and gave him a cold greeting before moving away to talk to Donna and Harlow's dad. I frowned, wondering what was up his ass all of a sudden, but Jet didn't seem to notice.

After approximately sixteen hours of cameras and phones in our faces, the parents finally waved us off, and we piled into a limo after saying bye to Harlow and Easton.

As soon as the car was moving up the drive, Hendrix

turned to Donna. "Your tits look *amazing*!" He released something between a groan and a whine, and we all busted out laughing.

"How long have you been holding that in?" Turner teased as he popped the cork on a bottle of champagne.

"Since they started bouncing down the stairs." Hendrix adjusted his junk and stared at Donna's boobs, getting his fill now that the parents weren't around.

"Excuse you, we did not bounce." Mena crossed her arms. "We floated down the stairs like ladies."

"Yeah, I'm pretty sure he's referring to Donna's boobs," I said before taking a sip of champagne.

We laughed and joked all the way to Fulton Academy. The school could more than afford to hire out a venue for the prom, but why bother when we had a ballroom already? Because no one at our school would be seen dead wearing designer formalwear inside a high school gym.

Nicola squealed when she saw us and gushed about our matching dresses. We joined our friends at our table, and not long after, I felt my phone vibrate. It was one minute past the hour, and there was a message from Mom.

She'd sent a selfie, a spacious powder room in the background. I smiled and sent one back.

The night seemed to be going by in a flash. Everyone was in a good mood, there was no drama, Mom kept checking in as promised. There was food and (spiked) punch, Headmistress Perry gave a speech, and we danced.

When a slow song came on, Jet pulled me into his arms. I wrapped my arms around his shoulders and gave in to the cliché prom moment as we swayed from side to side.

"You are so damn beautiful." He looked me right in the eyes as he said it, drawing me a little closer.

"Thank you," I whispered and rested my cheek on his shoulder. I was responding to his compliment, but I was thankful for so much more. He'd been there for me when I hadn't even realized I needed him. He made me feel safe. I was thankful for *him*.

The official prom ended not long after, but in true Devil-bend fashion, the party was set to go on. Nicola was hosting an afterparty at her place—a penthouse apartment in the tallest building in Devilbend.

We all piled into the limo once more, a little more disheveled than we'd arrived but in high spirits. Drew and a few of the football team guys joined us for the ride, so the car was rowdy.

It still didn't stop Donna and Hendrix from making out as if no one was there. Mena and Turner were giggling about something, their heads together.

I pressed my body against Jet's side, and he gripped my thigh.

"I miss you," I breathed against his ear, then gave it a little nibble. His chest rose with a deep breath.

"I'm right here, beautiful." He turned to capture my lips in a soft, lingering kiss.

"I know, but . . ." I sighed. I saw him every day at school, but everything had been so hectic with exams and my mom that we'd hardly had any time together. I was so ready to get into his pants. "My mom and Cal are still at that party, which means the house is empty."

"Hmmm?" He flashed me a little smirk.

"Do you want to just ditch the party and go back to my place?"

"Nobody's ditching anything!" Hendrix shouted before Jet could reply. We'd come to a stop, and everyone was getting out of the limo. Hendrix wrapped an arm around Jet's neck and practically dragged him out onto the street.

I threw Donna an unimpressed look. "You couldn't distract him with your tits for just a few minutes longer?"

She just shrugged. "Come in and have a few drinks with us before you bail to get laid."

"Yeah, come on, Amaya. You can get dick anytime. Prom only happens once." Mena held her hand out to me.

With a sigh and an eye roll, I let her pull me out of the car.

We went up to Nicola's, where the party was already pumping. Every time a new group of people came through the door, everyone would cheer and hoot as if celebrating some epic win. I supposed we were. We'd survived high school—that was something to celebrate.

I had a few drinks and hung out with my friends, but once everyone was distracted, I went looking for Jet.

I found him in the far, shadowed corner of the balcony with his phone pressed to his ear. He frowned and murmured something to whoever was on the other end before noticing me meandering toward him.

He held his arm out, and I settled into his side.

"OK. I gotta go. Bye." He hung up and planted a kiss on my forehead.

"Everything all right? Who was that?"

"Yeah . . ." He looked uncertain for a second but shook it off. "Nothing that can't wait until tomorrow. Look what I found." He gave me a cheeky look, glanced behind us at the raging party, then pulled open a sliding door and tugged me into a dark room.

I giggled, feeling a little naughty that we'd entered a room that looked off-limits. "What is this place?" I could just make out a desk, a couch, shelves filled with books and knickknacks.

"I think it's Nicola's mom's office." Jet shrugged. "The door is locked, but they must've forgotten the one to the balcony." He flicked the lock. "But that's locked now too."

I launched myself at him. All I'd wanted all night was to

be alone with him, and now that I finally was, I wouldn't hold back.

He grunted as I collided with his chest, but recovered quickly to wrap me in his arms. I kissed him hard, my tongue demanding that we go deeper. He obliged with enthusiasm, our mouths devouring. He'd lost his suit jacket and tie somewhere already, and I started attacking his buttons. I stepped out of my shoes and dropped my clutch as we shuffled toward the couch.

With a shove from me, Jet fell onto the cushions, and I didn't waste any time hitching up my dress to straddle him. He was hard already, and I ground my core against his erection, finally, *finally* getting the kind of attention I'd wanted all night—all week, if I was being honest.

"Fuck, I am so horny," I groaned as I rolled my hips and rubbed against him harder.

He replied with a deep moan from the back of his throat, his mouth busy at my neck.

"Please tell me you have a condom." My voice was breathy.

Jet lifted his hot mouth from my neck and gripped my hips. "Shit." He sounded pained.

"Dammit, Jethro!" I slapped his shoulder . . . then groped it. He was so solid and strong, and his muscles practically danced under my touch.

"I didn't think I'd need one."

"Neither did I." I hadn't been expecting to find a secret dark corner of privacy. "Stay right there. Donna and Hendrix will have some for sure. Or I'll just raid the bathroom. I mean, it's a party full of horny, drunk teenagers in a movie star's penthouse—I'm sure I can find a few spare rubbers."

I moved to stand as I spoke, but Jet grabbed my wrist. "Don't go," he whined.

"Jet, I may be horny and embracing all the prom night clichés, but I refuse to add teen pregnancy to the list."

"That's not what I meant." He pulled me back down into his lap. "Let's just slip out of the party. No one will notice now. You think your house is still empty?"

"Yeah, probably . . ." I grinned and leaned down to kiss him again. His hands cupped my breasts, and our hips began rocking once more as we started to get carried away. But then it occurred to me that I hadn't checked my phone in a while.

I sat up, glancing around for my clutch.

"What's wrong?" Jet asked, his eyes glued to where his fingers slowly teased the front of my dress down.

"Nothing, I just . . . can't stop thinking about my mom." I twisted the other way, struggling to see in the dark.

Beneath me, Jet froze and pointedly pulled my dress back up over my boobs. "Uh . . . what?" He chuckled.

I laughed and scrambled off his lap. "She promised to check in, and I'm just a little worried . . ." I spotted my bag and picked it up, digging inside for my phone.

It was thirty-eight minutes past midnight, and the last check-in text I'd received was at eleven. I had three missed calls, but they were all from Harlow. Ignoring the calls, I quickly texted my mom.

I chewed on my lip as I stared at the screen, waiting for a reply. She'd just forgotten. It was getting late. Maybe they'd already gone home and fallen asleep.

Jet appeared at my back, startling me. I'd been so focused on my phone I hadn't even heard him get up.

"Hey," he whispered gently, rubbing my shoulders. "What's going on?"

"My mom is at this party, and she hasn't checked in like she promised. I'm just a little worried."

"Why? She's with the Calvin guy, right? It's just a party."

My phone rang, but it was Harlow again. I sent it to voice

mail, not wanting to miss my mom's reply. Harlow was probably drunk and calling to tell me how much she loved me.

"It's at this evil woman's house, and there's a cult and shit . . ." I waved a hand over my shoulder. "It's a long story."

Jet just kept massaging my shoulders. He probably thought I was some crazy conspiracy theorist.

A text came in, but the relief had barely washed through me before worry pushed it right away. It wasn't from my mom. It was from Harlow.

"God, she's persistent tonight," I mumbled as I opened it.

H: Call me back ASAP! I couldn't sleep so I started looking at pics online from that party. And then something in my memory clicked so I looked it up. The guy your mom is with—his name is Calvin CLAYTON. He's Raine's son!

An image came through underneath the text—a posed picture of a younger Cal with Raine. It looked like a newspaper clipping, with a caption naming them as mother and son.

"Oh my god." Panic had me breathing hard as I shoved my feet into my shoes and ran for the door.

Jet was hot on my heels, asking worried and confused questions.

I dialed Mom's number as I fumbled with the locked door. With steady hands, Jet moved me aside and unlocked it, and I rushed out into the hallway. Thankfully, the office was near the front door and I wouldn't have to shove my way through the party.

The call went to voice mail. I redialed the number as I jabbed repeatedly at the elevator button. The doors finally opened just as the call went to voice mail again.

"Fuck!" I yelled at the ceiling before continuing to blow up Mom's phone.

"Amaya, you're freaking me out here." Despite his words, Jet sounded pretty calm, if deadly serious.

"Harlow just texted. Calvin is Raine's son."

"OK." Jet nodded, as if waiting for more.

"Raine runs BestLyf. She's a dangerous person, and that whole organization is fucked up! And he's her son!" The slow elevator and constant unanswered calls were getting to me—I felt frantic. "I just need to know she's safe."

Jet pulled me into a tight hug, and instantly I calmed down a little. "Everything is going to be fine. Where's this party? Let's go there and check on your mom."

I released a shaky breath of relief. He wasn't getting irritated or treating me as though I was losing it—even though I kind of was. He was going to come with me and help. "It's only two blocks away."

The elevator doors opened, and we rushed out onto the street.

CHAPTER TWENTY

EVEN THOUGH MOM HAD CALMED MY FEARS ABOUT THE party, I'd still figured out where Raine's building was and how to get there from school and from Nicola's. So I didn't waste time looking it up—I just ran. I cursed the Louboutins on my feet but didn't bother taking them off. I spent more time in heels than I did barefoot; removing them wouldn't make me any faster.

As we turned the corner—the building entrance just a few feet away—my phone rang.

"Mom!" I yelled into it as soon as I accepted the call, coming to a stop.

"Amaya?" She sounded as panicked as I felt. "What's wrong? What happened?"

"Are you OK?" I was panting, and even Jet was breathing a little heavier next to me as he rubbed my back.

"Am I OK? I have, like, a thousand missed calls from you! What is going on?" The party noise in the background lowered significantly. She must've just stepped into a quiet room, but she was definitely still at Raine's.

"Can you please come downstairs?"

"Downstairs? Are you here?"

"Yes. I'm outside the building. Can you come out, please?"

"I'm on my way. Don't move." She hung up before I could insist she stay on the line. I went to call her back but decided against it. I didn't want to delay her for even a second.

I paced the sidewalk, my feet beginning to throb now that I'd stopped running and my body was catching up. I ignored them. Jet said something in soothing tones, but I ignored that too. I ignored everything and just paced while I watched the entrance to the building.

After what felt like hours of torture—but was probably merely a few minutes—Mom rushed through the brightly lit lobby and out onto the street, her eyes searching.

We ran into each other's arms. She squeezed me so tightly it almost hurt, but I finally felt as though I could breathe.

"You're scaring me, sweetheart," she said as she finally pulled back, scanning my face. "What's happened?"

"You didn't check in," I croaked, and it sounded pathetic. I sounded like an irrational child.

Mom blinked slowly, then sighed. "Seriously, Amaya Ann? I was having fun at a party. I am sorry I forgot to text you. But holy shit, you just gave me a heart attack." She turned to Jet. "Why didn't you stop her from coming all the way down here?"

He glanced between us, looking like a deer in headlights.

"It's not just that." I drew her attention back to me. "It's Calvin. I just found out and then you weren't answering and I panicked."

She frowned in confusion. "What about Calvin?"

"He's not who you think he is, Mom."

"What?"

"He's Raine Clayton's son." I dropped the bombshell, but it didn't seem to hit its mark.

"Yeah, I know . . ." Mom's frown deepened. Shit, maybe

she didn't fully appreciate the danger she was in, or maybe they had her brainwashed—my worst fucking nightmare.

"Viv?" someone called from behind me. "Is that you?"

Mom stepped around me, putting on her people-pleasing smile as she looked down the alleyway that ran down the side of the building.

"Ella? Nessa?" she called to the two women waving at her. "I didn't see you upstairs."

"Oh, we just got here! Come have a drink with us," the second one called, gesturing for Mom to come join them.

"I'm just talking to my daughter. I'll be up soon." Mom turned to face me, effectively dismissing her two drinking-buddy friends.

Whatever she'd been about to say was cut off by the screech of tires.

I turned just in time to see two men step out of an average-looking white SUV right across the alley. I'd barely had a chance to process the situation when an arm wrapped around my middle and yanked me backward.

I screamed.

The shrill sound cut through the warm night, echoing off the buildings.

Two men had my mom by the arms, and as I watched in horror, they shoved her roughly into the back seat of the car.

I screamed again, clawing at the arms keeping me prisoner—keeping me from my mom.

"Let the girl go!" a male voice shouted. A uniformed cop ran toward us from the same corner we'd rounded just minutes earlier. He had his gun drawn and pointed in my direction.

Immediately, I was released. I stumbled slightly as I shouted and pointed at the car. I didn't even know what I was saying, but I needed him to save my mom.

Mom started screaming at the same time, the sound muffled from inside the SUV.

The cop turned his gun in that direction. "Step out of the vehicle, now!" he shouted to the two men inside. Of course, they didn't. They took off, and the policeman fired, taking out a taillight.

One of the men leaned out of the SUV's window, and someone yanked me into the air and spun me around on the spot. Only as the sound of several gunshots rent the air did I realize it was Jet holding me. It had been him all along. He'd grabbed me out of the way when those men snatched my mom, and then he'd shielded me against the wall of the building when they fired at us.

Just as suddenly, his weight disappeared. I pushed off the wall, shaking.

Tires screeched again, and I cried out.

They had my mom!

I took a few running steps after the car, but it was pointless. They were gone. My mom was gone.

"Amaya!" Jet's voice stopped me in my tracks, and I turned around. "Stay with me."

He was crouching by the officer's prone form, holding his dress shirt over the bullet wound as the poor man writhed in pain.

"They're gone." His eyes turned soft as mine narrowed. "I need your help, beautiful. I need your help with this. Please."

I didn't want to help Jet. I wanted to run after my mom. But I couldn't possibly catch a speeding car, and the man on the ground was in real trouble. His arms hung limp beside him, and he'd gone really pale.

I stumbled over and dropped to my knees next to them. Jet took charge, guiding my hands to take over from his and press into the wound. The shirt was soaked, and my fingers felt disgusting in the warm, slippery blood.

"We need to call 911." My voice shook.

But I had no idea where my phone was, and I needed both hands to lean all my body weight into the bullet wound. Jet would have to call.

I looked in his direction, but he was already getting to his feet as he pulled the cop's walkie-talkie off his shoulder.

What the fuck was he doing?

He was going to leave me here, elbow deep in a dying man's blood. Just like everyone else. Everyone left me.

"Officer down!" Jet barked into the walkie as his eyes bored into mine. "Corner of Second and Willow. Two armed perpetrators in a white Toyota RAV4 driving south on Park." He rattled off the license plate number, staring me down as the truth came crashing down around me.

CHAPTER TWENTY-ONE

I'D BEEN SCRUBBING MY HANDS AT THE STATION'S bathroom sink for a solid ten minutes, but I just couldn't get the blood out from under my nails. I needed a nail brush to really get under there, and even then . . . I blew out a breath and leaned against the porcelain, the water still running.

Who was I kidding? I was going to have to get a manicure, a whole new set. The thought had barely entered my mind before guilt hit me like a punch in the gut. Avoiding my own reflection in the dirty mirror, I squirted more soap into my hands and started lathering again.

A man had nearly died, and here I was worried about my manicure. I was disgusted with myself.

I scrubbed harder, digging under my nails with my other nails.

Jet placed a gentle hand on my shoulder—barely a soft graze—but I startled anyway.

"Hey," he whispered, dragging his hand down my back.

I shook him off. "I need to wash my hands."

He sighed, then shifted until his front was at my back, his arms coming around me.

"You've been washing your hands for ten minutes. Enough." He said it in a gentle, coaxing tone, but his hands closed around my wrists, and he rinsed my hands for me.

I pushed away from the sink, fully intending to wrench out of his grip, scream at him, kick, punch, *something*. But once I was leaning back into him, all the fight drained out of me, and to my horror, my vision blurred with tears.

Don't cry. Don't cry. Don't cry.

Jet shut the water off and ripped a good chunk of paper towel from the dispenser. The brown paper felt rough against my hands, but he was gentle, patting them dry gingerly, even getting between my fingers.

He dropped the wadded-up towel in the sink, then gripped my shoulders and turned me to face him.

"Amaya," he whispered. So much emotion filled his voice, regret and conviction somehow riding the three syllables of my name.

"Don't," I rushed out. Fucking great. Now my voice was shaky too. I cleared my throat and tried again. "Just don't ask me if I'm OK. I fucking hate it when people ask that. Shit's fucked up. No need to pretend otherwise."

He rubbed my arms up and down, shoulder to elbow, and pulled me in for a hug.

I was too weak to resist. I told myself I'd react the same way if it were anyone else offering me a hug after this nightmare of a night, but that wasn't true. Despite the fact I now knew Jet had been lying to me about many things, I still felt comforted by him—his fresh smell, his sure arms around me, his firm chest under my cheek, his breath fanning the top of my head.

He'd put on a blue T-shirt with the police logo on it. His dress shirt would be totally ruined from all the blood.

I wrapped my arms around his middle and let him hold me, because it was what I needed in that moment. His strength grounded me; my breathing matched to his until the infuriating urge to cry subsided. I refused to shed tears during the conversation we were about to have.

"We don't have to talk about what went down tonight if you don't want to," he said, his arms still tight around my back. "But we do need to talk about what you learned because of it. About who I am."

My time to pull myself together was up. Because he was right—no way in hell was I leaving before I got some answers.

I extracted myself from his embrace and leaned back against the sink. With no idea where to start, I just stared at him. He was the one who had been lying to me from the first time I laid eyes on him—he could explain himself.

He licked his lips and straightened his spine. "I'm an officer with SFPD."

I rolled my eyes. No shit.

"I've been a beat cop since I graduated from the academy, but last year I applied for a spot on a task force, and I got it. It didn't take long for the task force to turn into something much bigger than anticipated. Suddenly, I was in a job that required secrecy, and most of the people I was working with were feds. I mostly just pushed papers, did grunt work for the detectives, but I was happy to be involved."

"I don't need your life story. How the fuck did you end up at my school?" I was being a total bitch, but I'd had one hell of a night, and I felt betrayed. I just wanted to know what was going on.

Jet narrowed his eyes—just slightly, just enough to tell me he wasn't going to take my shit. That was why I liked him so much in the first place.

"Amaya, you need to understand that it's not like I set out to fall for you and deceive you. I was doing my job. I'm telling you way more than I have to, because I want you to know me. I want to be real with you."

He was falling for me? I crossed my arms and chewed on the inside of my cheek. I refused to melt into him before he finished explaining himself. I wasn't about to let him hurt me again if I could avoid it.

Jet dragged a hand down his face and powered on. "A couple of months ago, my superior officers offered me an undercover gig. Some shit had gone down at a private school in Devilbend, and they wanted to see if they could get more info."

"Irene Richards," I said. That whole situation with Harlow and Easton and all the blackmail and threats was insane. It had solidified for us how sinister and dangerous BestLyf was. But then Irene conveniently died in jail before they could get more information from her, and we had to just go on with our lives, keeping our mouths shut and hoping the police did something about it. I guessed this was it.

Jet stared blankly at me, then, reluctantly, gave me a tiny nod.

"I'm guessing one of your superior officers is Detective Hopkins? You're on the BestLyf task force."

He sighed. "There's only so much I can tell you."

It was as good as a confirmation. What the hell else could possibly be happening at Fulton that they decided to set up a *21 Jump Street* situation?

"Anyway, they offered me the chance at a promotion. They said it wasn't an ideal situation due to my lack of experience, but they needed to move on it soon—before the school year ended—and I was the only one who could pass as a teenager." He grimaced, not too happy about his youthful appearance, but I could see why they chose him. As much as I'd questioned his scholarship and transfer so late in the year, I never thought he could be *that* much older than us. He had that round baby face with the dimples and the full, pouty lips.

"So why did they stick you in Devilbend North if you're supposed to be getting in with the rich and famous?" I asked.

"We came up with the scholarship story because I needed to be at Fulton and hanging around you guys, but I couldn't have anyone too interested in me."

"Like the kind of people interested in kids of the rich and famous." If BestLyf dug too deeply because he seemed like a good recruit, his cover would be blown.

"Beauty and brains." He grinned at me, letting those dimples come out to play.

"Don't." I pointed a finger at him. "Do not flirt with me right now. I'm so mad at you."

His grin fell, the serious face replacing it. "Fair enough. There's really not much more I can tell you, but considering what you witnessed, I was given permission to at least clue you in on the basics. Keeping that in mind, do you have any questions?"

I had so many important, relevant questions, but instead I blurted out the first thing that occurred to me. "Wait a minute. Is this why you wouldn't touch me with a ten-foot pole until my birthday?"

He rubbed the back of his neck, looking sheepish. "The age of consent in the state of California is eighteen. It would've been fine if I was actually your age but . . ."

"How old are you?" Oh, Jesus, Allah, and Buddha, had I been getting it on with some middle-aged man?

"I'm twenty-five." Jet pulled his wallet out and showed me his ID. It proved his age, the date right there under his name —Jethro Collin Burns.

"Well, at least your first name is actually Jethro."

"I really am sorry I lied to you." He stuffed his hands into his pockets. "But I was just doing my job. I didn't come into this looking for a relationship."

I stared at him, feeling myself harden inside and out,

prepared for the blow. My voice was even, almost monotone, when I spoke. "Right. So this was just part of your cover then. At least I know where I stand now."

Walk away! I screamed at myself in my head, but my feet didn't obey before his hands were on me again.

"Amaya, no." He gripped my shoulders and looked me right in the eyes. "I never intended to get personally involved with anyone, but I did. I was stunned by your beauty as soon as I saw you, and every time we interacted, I knew I was in more and more trouble because I can't get you out of my fucking mind. It was killing me to lie to you. Please, please . . ." His voice shook as he pulled me against his chest.

God dammit but I believed him. I returned his embrace and let myself melt into him again. He had no logical motive to try to manipulate me by declaring his feelings, not now that I knew everything.

"So, what now?" I mumbled into his chest.

"I still have a job to do," he said against my hair. "And to be able to do it effectively, I need you to keep what you learned to yourself."

I stiffened against him, my mind racing. I hadn't really thought about it yet, but of course I was going to tell my friends. My mother had been abducted, I'd been through something traumatic, and all our worst fears about BestLyf were confirmed. They had a right to know the gravity of the situation. There was no way to keep Jet's true identity out of it.

"I have to tell a few friends, Jet. They need to know. And I need them."

He held me out at arm's length and sighed, his face full of disappointment. "I can't let you do that."

"Let me?" I shrugged his hands off. I wasn't sure how much more of this roller coaster I could handle.

"You know what I mean. We can't risk my identity and

purpose at Fulton getting out. I'm so close to getting the info we need. And I'm not saying you can't ever tell your friends about us, about it all. Just not yet. I want to be with you, Amaya, more than anything I've ever wanted in my life. After this is all over—"

"I have no one." I cut him off. "Do you understand what you're asking? Those girls are my family. My mom . . ." I clenched my teeth and shoved the overwhelming emotions down. I refused to cry. I'd been a fool to let my guard down with him moments earlier. I wouldn't make that mistake again.

"You're not alone, beautiful. You have me." He moved forward as though to pull me into another embrace. I stepped aside and gave him a hard look.

"No, I don't. You just said it—you want to be together once this is all over. How am I supposed to believe you're not just telling me bullshit so I'll keep my mouth shut?"

He pressed his lips together. I could see frustration rising to meet my defensiveness. I didn't give a shit.

"Come on," he said. "You know that's not what this is. I want to be with you, but I can't risk years of work and the resources of an entire task force, the opportunity to take down some seriously bad people, on some teenage gossip."

I reeled back, momentarily shocked at his dismissive tone. He had no idea what we'd been through because of BestLyf. How dare he insinuate I was being immature or unreasonable after the night I'd had?

The outrage simmering in my veins gave me the strength I needed. I was done with this conversation, this night, and quite possibly, this man.

I stepped up to him and rolled my shoulders back. "Fuck. You," I said in an even, firm tone. Then I walked past him and out of the bathroom.

"Amaya! Wait!" he called after me as I stomped through the station and outside.

I pulled my phone out and swiped away the dozens of missed calls and text messages from my friends. I paused with my thumb over the ride-share app. I needed to get the fuck out of here, but at this time of night, it could take a while to get a ride. Plus, I really didn't want to get into a car with a stranger while my clothes were covered in drying blood.

Chewing on my lip, I glanced behind me. The station was lit up, everything clearly visible through the glass doors. Jet stood a few feet away, speaking to an older man. He kept glancing at me, as if I'd vanish if he didn't keep me in sight. Maybe I would. Maybe it would be better if I did.

The older man started walking away, and Jet threw me one more look, loaded with longing and unspoken things, then reluctantly turned to follow.

I paced the area in front of the door and called Donna.

We never called one another unless it was an emergency. If I'd been woken at two in the morning by a phone call from any of the girls, I'd immediately know it was serious.

Donna picked up on the first ring.

"Amaya? What's wrong?" She sounded a bit winded.

"Hey, D. I need a lift. Can you pick me up?"

"Where are you?"

"Police station downtown."

"I'm on my way."

Just like that. No questions asked.

The roads were dead at this time of night, and I had to pace the entry for only about ten minutes before a pearlescent white BMW pulled up out front. I jogged down the stairs as Donna got out of the car and gawked at me over the top of it.

"Holy fuck, Amaya, what—"

"I need to get out of here. Drive. Please." I cut her off,

stopping her from coming around the car and wasting time. She got back behind the wheel and took off as soon as my door closed.

I leaned my head against the seat and squeezed my eyes shut, taking a deep breath. Donna drove in silence for a few minutes, but I couldn't blame her when she started to push for answers.

"You don't have to talk about it right now." Her usually sure, firm voice was soft in the dark car. "But I need you to tell me if you're hurt, at least."

I opened my eyes to see her dividing her attention between the road and my bloodied prom dress.

"Physically or . . ." I waved my hand, looking for the right word. "Existentially?"

"Both?"

"The blood is not mine." I dug around in the glove compartment for the packet of cigarettes I had stashed there. Now that I felt safe, calm, I needed something to occupy my mind so I wouldn't think about all the blood, my mom . . .

"OK." Donna nodded and literally bit her tongue. It was killing her not to grill me for details. It actually made me smile a tiny bit as I lit a cigarette and lowered the window halfway.

Donna wouldn't usually let me smoke in her car, but even she could tell this was a special circumstance.

I pulled deep on the cigarette, feeling the smoke burn my lungs, then held it in for a second before blowing it out the window. The massive drag made me feel slightly lightheaded. Or maybe that was the shock setting in.

"I'm sorry for waking you." I took another drag, staring out the window at the trees flying by as we neared our neighborhood. "Thank you for coming to get me."

"Always," Donna said without a beat of hesitation. "You'd do the same for me."

I nodded. No doubt. I'd drop everything for my three closest friends without a second thought. They were my family. After tonight, maybe the only family I had left.

The next drag was harder to force past the lump in my throat.

"You didn't wake me up anyway," my best friend said, and I remembered that everyone had been at Nicola's afterparty.

"Shit, should you even be driving?" I knew for a fact she'd been drinking at the party.

"It's fine. I haven't had anything to drink for hours. I'm sober as fuck."

Hours. It had been hours since my mom was kidnapped. She could be anywhere by now.

CHAPTER TWENTY-TWO

DAWN WAS BREAKING AS WE PULLED INTO THE MEADS' driveway. Everything had that muted bluish tinge to it—a new day around the corner.

I didn't want it to be a new day. I had no fucking clue what to do now, and every bit lighter that it got, the more stark that reality became.

Donna and I walked into the house through the side door to the garage—only to find a crowd of people waiting for us.

"What the fu . . ." I trailed off to swallow the lump in my throat. Harlow and Mena immediately stood from where they'd been sitting together at the bottom of the stairs. I'd known they'd be here—we'd planned to all spend the night—but I hadn't expected the others.

Hendrix was leaning on the banister, Turner was sitting on the stairs behind Mena, and Drew sat in the accent chair in the corner. Even Easton was there, still in his nice slacks and shirt. The others had changed into casual clothes, but they all looked exhausted. The girls still had their makeup on.

"Jesus, guys. You have no chill," Donna grumbled.

"Yeah, well, you're the one who wouldn't let us come with you to pick her up." Mena huffed.

"Like you had any chill when you were playing dictator and telling us all what to do earlier?" Harlow raised a brow.

The two girls went to pull me into a hug, but I took a step back, acutely aware of the drying blood all over me.

That was when they saw it too. Harlow gasped and Mena's eyes filled with tears.

"It's not her blood," Donna said softly.

"What are you talking about? Why's everyone here?" I asked.

"We've all been out looking for you, A." Drew slumped forward to rest his elbows on his knees.

"You have?" I gaped at them as the girls decided they didn't give a shit about the blood and pulled me into a hug anyway. I extracted myself quickly. It was hard to fight the emotions welling up when they were hugging me like that.

"Nicola saw you running out of the party looking panicked with Jet chasing after you," Hendrix explained. "And no one could get a hold of you for hours. We were worried."

"Oh." I didn't know what to do with this. They'd all been so worried that they ran around town looking for me. And now these amazing people were all here, making sure I was OK after a sleepless night.

I took a shuddering breath, struggling again to keep my emotions under control.

"Where's Jet?" Donna asked, her expression not giving anything away.

"At the police station still, I assume," I said.

There was a loaded pause, and a few of my friends couldn't help looking at the blood all over me.

Easton broke the silence, surprising me with his question and his deathly calm tone. "Did he hurt you?"

I shook my head but had to take a moment before

answering. Because he had hurt me, just not in the way they were concerned about. "No. He saved me. But he lied . . ."

"Lied about what, hon?" Mena asked gently.

"Uh . . ." I suddenly felt so fucking overwhelmed. I looked around wide-eyed at the people who cared about me most, and stuttered. I didn't want to say it. If I didn't say it, I could pretend for just a little while longer that none of it had happened.

My gaze met Turner's and stuck. Whatever he saw in my eyes made him sit up straight.

"This has something to do with BestLyf." It was a statement, his voice certain.

I nodded, and he got to his feet to stand before me.

I kept my eyes on his. I couldn't look at anyone else—they wouldn't really understand. But Turner would. He'd lived this nightmare already.

"They took my mom," I wailed, and the emotional dam finally broke. I caught a glimpse of Turner's devastated expression before my vision blurred, and he pulled me into a fierce hug.

———

I woke up the next morning with a start, the horrible events of the previous night rushing through me as violently as wakefulness. I couldn't even have that second of disorientation where your brain takes a moment to catch up.

"You're OK. You're OK." Mena rubbed my shoulder, sitting down next to me on the couch. "You're at Donna and Harlow's. You're safe."

I drew my knees up to my chest as my heart rate slowed down. I must've fallen asleep on the couch after telling my friends all the gory details of my eventful evening. Fuck Jet for telling me to keep my mouth shut. My friends and I had been in too many situations where secrets blew up in our faces. I may not have been the most intelligent one in our friend group, but I was smart enough to learn from mistakes. I'd told them everything.

Afterward, I'd scrubbed my face and put on borrowed sweats, but I couldn't even remember drifting off. I must've just crashed once the adrenaline vacated my body.

They hadn't left me all alone though. There was an extra pillow and blanket on the sectional where Mena must've slept. Turner was in one of the armchairs. He didn't look as if he'd slept at all.

"Hey, Amaya." The girls' mom walked into the living room with a sad expression on her face.

"Good morning, Emily. Thanks for letting me crash."

"Of course. You know you're always welcome." She sat on my other side and brushed my tangled hair over one shoulder. Such a motherly gesture. I sat up and stretched so I wouldn't cry. "The girls told me what happened. Sweetheart, I'm so sorry."

All I could do was nod and frown down at my lap. What the hell was I supposed to do now?

"I want you to come stay with us a while, all right? And I won't take no for an answer. I don't want you alone in that big house. Especially not now."

I nodded again and managed a croaky "thank you."

"Are you hungry? Magda is nearly finished getting breakfast ready."

The Meads' housekeeper put on an epic breakfast spread, but I wasn't sure I could eat anything. "Maybe just some coffee to start?"

"Sure. You take your time and come get some when you're ready." With that, she left, passing Donna and Harlow on her way out.

"We didn't tell her about Jet," Harlow rushed out as soon

as her mom was out of earshot. "Just about how . . . yeah . . . what happened with your mom."

"It's OK." I sighed. "I don't give a shit about keeping his secrets anyway. He can stick them up his tight ass."

"There's my girl." Donna grinned at me.

Turner got to his feet and stretched. "I gotta go home and shower. Get some sleep. I've got a shift tonight."

"Thanks for staying. You didn't have to do that," I told him honestly. I was surprised he'd stayed, but I appreciated it more than I knew how to express. Drew and Easton had left before I got into the details. Hendrix had stayed and was probably still snoring in Donna's bed.

"It was nothing." He shrugged, and Mena walked him out.

I took some time to clean up and head into the breakfast area off the kitchen. Richard Mead had joined the rest of his family, and Hendrix looked as if he'd just dragged his ass down the stairs, while Magda bustled around making sure everyone had what they needed. She placed a steaming mug of coffee in front of me before I even had to ask for it.

"Thank you." I smiled up at her, and she gave me one of her stoic Magda looks and a firm squeeze of my shoulder. I sipped my coffee in silence and watched them all eat as a family.

Would I ever have a family? Or was I doomed to walk through life alone? My dad died when I was a kid, and my mom may as well have died the same day—that was how absent she'd been in my life. Then when it seemed as if she might finally get her shit together, she was taken. And the guy I was falling for wasn't even who he said he was.

Was it me? Was I the problem?

Thank fuck for my best friends. They were the only constant in my life. The only people I could truly rely on.

"I'm gonna head back to my place," I announced, getting to my feet. I appreciated them more than they'd ever know, but seeing them all just . . . *be* together was starting to get overwhelming.

Seven frowns were aimed my way, but it was Richard who spoke. "I insist that you stay with us, Amaya. We want to support you. We want you here."

I gave him a brittle smile. "I know. I will. I just want to go pack some things and . . ." I cleared my throat. "Honestly, I just need a bit of time alone."

Thankfully, no one insisted they come with me, but Donna did drive me home. It may have technically been next door, but both our properties were huge, and it would've taken me a good twenty minutes on foot.

The house was deathly silent when I let myself in. Maybe I was just being dramatic, but it felt empty—barren—in a way it never had. Not even when Mom would disappear on days-long benders.

Two champagne flutes rested on the console table in the foyer, a small bit of flat champagne still sitting at the bottom of one. Mom and Calvin must've had a drink before leaving last night. The other glass had her favorite shade of pink lipstick on the rim.

I picked it up and stared at the imprint of her lips on the glass.

Then I threw it against the wall with a pained, frustrated growl. It shattered, the jagged pieces tinkling on the marble floor.

Everything about this was *total fucking bullshit*. Angry tears stabbed at my eyes as I jogged up the stairs. It was so unfair.

Movement out of the corner of my eye made me freeze at the top of the staircase. I swiped away my tears so I could see properly and nearly called out.

Don't be a fucking horror movie bimbo, Amaya.

Whatever had moved was in the general area of my mom's bedroom. And I knew for a fact she wasn't in there.

The smart thing to do would be to go downstairs and get the hell out of this house. I'd come back with someone later—maybe a whole group of someones. Hell, I could get Drew and the entire football team down here if I really wanted to.

But before I could do exactly that, a head peeked out from behind the door to Mom's bedroom. When he spotted me, Calvin came fully out into the open.

"Amaya! Thank god!" He tucked something into his belt as he rushed toward me.

That was a gun. I'd seen enough of them to know that was a damn gun.

"What the fuck are you doing here?" I yelled. I didn't know why—it wasn't as though any of my neighbors' houses were close enough to hear me scream as I got murdered.

His steps faltered—he genuinely looked confused. I saw my opportunity and ran back down the stairs.

"Amaya!" he called after me.

I didn't turn to check if he was chasing me. I just ran for the front door. I flipped the lock, grabbed the handle, and yanked. It opened an inch before Calvin caught up and slammed it closed again, and I screamed.

He backed up, hands held up in front of him, eyes wide. "Amaya. Amaya! I'm not going to hurt you."

"Then why the fuck did you chase me down the stairs?" I screeched.

"Because I need to talk to you. I'm trying to keep you safe." He glanced out the window next to the door.

"Oh, like you kept Mom safe?" I gritted out, breathing hard. Now that flight was no longer an option, my body seemed to be preparing for fight. Too bad there was nothing close by I could use as a weapon. I'd just knee him in the balls.

But Calvin deflated before my eyes, his shoulders

slumping and his head falling to his chest as he stumbled backward—away from me. He leaned heavily on the banister.

I glanced at the door. This was my chance to run, but . . . was he crying? His shoulders shook, and when he wiped at his cheeks with the back of his hand, I realized he was indeed crying.

"I didn't think she'd go this far," he said under his breath, but I still heard him.

"Who? Mom?" I took a step closer, no longer interested in running away. Not if he could tell me something about where my mom was. "Where's Mom? I know you know."

He looked at me with a devastated expression. "I swear I don't. I wish I did."

"You have to know something," I spat. "You're Raine's son, aren't you? You run illegal shit for her. Don't deny it. I saw you with Shady. BestLyf took my mom, and you're going to tell me where the fuck they took her so I can get her back."

Calvin slowly straightened, steel entering his spine as his tears dried up. He fixed me with a much calmer look. "Yeah, I'm her son, but I've been slowly pulling out of the illegal shit, *all* of the shit." I scoffed, but he continued. "You don't have to believe me. That's OK. But I do have to keep you safe, Amaya. It's what your mother would want. It's what I want. Now, I want you to go pack a bag. Quickly. I'm going to take you somewhere safe."

I gaped at him. "Are you insane? I'm not going anywhere with you!" I wanted him to tell me where my mom was so I could save her—not take me to her so we could both end up . . . I couldn't think that final thought. I refused to go there.

"Amaya!" It was the first time I'd heard Calvin raise his voice, and it startled me. It was a stark reminder I was alone with a dangerous man.

Before I could even glance at the door, think about

running again, it burst open. The glass in the windows on either side of the door rattled with how hard it slammed open as Jet rushed inside, gun at the ready. Within a second, he assessed the situation, placed himself in front of me, and pointed the gun at Calvin.

"Hands behind your head," Jet barked.

"Seriously, Burns?" Calvin sighed, holding his hands out at his sides. "Drop your gun."

"Hands. On. Your. Head." Jet's voice was icy calm.

Calvin gritted his teeth but did as he was told. "This is a waste of time. I hope you have a warrant to enter my place of residence, officer."

"It's detective. And I heard shouting. I had reason to believe someone was in danger." Jet tilted his head to the side just slightly, not taking his eyes off Calvin. "You OK?"

I nodded, then realized he couldn't see me and said, "Yes."

"Anyone else in the house?"

"No," Calvin and I said at the same time.

"Am I under arrest?" Calvin asked, his tone impatient.

"That's yet to be determined." Jet lowered his gun, relaxing slightly as he went to Calvin and searched him. He took the other man's gun and placed it on a side table out of reach. "You have a permit for that weapon?"

"Yes, sir." Calvin seemed to have reached the end of his rope. He turned to address me. "Unless this jerk arrests me in the next three minutes—which he won't—I'm getting out of here. Please come with me."

"No." I shook my head and took a step closer to Jet. I may have been mad at him, but at least I knew I was safe with him. At least I could be positive he didn't have anything to do with my mother's kidnapping.

"I'm just trying to keep you safe. You need to trust me."

"I don't need to do shit."

"She'll be perfectly safe with me," Jet said, angling his

body to shield me. "Now, I'm not placing you under arrest, but we have been trying to get a hold of you since last night."

Calvin scoffed. "Yeah? Well, take a hint. I don't want to talk to any of you. They have the woman I love, and I'm going to do whatever it takes to get her back. Deal's off. Last chance, Amaya." He fixed me with an expectant look. The kind of look a parent would give to a child, expecting them to make the right choice.

"Just leave." I sighed, feeling drained again.

With a resigned nod, Calvin picked up a duffel I hadn't noticed by the door and marched out.

Once the sound of his car starting reached us through the gaping front door, I turned to Jet.

"What deal is he talking about?" I asked.

For a split second he looked as if he was fighting some kind of internal battle, but then he pressed his lips together, and I knew he'd tell me nothing. Just like last night. Just like since the day I'd met the asshole.

I shook my head and rushed back upstairs.

CHAPTER TWENTY-THREE

I LOCKED MYSELF IN MY ROOM AND RAGE-CLEANED. AFTER a good half hour, there was a knock at the door.

"Amaya?" Jet called. "Can you come out, please? We need to talk."

"Fuck off!" I shouted and threw whatever was in my hand at the door. My pen cup smacked against the wood, and pens and pencils scattered everywhere.

"Real mature, Amaya!"

I held up both middle fingers at where I imagined him standing.

After a beat, he let out such a deep sigh I could easily hear it from inside my room. "I'll be downstairs when you cool down."

His footsteps retreated, and I glared at the door. I considered climbing out the window and making a run for it, but he'd hear my car and just follow me to the Meads', so I decided to wait him out instead.

I cleaned my room until it was so tidy it looked as if no one lived there. Then I texted the girls to tell them I was taking more alone time and locked myself in the bathroom. I ran myself a bath and took my sweet time in there. I shaved my legs, washed my hair, did a hair and face mask. I even soaked off my nail extensions. I couldn't stand looking at them, even though I'd gotten them as clean as new. All I could see when I glanced at my hands was the blood that wouldn't come out from under my cuticles.

I ate the three granola bars I'd found in my desk and smoked several cigarettes, but by midafternoon I was starving.

It had been hours since I'd told Jet to fuck off through my door. Surely, he'd given up and left by now. Clean, dry, moisturized, and in comfortable sweats, I poked my head out the door. The house was silent. I made my way downstairs quietly, keeping an eye and ear out for him . . . or anyone else.

He'd really left. I couldn't believe that jerk had actually left! Yes, I'd told him to fuck off, but I didn't want to be alone in this fucking house after the last twenty-four hours. Ugh!

But then, as I made my way to the kitchen, I spotted him. He'd fallen asleep on the living room couch. His shoes were off, one arm thrown over his eyes, his mouth slightly open.

A pang of some emotion shot through my chest. I simultaneously wanted to curl up with him and smother him with a pillow while he was vulnerable. Instead, I saw an opportunity to get away.

Deciding I'd eat at the Meads', I turned to tiptoe back to the front door.

"Don't even think about it." His voice was firm and clear, if a little croaky.

I squeezed my eyes shut and huffed before turning around and heading to the kitchen. If he refused to leave, then I'd just pretend he wasn't here.

As I pulled leftover pasta from the fridge, I could see him out of the corner of my eye—sitting up, rubbing his eyes, checking his phone. Dammit! He really had been asleep for a while, and I might've been able to sneak past him if I'd just come downstairs sooner.

I glared at the microwave as my food turned inside.

"Amaya," Jet said gently, carefully, as he leaned on the counter. The microwave beeped. I grabbed my hot-ass bowl with the lukewarm food inside and made my way out to the patio table.

Not taking a hint, he followed me out after a few minutes with a sloppily constructed sandwich on a plate.

"Sure, help yourself to anything in the kitchen," I dead-panned before shoveling pasta into my mouth.

"Thanks," he said around a mouthful of sandwich. "I'm starving. I've barely eaten all day. I think I needed the sleep more though. I never made it to bed. Just had a shower after I left the station and headed here. Good thing I did too."

I glared at him as he rambled. "Oh my god. I don't give a shit."

He just rolled his eyes, and for a while we ate in silence. The food calmed some of the rage deep in my belly—smothering it with carbs. I pushed the empty bowl away and closed my eyes, enjoying the warm afternoon sun on my face. Well, as much as anyone could enjoy anything after the kind of turmoil I'd had to deal with lately.

"Amaya. Look, I know you're . . ." He sighed. "A lot of things right now. Things I can't even imagine. But I do need to speak with you."

I kept my eyes closed. "As Detective Burns? Or as my ex-boyfriend?"

After a beat of silence, I opened my eyes just in time to see a hint of hurt and uncertainty in his expression. I got a sick kind of satisfaction from knowing that at least some aspect of this mess actually upset him.

"Both," he finally said.

"OK, detective." I sat up straight and folded my hands on

the table in front of me—all business. "What's the update on my mother's kidnapping?"

"We ran the plates, but they were stolen. We managed to track the vehicle using CCTV but lost it, so that's a dead end too."

I nodded, pursing my lips. "So that's it? She's gone. Nothing you can do about it? Cool. Thanks for the completely fucking pointless update. Bye now."

"We're exploring other leads. This investigation isn't over."

"What other leads?" I threw my hands up. "We both know it was BestLyf. They're behind this. Why aren't you searching their properties? Why aren't you arresting Raine Clayton?"

"It's not that simple." He gave me a pitying look.

"Don't patronize me," I snapped. "You may be seven years older than you pretended to be, but that doesn't make *me* a child, nor does it make me stupid. I know none of this is fucking simple. And I don't care. Do you get that? They have my mom! What are you doing to find her?"

He didn't rise to my ire, keeping a cool expression and replying in a calm tone. "We have a pretty clear picture of one of the men's faces from a security camera. We're trying to identify him. We're also planning to interview some people."

"Like who?"

"The police officer who was shot, once his doctors permit it. He may have seen something I didn't catch. We're also trying to get in touch with people who were at the party, but it's proving difficult."

"Yeah, I bet it is." Of course Raine and anyone associated with BestLyf would be dodging the police. Bunch of brainwashed assholes.

"We'd also like to speak to the two women your mother

spoke to just before she was attacked. Do you happen to know who they are?"

"Yes." I nodded and grabbed my phone. I knew those two bitches all right. I gave him their names and phone numbers, but I didn't know where they lived.

"Thank you. This is helpful." He focused on his phone for a while, probably sending all the information to whoever would look into it.

"Why aren't you guys busting down their doors?" I asked quietly, spinning my phone on the tabletop. "They kidnapped a woman. Isn't that enough?"

Jet sat back in his chair heavily and rubbed his face. "I wish it was."

I scoffed. I wanted to argue more, rage at him, but I knew it wouldn't get me anywhere. I felt utterly defeated.

"Is that all, detective?" I wanted to be alone for a while longer before heading next door.

"Officially—"

I cut him off by pushing my chair back, then collected our plates and headed inside. He followed me.

"I don't want to talk to you about anything else," I said, not looking at him as I dumped the plates in the sink. "If you have any more information about my mother's kidnapping or if I can help in any way, please send someone. You know where the door is."

"Fine then." I could hear the edge of frustration in his reply. "Strictly professionally then, I'm not leaving."

I spun to face him. "What?"

"I spent half the night convincing my superiors that you needed to be under protection. I couldn't convince them to approve a safe house, but they conceded to having an officer with you for the next few days—at least until we know more."

"OK, then have them send an officer to the Meads' place. I'll be staying there for a while."

"I volunteered for the assignment."

I groaned. Of course he did.

I contemplated going to the Meads' anyway and making him sit out in his car, but I didn't want to bring this bullshit to their door. The drama with Jet was irritating, but if an argument really could be made that I needed armed protection, that was a whole other ball game. I couldn't go if there was a chance of danger following me.

Glaring at Jet, I called Donna.

"Hey, girl!" she answered on the second ring. "Was starting to think you'd drowned in that bath. You heading over?"

"Hey. Actually, I'm going to stay home." I gave her a rundown of the situation. Naturally, she still insisted I come stay with them. Then Harlow got on the phone and tried to do the same. Even Emily interjected, taking the phone from her daughter to speak to me. She demanded I put Jet on, and he answered multiple questions politely and professionally. He even recited his badge number.

I had to turn away to hide the smile that brought to my lips. It was nice to have someone looking out for me.

After we hung up, I went back to my room and back to ignoring Jet.

Not even half an hour had gone by when the doorbell rang, immediately putting me on edge. Poking my head out of my bedroom, I was grudgingly thankful to see Jet going to the door with his hand hovering over the gun at his hip.

But it was just Emily Mead. I took a moment to tuck the emotion and amusement away before heading down.

She'd brought over a clearly store-bought pie, saying she was dropping off a home-cooked meal for me while suspiciously eyeing Jet. I reassured her I was OK, and she left.

The pie was from an artisan bakery nearby, and it tasted delicious. I had it for dinner and didn't offer Jet any. He helped himself to some anyway. Jerk.

I went to bed early, determined to avoid him, and tried to read. But I had trouble focusing on the words and sentences. My mind was racing.

I couldn't stop thinking about my mom and where she might be. If she was OK. If I'd ever see her again. Then some alarmed voice in my mind would cut in with horror scenarios that included masked men barging into the house, shooting Jet dead, and taking me.

Every little sound from outside, every shift of the house, put me on high alert. I was a fucking mess inside, and I didn't have the adrenaline crash and absolute exhaustion that had made me pass out the previous night.

A little before midnight, I gave up trying to sleep and slowly padded my way downstairs.

I didn't want to admit to myself I was looking for Jet, but I was. I felt so alone, and he was the only other person in the house.

All the lights were out, but the telltale flicker of the TV in the front room lit up the foyer, so I headed there. This room was a bit more formal than the open-concept space at the back of the house with the kitchen. It wasn't used as often, but it was expertly decorated in creams and royal blues. The TV—normally hidden behind built-in cabinet doors—was on with the volume down. I didn't even register what was playing; I just headed for the couch under the window and folded myself into the corner, leaning against the armrest.

There was a whole other three-seater on the opposite side of the coffee table, and a comfy armchair, but I'd plonked myself down next to Jet. He sat reclined in the couch's other corner, a throw blanket over his lap.

He tracked my movements carefully but didn't try to talk to me. I was more thankful for that than he knew. I didn't want to talk. I wanted to sit in silence and just be. Only not by myself.

I turned my face to the screen but didn't even remotely pay attention to what was on it. Jet was looking at the screen too, but I could sense his focus on me.

After a beat, he sat up, draped the throw over my lap, and leaned back into his spot.

He'd changed out of his slacks and shirt and tie. The sweats and ribbed tank he had on now made his shoulders look even bigger than they were. He looked like the Jet I knew—the one I'd been falling for—in his casual clothes. It made my heart ache.

He was sitting right next to me, and I missed him so damn much.

Life was a fucking bitch sometimes.

I tried to spread the blanket so we could share it, but it was way too small. With a resigned sigh, I scooted closer and draped it over both our laps. Our legs were touching.

The whole thing was ridiculous. Neither of us really needed a blanket on such a warm night anyway. But I was still in the whole self-denial stage. The blanket made it easier to pretend I wasn't trying to get closer to him, because it hurt to have any distance between us.

He draped one arm over the back of the couch and looked at me, still not saying anything. His expression held no judgment, no expectations. He was just . . . open to whatever I needed.

Not allowing myself to think about it, I leaned sideways and settled into his side. After a beat, he gently wrapped one arm around me.

In a corny moment worthy of a Lifetime movie, we both released a small sigh, relief palpable in the sound. Why did it feel so damn good to be in his arms? He made me feel so safe. Despite all the bullshit keeping me up, I actually felt calm. He made something deep inside me, something intrinsic, believe everything would be OK.

But the practicalities of everything going on just wouldn't let up.

"What's going to happen to me?" I asked, my voice small.

He leaned back to look at me. "What do you mean?"

I started fiddling with the hem of his tank. "I don't know. Like, what am I supposed to do now? What if Mom needs to be in the hospital for a really long time? What if they don't find her . . ." I couldn't even go there. "I know I've had to learn to be really independent, but fuck. This is different, Jet. Is the house mine now? What about all the other assets? I don't even know who our lawyer is. I can't do this."

"Yes, you can," he said, not a hint of uncertainty in his voice.

"Jet, what's going to happen?" I asked again.

He stared me down, a million complicated things in his gaze. "I don't know, princess," he finally answered. "No one ever really knows what's going to happen. Life just doesn't work that way. But what I do know is that you won't have to deal with it alone. You have the fiercest, most supportive friends I've ever seen. I have no doubt whatsoever that they'll be ready to do whatever you need. And I know shit between us is . . . uncertain right now, but I'm not going anywhere. Not until I'm absolutely sure you're safe. Not as long as you want me around."

"I don't want you around," I declared, gripping his tank in a tight fist. I appreciated what he was saying. I'd needed the reminder that I had people in my corner. It soothed some of my panic. But I didn't want to dwell on it.

My head was all over the place—wanting to sit in silence one minute, then wanting to talk the next. Wanting him gone, then searching him out. Asking questions, then deflecting when he answered them.

"You sure about that?" Jet raised one eyebrow, glancing pointedly at where I was clutching his clothing.

"Positive." I met his eyes, still gripping the fabric in my fist.

"Then let go, Amaya."

The challenge was clear in his intense stare, but I didn't want to let him go. Not really. Not in this moment or in the bigger-picture context.

So instead of pushing him away, I pulled him closer and kissed him hard.

CHAPTER TWENTY-FOUR

His hand threaded into my hair, and he met the challenge with gusto. Our tongues battled for dominance, teeth clashing.

We were both desperate—maybe for different reasons, but the resulting intensity only amped up. I poured all my desperation, all my frustration and uncertainty, into him. He took it all and then some, giving me exactly what I needed. As he always did.

I yanked on that tank top, and he helped me get it off, putting his glorious body on display. I straddled him as I took off my own pajama T-shirt. He was already hard for me, and I ground myself on his erection. Lightning sparks of pleasure shot through my body, driving me to keep rolling my hips, keep chasing that feeling.

Jet sat up, his hands splayed on my back to keep me from falling backward. His hot mouth trailed messy kisses and scrapes of teeth down my neck until he reached my breasts. They weren't big, but I'd never had any complaints, and Jet groaned as that mouth of his closed around a pert nipple.

He grabbed my ass with one hand, his other holding me

close to his mouth as he got his fill of my tits. His hips gyrated, moving with me as I rubbed myself on his hardness, getting that friction right on my clit.

It was heady, this feeling—addictive—having him hold me as I chased my pleasure on his lap. But I'd never been one of those girls who could come from dry-humping. Fun as it was, there were still too many layers of clothing between us.

I angled his head back so I could kiss him deeply, then scooted backward. My core clenched at the loss of friction, but I dropped to my knees on the soft carpet anyway. A wet patch showed on his sweats—a darker spot of gray right over the outline of his dick under the fabric. Evidence of how turned on we both were, how hot we were for each other.

Jet sat up, his body following mine, but I stopped him with a firm hand to his chest and shoved him back against the cushions. He looked so damn fuckable, lounging back with his knees wide and his smooth chest heaving, those eyes dark and needy.

I did that to him. I had him looking dazed and crazed with lust, and that made me near euphoric. It was proof I still had control over some things. I still had agency.

Seizing the hem of his sweats, I pulled, and he lifted his hips for me. He wasn't wearing any underwear, and his cock sprang free, slapping against his toned abs. I shoved his pants down to his ankles, and he kicked them off.

The hair on his legs was coarse as I ran my palms up his shins, then added more pressure as I moved up the thighs. His dick twitched when I dug my nails in closer to his groin. I caressed his thick length with my palm, from base to tip, spreading the bead of pre-cum with my thumb. His cock felt so hard in my grip, hot and firm, and I wanted to lick it.

I'd never really been into sucking dick. It was fun to read in my romance novels, but anytime I'd come face-to-face with one, I'd turned my nose up at it. I just didn't see the appeal.

But I wanted Jet's cock in my mouth. I wanted to taste him so badly my mouth watered.

Gripping him firmly at the base, I slid my tongue up the underside all the way to the swollen head. That part was softer against my mouth. I ran my lips over it gently, then licked the salty pre-cum off them. Raising my eyes to watch him, I opened my mouth and sucked Jet's hard cock into it.

He struggled to keep his gaze locked on mine as his eyes rolled and he released a low groan.

The sound made me clench my thighs. The sight of how much I could affect him with nothing more than my mouth sent a rush of desire shivering through my body.

I sucked him off slowly, taking my time and absorbing every hitch of his breath, every twitch of his abs, every little reaction to what I was doing to him. I may have been the one on my knees, but he was at my mercy. There was something perversely gratifying about the knowledge that I could clench my jaw and bite into his cock at any moment, that he trusted me enough not to. Something addictive about learning which movements elicited the best reactions.

"Fuck, beautiful." He groaned. "I'm gonna spill down your throat if you don't stop that."

I sat back, licking my tingling lips as I contemplated the idea. I wanted him to come in my mouth. Just the thought of being able to make his body do that had more moisture seeping out between my legs.

Jet just sat there, breathing hard, his swollen, glistening cock on his belly as he waited for my next move. He was totally letting me take the lead.

I decided to indulge in my newest fantasy another day. I needed him inside me *now*. We'd waited for so long, and I didn't want to wait any longer.

I got to my feet and pushed my sleep shorts and underwear down in one go.

Jet's head tipped back against the cushions as he gazed up at me. I stood before him completely bare.

He'd made me feel stripped bare more times than I could count—completely emotionally exposed. This time, I'd bared myself to him intentionally. It was *my* choice. And he was just as bare for me. He was spread open and willing, waiting for me to take what I wanted from him—body and soul.

I moved to straddle him at the same time he leaned over to grab his wallet off the coffee table. He ripped a condom out and rolled it onto his length while I caressed his shoulders, letting my tits hang in front of his face.

He darted his tongue out to lick a nipple, then leaned back once more and gripped his dick at the base.

I shifted closer, holding on to the back of the couch for balance as I positioned myself. With our gazes locked, I sank down onto Jet's cock. I was so ready, so wet, that he slid in easily. I sighed at the feeling of stretching, the welcome intrusion of his body into mine.

Jet sat up and wrapped his arms around my back, and I spread my knees as wide as they'd go. For a few moments we just stared at each other, not moving, just feeling this wonderful sensation of togetherness. Our foreheads touched, and we breathed each other's air. The pressure, the urge to move, built up and up inside me until it was impossible to ignore.

I rolled my hips.

A surprised gasp of pleasure escaped my parted lips at how fucking good it felt. I was hyperaware of every inch of him inside me, every little twitch of his legs, every shift of his body against mine.

I tilted my head to the side, and our lips met in a deep, all-consuming kiss. We started to move, our mouths and bodies flowing in rhythm. His tongue licked at the inside of my mouth just like his cock was caressing the inside of my pussy.

I'd never had sex like this. The position, sure, but not this intensity. With the deep emotions between us, it felt as if he was reaching places deep inside me—places no one else could reach.

I guessed sex was like that when you loved the person you were having it with.

The realization made me gasp, but Jet didn't notice. He leaned back on the couch and gripped my hips, his eyes fixed on the spot where our bodies connected.

The new angle made me moan, and I decided to ignore the realization about the man between my legs. Just for now. Just while I enjoyed these feelings in the most physical, carnal way.

I grasped the back of Jet's neck with one hand and propped the other on his knee as I started to fuck him in earnest.

He caressed my body, dug his fingers into my hips, and thrust up to meet my movements. But for the most part, he lay back and let me take what I needed. I lost myself in the feeling—yes, the pleasure between my legs, but also the satisfaction of being in control. His strong body was splayed out below me as I rode his dick harder.

My entire lower body started to tingle as his pelvis slammed against my clit with every stroke. I ground myself on him, feeling him deep inside me, and surrendered to the pleasure. The heat at my core burst, carried by those tingles up my chest and into my head, running down my arms.

The orgasm seemed to go on and on but was no less intense for its duration. I moaned and writhed through it while Jet kept thrusting upward, shoving me down onto his thick cock with a bruising grip on my hips.

I released a sound somewhere between a sob and a laugh as it finally faded.

"You are so fucking beautiful when you come," Jet whispered, his voice strained. He brushed messy hair off my sweaty forehead and peppered gentle kisses all over my neck and shoulders.

I couldn't speak, so I just hummed as I struggled to catch my breath.

Jet gave me a few moments to recover before he moved. He held me tightly to his chest and stood up from the couch with ease. As if he wasn't tired from the sex so far—as if I weighed nothing.

I gasped in surprise and wrapped my tired limbs around him. Still buried inside my dripping core, he walked across the room, through the foyer, and up the stairs to my bedroom.

By the time he lowered me onto my bed and settled himself on top, I was writhing against him once more. The way he'd carried me through the house, his strong arms keeping me safe and still firmly on his dick, was sexy as hell. And the movement of him inside me as he'd climbed the stairs had me squirming.

He hitched one of my legs up high and let the other fall open on the bed. Then he positioned himself just so, one knee bent higher than the other, and pulled almost all the way out. His eyes did that fluttering, rolling-into-the-back-of-his-head thing again as he slid all the way back in. He did it a few more times—all the way out, then all the way in—slowly, feeling every inch as my pussy clenched and pulsed around him involuntarily.

His hips started to pump faster and faster. I was so wet and messy the sound coming from between us was obscene as it mingled with our moans and grunts. I clawed at his back, feeling his lithe muscles move, wanting to draw him closer.

He kept pounding into me until his movements became as sloppy as the sounds of our fucking. Then every muscle in his body went tense as he moaned long and loud, his hips slamming home one last time as he came hard.

My second orgasm took me by surprise. It was just as intense as the first, but it burst through me with such unexpected force that I screamed.

It took us a long time to catch our breath. We were spent and sweaty, but we remained tangled together, kissing and nuzzling and holding each other. It was downright fucking romantic, and it made me think of my earlier realization that I loved him.

Thankfully, I was too tired to freak out about it. Even more thankfully, Jet was alert enough to go to the bathroom and clean up, then return with a warm, damp towel. He gently and lovingly cleaned me up too. Then he crawled into the bed and covered us with the sheets.

"I love you," I murmured before I could stop myself. I was half-asleep, and the words just tumbled out onto the soft sheets between us. I kept my eyes closed to give myself an out. If he mentioned it the next day, at least I could pretend I had no recollection of saying it.

Jet placed the softest, gentlest kiss on my cheek before replying. "I love you too."

There was no doubt or uncertainty in his voice.

I snuggled into his side and smiled against his warm, bare shoulder. I was terrified to say it to him with my eyes open, in the stark light of day, but even more, I was excited. Because I did love him, and as scary as it was to say, it was worth the risk to hear him say it back, to know he meant it.

CHAPTER TWENTY-FIVE

I WOKE UP WITH JET'S ARM DRAPED OVER MY WAIST, THE
sheets tangled around our legs. Maybe it was the comforting
presence of a strong body at my back, or maybe just that the
trauma was no longer so fresh, but I didn't jerk into wakefulness in a panic as I had the day before. I had that hazy
moment of blissful ignorance. My brain was slower to wake
up and, therefore, slower to remember the situation I was in.

I thought I'd wanted this moment of respite when I woke
up yesterday, but now that I was having it—and the crash of
emotions that came when the memories rushed back in—I
realized I'd been an idiot. This was so much worse. It was like
experiencing it all over again.

Jet must've felt my body stiffen, because he tightened his
grip on me and kissed the back of my head. *I've got you*, he
seemed to be saying without words.

"Are you supposed to be sleeping on the job?" I asked.

He yawned before answering. "There was a patrol car
parked out front until six. I've been on shift and awake since
then. Don't worry, you're safe."

I didn't know what to say to that. I didn't feel safe—physically or emotionally. I had no idea where we stood, and I didn't have the emotional bandwidth to even think about it.

Instead of trying to come up with a response, I got up and headed for the shower.

My bedroom was empty when I got out, and as I headed downstairs, I could make out several voices coming from the kitchen.

"Bullshit!" Harlow dragged the word out as she yelled it. I could make out Donna's voice next but not what she was saying.

Keeping my steps light, I crept toward the kitchen. As I rounded the corner, the scene and conversation came into focus.

Jet was sitting at the island, and Donna, Harlow, and Mena stood on the opposite side with their arms crossed and their stares lethal. They were tearing him a new one.

I almost felt sorry for him.

"Do any of you seriously think I intended for any of this shit to happen?" Jet asked, sighing deeply. My friends remained silent. Only a brief glance from Mena told me they knew I was there. "I was supposed to go in, make friendly with the students, and dig up information. My assignment wasn't to single out Amaya, or to fucking fall for her. Jesus, they could have my badge for this if they really decide to throw the book at me. The only thing that's saving me is the fact she was eighteen before anything happened —and that everyone's too damn busy to worry about ethical gray areas right now. I didn't set out to hurt anyone. Especially her."

"Yeah, well, you did," Donna declared, her no-bullshit lawyer face on. "And it would serve you right if you did lose your job."

Jet laughed, kind of maniacally. "I'm not sure I even care anymore. All I've ever wanted was to make detective, and I did it with this task force, but all I can think about is Amaya

—being with her, seeing her safe and happy. I love her, and I just want this bullshit to be over."

"So, what do you expect us to do now?" Harlow popped her hip, full of attitude.

"Leave," Jet said, sounding impatient. "None of you should be here right now. And since we all want the same thing—to be there for Amaya—maybe cut me some fucking slack."

"Don't use that tone with my friends," I snapped, walking into the kitchen.

Jet sat up ramrod straight, his eyes doing a quick scan of my body. "You should've heard how they were talking to me earlier."

"They're protecting me." I shrugged, getting a bowl of cereal ready.

"*I'm* protecting you," he argued.

"I don't need your protection."

"You just said your friends were protecting you!"

"I meant it figuratively. Like, emotionally and shit. You're saying it literally, and I don't think it's necessary." I'd spent my entire shower thinking about this. "I don't think I'm in any danger. They must have taken Mom because of whatever she got mixed up in at BestLyf and maybe because of Calvin. They might be after him too—he was pretty twitchy yesterday—but I don't think they give a shit about me. I've had nothing to do with anything. I didn't even connect the dots that Mom was mixed up with these whacks until the other day." God, was that only the other day? It felt like a year ago, and it wasn't lost on me that my panic in that moment had been warranted.

"You sound like Hopkins," Jet grumbled. The girls and I exchanged glances at the mention of the detective Harlow had dealt with after all the craziness with Irene. At least we could be sure Jet was reporting to Detective Hopkins now and was on the same task force.

"So, Hopkins didn't think I needed protection either, huh?" I shoveled cereal into my mouth, slurping and crunching it obnoxiously.

"No. No one thought it was worth our limited resources." He scoffed.

"But you convinced them otherwise?" Mena pushed.

"Yes. Because I refuse to leave Amaya unprotected and vulnerable."

I sighed and gave the girls a pleading look. *What am I supposed to do? Yeah, he lied, but he has a pretty good excuse for it. And he loves me.*

Donna raised a single eyebrow, only slightly. *He's definitely saying all the right things, but I still don't like that he lied to you.*

I rolled my eyes. *I know! Same. But . . .* I bit my lip and glanced at him. *He's so cute though. And he's being all protective. And I think I love him too.*

Mena bounced on her toes and grinned as she gave me a meaningful nod. *Aww! You love him? I think you should forgive him. I think you already have. You guys are so cute.*

I bugged my eyes out at her. *Stop!*

Harlow slowly crossed her arms and stared at me until I met her gaze. Her lips rose into a smirk, and she glanced between me and Jet before fully grinning. *You guys totally did it.*

"Shut up," I said out loud, pointing a finger at her.

Jet looked between us, a deep frown on his face. "What have I missed?"

The girls and I burst into laughter, which made Jet even more confused. It was a wonderful little release of tension.

"You're in luck." Donna put him out of his misery. "We discussed it, and we've decided you're forgiven."

Harlow came around the island and sat down next to him, giving him a pat on the shoulder. "We just want what's best for our girl, and you seem to be it, so yeah. You're forgiven but not off the hook."

"Think of it as a probationary period." Mena leaned on the counter. "Don't fuck it up."

"Huh?" Jet pinched the bridge of his nose. "You discussed it? Discussed what? And when?"

Harlow tapped her temple and bugged her eyes out at him. "We have ESPN."

The girls chuckled at her joke and Jet's continued confusion, but I couldn't find it in me to be happy. Even the laughter from a few moments earlier—the laughter I'd been so grateful for—had me feeling guilty. I had no business laughing while my mom's life was in danger.

Jet's warm fingers wrapped around my hand, pulling my attention back into the room. He gave me a tentative tug, and I went willingly into his embrace. He held me tightly for a moment, his strong arms around my back, his knees on either side of my hips where I'd stepped between them.

I breathed him in, let his fresh, bergamot-tinged scent ground me.

"Amaya." He tenderly brushed my hair back from my face and opened his mouth, no doubt to say something comforting. Some bullshit placating comment I just didn't want to hear.

"I need to do something," I rushed out before he could. "Please, Jet. I know you can't tell me any of your super-secret, classified cop information or whatever, but I can't just sit around and worry. It's killing me."

"I can only imagine how hard this must be, princess." He gave me that puppy-dog face—the one that told me he wasn't going to give me what I wanted, but he also didn't want me to be mad at him. "But I won't do anything that will put you in danger."

I stepped out of his embrace but kept a hand on his

shoulder. "I'm not asking you to. I'm just asking you to talk to me. We've been dealing with BestLyf bullshit all year. There has to be something we know, something we can do to help, even if it's the smallest little detail . . ." I wasn't even sure what I was saying anymore, what I was asking.

"Why have no arrests been made?" Donna asked. She could tell I was floundering, and she got right to the point. God, I loved her.

"They don't have enough evidence or something." I huffed. Jet had explained this yesterday.

"What does that mean?" Donna pressed.

"We've been building a case against—" Jet stopped himself, clearly fighting an internal battle. He wanted to tell me more, but his sense of duty was strong. "We've been building a case. This has been in the works for some time— over a year. Those in charge don't want to make a move— and alert *anyone* to the level of the investigation—unless we are positive that what we have is airtight. Do you understand? We want to do this once, do it well, and make sure it sticks."

"Kidnapping isn't enough?" Donna asked. "It happened in front of two police officers. How is that not enough?"

"It's a crime, certainly, and it's being taken seriously. It's being investigated."

"And off the record?" Harlow leaned forward, and we all held our breath, waiting to see if he'd break and give us more info.

Jet pressed his lips together so hard they went white. Then he released a massive breath and hung his head, and I knew we had him.

"Off the record, we know this was BestLyf, probably at the direct order of Raine Clayton, but we don't have enough to tie it all together. It's not like Raine jumped out of that car in her cocktail dress and shoved your mom into the trunk herself." I winced at the visual, and he gave my hip a squeeze. "Sorry."

"It's OK." I waved him off. "What would be enough? What do you have now? Maybe we can help you find the evidence you need."

"I can't go into specifics of what evidence we already have." Four feminine, exasperated sighs filled the air, but Jet just raised his voice slightly and kept speaking. "And not just because of legal reasons. It's too complex, too many different angles and connecting stings to go over. Some of it may be related to your mom's kidnapping, but none of it may be. The best approach is to find her—solve this crime—and see if we can connect it back to BestLyf."

"How would we connect it back to BestLyf?" Mena asked.

"You wouldn't do anything. We—as in, the police—would need solid evidence."

"Like . . ." Donna made a beckoning gesture that invited him to go on.

"Like tracking down the car and having it be registered to someone in BestLyf, but the plates were stolen and we can't find it. Like arresting the two assholes who grabbed her and getting their confessions, but that's been a dead end so far. Like getting confirmed correspondence between Raine and the kidnappers saying, in no uncertain terms, 'go steal this person.' Like finding your mom in a building owned by BestLyf or Raine Clayton."

"Can't you just search all the properties owned by Best-Lyf?" I asked.

"On what grounds?" He gave me a desperate look and shook his head, dejected.

"What if you knew where Vivian was being held?" Donna suggested. I could see the wheels turning in her head.

"Then we would be able to go get her, assuming the information was solid."

"How solid? What if it was from an anonymous source?"

"It would need to be a very reliable source or come with very convincing information. Especially if the property happens to be tied to BestLyf."

"What are you thinking, D?" I asked.

"I'm thinking we know a lot of people in high and low places, and it's time we start getting in touch."

"I have a list of BestLyf-owned properties," Harlow announced, pulling her laptop out of a bag on the floor. "And those owned privately by BestLyf members. Although that second list is still being compiled."

"What?" Jet gaped at her. "How? Compiled by whom?"

"I can speak to Jayden. I don't think he'll know anything, but it's worth a shot," Mena said.

"Mena, no. You don't have to do that." I shook my head. He was her bully, and she'd just offered to casually call him and ask about a major crime that had recently been committed.

"I know I don't. But it's OK. I'm OK. I got this." She gave me a confident smile and pulled her phone out, walking over to stand by the window.

"I'll try Will. He fucking owes me." Donna pulled her phone out too, ready to call her piece-of-shit ex.

Harlow clicked away at her keyboard, probably talking to some hooded figure in a dodgy corner of the internet.

My throat got tight as I watched them go into action. For me. I'd lost track of the number of times I'd cried or held back tears in the past few days. I truly had the best friends in the world.

I made a fresh pot of coffee and called Nicola. Our friend's mom was a famous actress and had been involved with BestLyf for years. Nicola herself constantly talked about the youth program. They may have been too entrenched in the whole web, but I figured it was worth a shot.

For the rest of the morning, we made phone calls and had unpleasant and sometimes boring conversations.

Jayden didn't know anything, but he did give Mena the number of one of his dad's friends who used to be at BestLyf but was firmly in the "they are the devil" camp now. We couldn't get through to him, but Jet took the information and passed it on to his colleagues to look into—anyone who hated BestLyf could be helpful in providing information to bring them down.

Will was a dick on the phone. I could only hear Donna's side of the conversation, but I could tell she was losing her patience. In the end, he gave us a few addresses in the surrounding Devilbend area—places that had been used for the illegal fights his dad ran.

My conversation with Nicola was pointless and painful. She'd heard about my mom's kidnapping and was being a supportive friend—asking questions, offering to come over. I didn't know how to come out and say, "Hey, does your mom know any places where her self-improvement cult might be holding my mom hostage?" and I couldn't figure out how to bring up BestLyf in a roundabout way.

Harlow had a whole army of hackers using definitely illegal means to look at security camera footage around the list of addresses she had. But there were a lot of addresses, and it was taking forever.

Jet had moved to the other side of the room and would cover his ears anytime Harlow opened her mouth. His attempts to avoid seeing or hearing anything illegal would've been amusing if I weren't in an almost constant state of panic.

"Thanks for trying, guys," I said, feeling defeated as I passed around the Chinese takeout we'd ordered for lunch.

"We're not done." Harlow covered my hand with hers. "I still have my guys checking the addresses."

"Lalalala!" Jet covered his ears and yelled over her. I smacked him, and he got back to slurping his noodles.

"I do have one more idea but . . ." Donna chewed her lip. "It might be more trouble than it's worth."

"Then it's probably not worth it," Jet supplied unhelpfully.

I sighed. "Shady," the girls and I all said at the same time, and I nodded at Donna. "Do it."

At this point, I'd make a deal with the devil himself to get my mom back. Shady couldn't be any worse.

CHAPTER TWENTY-SIX

DONNA TYPED OUT A MESSAGE, AND WE ALL TRIED NOT TO watch her phone as we ate. By the time we finished, he'd replied, and another half hour later we were pulling into the parking area of Oak Hill Park to meet him.

"This is so dumb. I can't believe I'm letting you do this," Jet grumbled, gripping the wheel tightly.

I huffed. "You're not *letting* me do shit. I was going to do this with or without you."

"I know," he gritted out. "That's why I'm letting you do it."

He'd insisted on coming but tried to talk me out of it the whole way there. We'd been bickering the entire drive, but I was secretly glad to have him by my side. Every time we interacted with Shady, we walked away with one of us owing him something. Being in debt to a criminal like him was stressful as fuck.

It took us a while to find a spot in the almost-full parking lot. It was a beautiful summer day, if a little hot, and people were out enjoying it. Several groups had picnics set up in the shade of the tall trees, and a couple walked up the hiking path and disappeared around a bend.

The five of us wandered over to the main path. I did my best not to run and look as frantic as I felt. Harlow still had to grip my arm hard a few times to stop me from rushing ahead.

Where the hell was that deviant?

All I could see were families and groups of friends having a fun day. No tracksuits as far as the eye could see.

"Donna." I sighed.

She gave me a small smile. "I already texted him."

Jet mumbled some more about what a bad idea this was.

A few minutes later, Shady emerged from the same path that the hiking couple had gone down. He was in shorts and sneakers but still wore a loose-fitting, lightweight tracksuit on top. Even with it zipped only halfway, the sky-blue garment looked out of place in the heat of the afternoon. No more than the two chihuahuas he was walking, though.

He sauntered up to us, two diamanté-encrusted leads clutched in his fist as the little dogs pranced obediently by his side.

We all gaped at the tiny dogs. Shady's unimpressed glower didn't waver.

He also didn't stop. Just walked right past us toward the parking lot.

"Shady! What the hell?" Donna called after him, and he stopped, looking over his shoulder.

"Hey, girl." He gave Donna a sleazy smile. "You looking fine, but I gotta get these two rats home. They need their nap."

One of the "rats" yipped, and they both wagged their little tails as they stared up at him.

"You said you'd talk to us." Harlow huffed.

"I said I'd talk to *her*." Shady pointed at Donna. "Now, I

expected her to bring you three. But you should all know better than to bring a cop along for a ride with me."

For a moment, no one spoke, and the corner of Shady's mouth quirked up into a satisfied smirk.

"Jet? He's not a cop. He's just my boyfriend." I laughed, hoping I wasn't laying it on too thick.

"Yeah, he goes to our school," Mena added.

"You four should know not to bullshit me." Shady shook his head like a disappointed parent, but I didn't miss the malice in his gaze. He was pissed. I wasn't too proud to admit that scared me. He was a dangerous man.

"It's OK." Jet waved his hand dismissively. "Yeah, I'm a cop. But the reason why Donna reached out to you stands. My occupation is irrelevant."

Shady scoffed. "The fuck it is. I've got nothing to say to any of you." Both the chihuahuas barked. Then one of them sniffed the ground and squatted to start pushing out a poo.

"I'm not interested in whatever petty shit you've got going on," Jet snapped. He stood with his hands in his pockets, casual to anyone looking over from a distance. But his shoulders were back, his feet planted, his eyes hard. The air of authority about him had my heart skipping a beat. "I'm not here to arrest you. We just want some information. Give it to us, and we can all get on with our days and pretend like this little picnic never happened."

Shady folded his hands in front of his body and cocked his head to the side. The two men shared an extended stare-off, sizing each other up or whatever. The girls and I shared exasperated looks.

"What's in it for me, pig?" Shady finally asked, licking his bottom lip as if he could taste the leverage he was about to have over a cop.

"How about I don't arrest you?" Jet said.

Shady threw his head back and laughed. "For what? I'm

just out here walking my buddy's dogs, enjoying this glorious day."

"Refusing to assist a police officer."

"I'll be out before dinnertime."

"Not picking up after your dogs." We all looked down at the little pile of poo next to Shady's foot. The chihuahuas cocked their heads and started wagging.

"Not an arrestable offense." Shady produced a poo bag from his pocket with a flourish. He bent down, scooped the poop, and tied the little baggie off expertly.

"True. You clearly know the laws." Jet nodded, and Shady shrugged with a smug smile. "And since you're so knowledgeable about the laws, then I'm sure you're aware of the ones around carrying a concealed weapon. How about I arrest you for that handgun tucked into your ugly shorts? Hmm?"

Shady ground his teeth.

I had an irrational urge to drag Jet into the bushes and get him naked. The way he was handling a man who scared the crap out of me was such a turn-on.

"Have you got a permit for that weapon? Anything else on your person I should be aware of before I search you? How about that black SUV with your two buddies sitting in it watching our every move? Anything inside that vehicle that might be illegal?"

"What the fuck do you want?" Shady snarled, glaring at us girls.

Jet removed his hands from his pockets and got in Shady's face, any semblance of casual calm gone. "Don't look at them. Don't even fucking think about them. Look at me."

Shady glared at Jet instead but didn't step back. The dogs barked and growled, getting worked up.

"Call off your dogs," Jet demanded.

Shady clicked his fingers. "Sit." The little doggies sat and calmed down immediately.

"The other ones."

With a sigh, Shady gestured dismissively over Jet's shoulder. I whipped my head around just in time to see two men climbing back into a black SUV.

"Now, you give us some information, and you're free to go. It's as simple as that." Jet stepped out of Shady's space and stuffed his hands back into his pockets.

"What information?"

"Two nights ago, a woman was kidnapped from downtown Devilbend. I want to know where she's being kept."

"Are you out of your goddamn mind?" Shady scoffed. "You know how many people get snatched every damn day? How am I supposed to know where one bitch is?"

"She was taken from outside Raine Clayton's private residence. She's dating Raine's son, Calvin Clayton."

Jet didn't spell out the obvious, and Shady's expression didn't give anything away. But we all knew that Calvin owned Davey's—the dive bar where Shady conducted a lot of his "business"—and that Shady had connections to BestLyf.

My heart hammered in my chest as Shady stood there with a stoic expression, probably weighing up who he feared more—BestLyf or the fucking police.

Without breaking eye contact with Jet, he pulled his cell out of his pocket and called someone. After two minutes of speaking in some kind of code to whoever was on the other line, he hung up and gave us an address.

———

As soon as Shady was gone, Jet called his superiors to report the "anonymous" tip regarding my mom's whereabouts. Then he went into full boss mode, ordering the girls to go home and declaring I was coming with him "for my own safety."

Of course, the girls wanted to come with me, but Jet

wouldn't budge. He insisted they get an Uber, then waited until they were safely on their way before walking me back to his car.

He took us to a squat building in Devilbend near the police station. With his hand on my lower back, he rushed me inside and up to a second-floor apartment. He'd told me on the drive over he was taking me to the base of operations for his task force, but I hadn't really thought about what to expect.

At least a dozen people were bustling around the apartment when we walked in, and after a moment, another three walked out from a back room. Desks and computers had been set up everywhere, and a fraying couch sat near the dated kitchen.

Detective Hopkins spotted Jet, glanced at me, and marched over to us. "Burns, what the fuck are you thinking?"

"She needs protection." Jet stood his ground against his boss. I did my best to look confident and not in the way. This was the closest we'd been to finding my mom—the closest I'd been to seeing BestLyf finally destroyed—and I didn't want to miss it.

"You just compromised this entire operation, bringing a civilian here!"

A few of the other detectives turned curious glances our way, but no one stopped what they were doing to watch. An air of business, of urgency, permeated the air.

"With all due respect, sir, she already knew of the existence of this operation, mainly due to your contact with Harlow Mead recently. We are on the precipice of a major breakthrough here. She's not going to get in the way of that."

"I want her out of here. Immediately." Hopkins put his hands on his hips, starting to go a little red in the face.

"Sir, please," I blurted, sick of just standing there like a naughty child while the adults talked. They both turned reproachful expressions in my direction. I squared my shoulders and channeled the kind of confidence Donna had when putting someone in their place. "They have my mother. I won't get in the way. I won't jeopardize this in any way. I'll just sit on that couch and be quiet until you tell me where to go."

"We have good information that Vivian Ellis is being held in a BestLyf-owned property," Jet said. "This could be what we need to get the rest. Amaya is the least of our worries right now."

With one last death glare at us both, Hopkins walked off. Was that a yes? Jet must've thought so, because he led me to the couch.

"Take a seat here. Let me know if you need anything, OK?" He rubbed my shoulders. "I'm going to head out with the others to get your mom. I need you to promise to stay here. You'll be safe."

"By myself?" I frowned.

He shook his head. "The analysts will be here. They're not trained to go in the field, but they're trained enough to protect you."

"OK." I nodded and looked around, wide-eyed. The buzz of activity was ramping up as people leaned over monitors, strapped vests to their chest, and checked weapons.

This suddenly felt too real. There were a lot of guns in one room, a lot of very determined-looking police officers.

"Hey." Jet caressed my cheek, drawing my attention back to him. "I love you."

"I love you," I whispered back as he gave me a kiss on the forehead. Then he rushed off to get ready.

I sat down heavily on the ugly couch and tried my best not to panic—or at least not to let it show. I must've done a good enough job, because no one paid me any attention as they rushed around.

In a matter of minutes, most of the people cleared out—
on their way to save my mom. Only two officers remained.
The man and woman sat at desks next to each other, each
with three screens in front of them. They were across the
room with their backs to me.

I updated the girls but was too nervous to read or even
scroll social media. I kept glancing at the door, as if the police
could have driven two towns over and returned with my mom
in the ten minutes they'd been gone.

I sighed deeply as I realized I was in for an excruciating
wait.

Unable to sit still, I got up and went to the window,
moving the curtains aside to peer down at the street below.
Everyone was just going about their business as if it was a
normal afternoon. I supposed it was for them.

"Hey! Get away from the window!" the dude analyst
barked, making me jump.

"Shit!" I pressed my hand to my chest. "Sorry. God."

"Be a good little girl and stay away from the windows,
OK?" He gave me the most patronizing look I'd ever been
subjected to before turning back to his screens.

I gave his back the finger but stepped away from the
window. All the windows had the blinds drawn, and I figured
there was probably a reason for that. But I still couldn't sit
still, so I wandered around the dingy room, looking around.
There wasn't much to see. Just peeling wallpaper and dirty
coffee mugs. Not a personal item in sight.

One of the desks was a total mess of notepads and folders,
with mugs and plates on top of them. I stacked the plates and
straightened the folders.

"Don't touch that!" This time it was the chick analyst
telling me off. "Jesus Christ, what kind of idiot are you? That's
classified, important information you're messing with."

"I was just tidying up," I gritted out.

"Well, don't. Just sit on your spoiled little ass and don't touch anything." She turned away without waiting for a reply. I flipped her off too and headed back to the couch. Why did they have to be so fucking mean? The hostility was next level.

I took my phone out to message the girls and complain about the bitchy analysts, but a text came in before I got a chance.

It was from Calvin. I sighed, not in the mood for more of him trying to convince me I should go somewhere with him for safety, but I opened it anyway.

And my stomach plummeted.

It was a short text, and a photo came through right after.

C: I have your mom. Come now and DO NOT tell your cop boyfriend about this.

There was an address at the end. The photo was of Mom. She had on the same dress she'd worn that night—the one I'd cobbled together for her—and bruises covered her face. She was lying down on some bed, passed out.

CHAPTER TWENTY-SEVEN

I CALLED HIM IMMEDIATELY. HE DIDN'T PICK UP. I CALLED again, and again no one picked up. Then another text came through.

C: Stop calling. Just come to the address. Alone.

Fuck that. Fuck him!

I sprang to my feet and ran across the room to the two analysts.

"Can you get in touch with Jet and the others?" I slapped my palm down on the chick's desk. She looked at it pointedly, then glared at me.

"What now?" The dude sighed dramatically as the chick flicked my hand off her desk as if it were a bit of moldy pizza crust.

"You need to call them and tell them they're going to the wrong place. I just got a text. My mom is not there anymore. Calvin . . ."

They weren't listening. They were laughing at me. At first trying to contain it, then outright laughing.

"Just wait for your boyfriend and let us do our jobs, little girl." The chick waved me off as if I were an irritating fly. They were clearly too far up their own asses to listen, and I didn't have time for this bullshit.

Without another word, I turned on my heel and rushed to the door. The dude called after me, swearing, but neither of them chased me down the stairs or out of the building. I called Jet on my way down, but he didn't answer his phone. Of course he didn't. It was probably on silent while he stormed an empty building with the other cops.

Out on the street, I looked up the address. It was a good hour drive out into the hills. I needed a car, but I'd come here with Jet. Dammit!

Pulling at my hair and growling, I turned on the spot in search of a solution. I could get an Uber home and grab my car, but that would add another forty minutes to my drive. I could go to the police station one street over. If the dickheads upstairs weren't going to take me seriously, maybe they would. But I dismissed that idea almost as quickly as it came. There was a reason the BestLyf task force was in a shitty apartment with the blinds constantly drawn—the police couldn't be trusted. Raine almost certainly had the local police in her pocket. What if they tipped her off? What if they tipped Calvin off? I couldn't risk him taking Mom away again—or worse.

Think, Amaya! What else is in the area? A few friends lived in the apartment buildings nearby, but the closest familiar spot was Exert—the gym where Turner worked. I jogged around the corner and up the block to the gym.

The young girl in activewear behind the counter smiled at me. I was a regular here, and most of the staff knew me.

"Is Turner here?" I rushed out before she could greet me.

"Uh, no." She looked worried now that she'd taken in my

panicked expression, my labored breathing. "He's not working today."

"Fuck. OK. Julie, right?"

She nodded, looking more uncertain by the second.

"Do you have a car?" I asked. "Is it here?"

"Yeah . . ." She frowned.

"Good. Can I please borrow it? It's an emergency."

"Um . . . I don't know . . ."

I resisted the urge to scream "IT'S AN EMERGENCY" into her face and took the pragmatic route instead. "Look, how much is it worth? Your car."

"Like . . ." She looked up to the ceiling. "Three grand, maybe?"

"OK. I'll give you five right now if you hand over the keys."

"What?" She bugged her eyes out.

"Five grand." I pulled my phone out and navigated to the payment app. "Right now, for your keys. And you can have the car back when I'm done with it."

When she continued to stare at me, wide-eyed, I waved my phone in her face. Finally, she snapped out of it and gave me her account details. After I'd transferred the money, she slid her keys over the counter to me, and I snatched them and ran for the back door.

"It's the red Mazda!" she called after me.

I found the red compact car, set my phone up on the holder and turned on navigation, then got the hell on the road.

All I could think about was getting to my mom.

Once I was out of downtown traffic and on the freeway, I tried calling Jet again. It just rang and rang until it went to voice mail. I left him a message, but—feeling paranoid—I didn't say the address or allude to what he was currently doing. Hopefully, my urgent tone and insistence he call me back immediately would be enough.

Then I called Donna.

She answered right away. "Hey, girl. What's happening?"

"Hey!" I froze, my mouth opening and closing, unsure what to say or how to say it exactly.

"Have they found your mom?"

"No, there's still no leads on that."

Donna paused for a beat. We both knew there was a very strong lead on that—we'd heard Shady give it to us just a few hours earlier.

"That sucks." Donna picked up what I was throwing down. "Let me grab Harlow and we can talk for a while."

She was telling me without telling me that her computer-nerd sister would know if my phone was tapped. Spying wasn't out of the ordinary when it came to our interactions with members of BestLyf. Harlow diligently checked our devices for spyware and whatever else, but it had been a while.

"No, that's OK." I was coming up to my exit and needed to focus on the road. But I wasn't dumb enough to go into a dangerous situation without someone knowing. Fuck Calvin and his demands that I come alone and tell no one. I was coming alone, but I'd make sure I wouldn't stay that way for long.

"I just wanted to check in, hear your voice. But I don't have time to talk. I'm on my way to that *appointment* I've been *avoiding* and I'm running late. They messaged me last minute, and I figured I'd go before someone else *took* it."

"Oh, OK. Do you want me to come meet you?" I could hear the edge of worry in her voice.

"Nah, but I can't get a hold of Jet to tell him I'll be late for our date. Can you try calling him when he gets off work? His phone is on silent, and I don't think he'll get my messages."

"Consider it done."

"Thanks, D."

"Love you, A." It sounded as if she was saying, *Be careful.*

"Love you too."

I hung up and concentrated on the winding roads. The address Calvin had sent was kind of remote, nothing but trees and the occasional driveway on either side of the road.

Finally, the GPS told me to turn into one of the driveways. My heart hammered in my chest, and I gripped the wheel even harder than I'd been clutching it the entire drive over.

The driveway was long and overgrown. I had to slow down to a crawl as the little car bumped along seemingly endlessly. Eventually, the road ended at a cabin that looked abandoned. Boards covered the windows, and weeds grew through cracks in the little porch. A pickup truck was the only sign there was anyone other than me here.

With a shaky breath, I got out of the car and walked up to the front door.

CHAPTER TWENTY-EIGHT

THE DOOR SWUNG OPEN, REVEALING A DISHEVELED CALVIN clutching a gun. He was wearing the same clothes he'd been in when I saw him last. His hair was a mess, his eyes bulging.

"Where is she?" I gritted out, painfully aware of the weapon in the unhinged man's grip. He scanned the area behind me.

"Amaya!" Mom called from somewhere within the house.

Acute relief slammed through me, mixed with the fear that had been a constant companion. The strange combination of feelings made me a little dizzy.

Calvin stepped out onto the porch, and I instinctively took a step away from him. But he hardly looked at me as he moved down the steps, still surveying the woods all around the dilapidated cabin.

I darted inside, desperate to get to my mom. It was dark, but a lamp provided some light in the far corner—right next to a couch where my mother was struggling to stand up. I sprinted to her and dropped hard to my knees.

She pulled me in for a hug. "A hug" didn't really encapsulate the way we clutched each other though. It was too mild a term for the level of intensity, for all the unspoken things contained in the space between our clasping arms.

I was wary of hurting her, but she squeezed me fiercely. It gave me some comfort to feel the strength in her grip.

"Mom, can you walk?" I asked in a harsh whisper, looking at the open door behind us.

"Yes, honey. It's not—"

"We have to move now. Before he comes back." I got to my feet and pulled on her arm. At the same time, I inspected the cabin for something I could use as a weapon. The open-plan space wasn't as shitty on the inside as it looked on the outside. There was a small, clean kitchen, a quaint round table with four chairs, and a fireplace next to the couch and armchair. Two doors on the adjacent wall probably led to a bedroom and bathroom.

"Before who comes back?" Mom got to her feet with a wince. I didn't know what hurt, but I winced too.

"Calvin." There were probably knives in the kitchen, but the fireplace was closer. I grabbed the poker from the pile of fireplace tools and wrapped an arm around Mom's waist. "He wandered out toward the driveway, but I don't know how far he went. We need to move."

But Mom didn't budge when I tried to get us hobbling toward the front door.

"Oh, honey, you scared me." She sighed, then lowered herself back down to the couch.

"What? Mom! Get up!" I yelled.

The door slammed, and I spun around to see Calvin standing inside. The gun was no longer in his hands, but I brandished the fire poker in front of myself anyway.

"Stay the fuck away from us!" I screamed.

He just stood there holding his hands up as if I were mugging him, a confused expression on his face.

"Amaya," Mom said gently. She covered my hands with

hers, gently pushing until I lowered the poker. "Calvin is not going to hurt us. He saved me."

Breathing hard, I let her words sink in. Now I was the one confused.

"What?" I shook my head and let Mom take the poker. She dropped it to the floor with a clang, and Calvin relaxed.

"I thought you messaged her and told her," Mom said to Calvin.

"I did." He dragged a hand down his face. He looked exhausted as he moved to the kitchen and put the kettle on— the old-fashioned kind that you heat on the stove.

"He sent me a photo of you looking banged up and dirty and told me to come here and not bring the cops." I started to take in more details as I spoke. Mom was no longer in her dirty dress from the photo. She had on baggy sweats and looked clean. Her hair was even still damp.

"Calvin." Mom sounded reproachful. "I told you to reassure her, not send her a ransom note!"

"I thought I was. It's been a very stressful fucking couple of days." He sighed and leaned heavily on the counter. "I'm sorry, Amaya."

"He saved you?" I asked Mom. I needed to have it confirmed again. "You're OK? He's not keeping you here against your will?"

"No, honey. We can leave if we want to."

"No, you can't!" Calvin sounded panicked. My anxiety spiked.

"Calvin!" Mom barked.

"Sorry, sorry. I just meant it's safer if you don't. I don't want anything to happen to you. We have to be very careful about our next move. But, no, I'm not holding either of you hostage or whatever."

"What the fuck is happening?" I collapsed onto the couch

next to Mom. She brushed my hair over my shoulder, and I leaned into her touch.

"Cal and I have been planning to get out. With you finishing high school and going off to college or traveling, we were putting things in motion to move away from Devilbend. The business I mentioned was a new chapter of BestLyf— somewhere the organization doesn't have a lot of members," Mom explained.

"Why? Mom, BestLyf is a cult. Please, you have to believe me. They're dangerous and they do all kinds of illegal shit."

"I know." She patted my arm, then frowned at me. "Wait, how do you know?"

A bitchy comment about how she'd know if she'd paid any attention to me over the last year was on the tip of my tongue, but I held it back. Old habits die hard. "Doesn't matter. How did you end up . . . here?" I gestured vaguely to her banged-up state and the time capsule of a cabin we were currently in.

"The new BestLyf chapter was supposed to be just a stepping stone. Once we had some distance from the headquarters in Devilbend and from Raine Clayton, we were planning to pull back from it and eventually separate ourselves from it entirely. We spent a lot of time making a plan, thought it out carefully, but . . ." She looked at Calvin.

"But my mother is a fucking psychopathic megalomaniac," he gritted out. The kettle started making a high-pitched noise, and he turned to take it off the heat, busying himself with making tea.

"Raine somehow got wind of our plan, and she didn't like it. She's very possessive of her son. And he knows a lot of things that could threaten BestLyf."

"Oh, you mean how they run a bunch of illegal businesses and kidnap and kill people regularly? Yeah, I can see how she might be worried about that getting out." I huffed.

They both gaped at me, and I shrugged, unfazed. I wasn't the one who needed to explain herself right now.

"So, what's the new plan then?" I asked.

Calvin placed two steaming mugs of herbal tea on the side table. "We lie low for a while. No one knows about this cabin. We take some time so your mother can recover, and we plan our next move."

The sound of footsteps on the porch had us all swinging our heads toward the door. There was a knock, and Calvin pulled his gun out.

"I told you not to tell anyone," he hissed at me. "Who did you tell?"

Before I could even reply, another knock sounded on the rickety wood. Then a woman's voice came through the cracks.

"Come on, Cali-boy, open the door for Mommy. I know you're in there!"

We exchanged looks, the blood draining from all our faces. It made the dark bruises on Mom's cheek and eye appear even more stark.

"Calvin! Open this door right now!" Raine shouted.

Cal held his finger over his lips in the universal sign for silence and went to the door. "Mom?" he called, putting on a surprised voice.

"Amaya," Mom whispered as she pushed me away. "Go to the door on the left and hide. Go now."

I got up from the couch, but instead of hiding, I picked up the poker again.

Calvin hid the gun behind his back as he unlocked the door and opened it a crack. He said something I couldn't make out. Then Raine laughed.

"You should know better than to lie to me, my stupid, sweet boy."

Loud banging and glass breaking made me jump. I brandished the poker in both hands, swiveling around. The sound was coming from all sides, and I didn't know which way to face, where the danger was coming from.

People flooded into the house. They came from all directions, shoving past Calvin through the front door, climbing through broken windows, rushing in from the bedroom. Some were women but most were men. They all wore casual clothes and wielded guns and menacing expressions.

I counted at least a dozen. Where had they even come from? How did we not hear a car coming up the drive? Did they creep up through the woods? Did I lead them here?

Too many questions to even process flashed through my mind.

Mom was suddenly standing, her back to mine. I leaned against her and swung the poker in a wide arc. The two mean dudes closest to us just laughed, pointing their guns at my head.

They had a point. What the fuck was I going to do with my stick against their guns?

I still held on to it though. It felt like the only thing giving me any strength in this fucked-up situation.

The intruders easily disarmed Calvin, outnumbered as he was, and one of the men shoved him. He stumbled and caught himself on the edge of the table, sending one of the dining chairs clattering to the floor.

Raine walked into the cabin calmly, her wedged heels thudding on the wooden floors. She was in blue linen pants and a loose white shirt with a chunky necklace, her hair neatly styled in a low bun—an ensemble that paired perfectly with her smug, beatific smile. It was as if she'd been on her way to brunch with other obscenely wealthy women of a certain age and had just popped into this remote, crumbling cabin in the woods on her way.

She paused just inside the door, took in the scene, and

wandered over to the dude who'd shoved Calvin. Swinging her arm wide, she smacked him on the side of the head.

The armed man, who was twice her size, just stood there and took it.

"Do not lay a hand on my son," she said, authority heavy in her voice.

"Sorry, ma'am." He hung his head, looking miserable and frightened at the same time.

"Are you OK, Cali-boy?" she cooed to her grown-ass son and caressed his head as if he were a toddler.

Calvin jerked away, disdain and hatred clear in his eyes.

She just folded her hands in front of her. "You're mad at me, I know. But, darling, I'm very disappointed in you too."

She looked at him expectantly, slowly raising one eyebrow. Calvin just kept glaring.

My arms started to shake from holding the heavy poker up in front of myself.

"Not ready to apologize then." Raine sighed. "I shouldn't be surprised, I guess, considering the lengths you went to in order to run away from home." She chuckled. "And here I am ruining your fun."

Was this a fucking game to her?

"Now, come on, get your things. It's time to go home." She smoothed the front of her shirt, unaffected by the deadly weapons in the room or how fucked up this situation was.

"How did you find us?" Cal asked. He sounded defeated.

Raine released one harsh laugh. "I thought you'd learned your lessons a long time ago. There is nothing you can hide from me. I know everything there is to know. I am everywhere, and my will is absolute. Now, you're trying my patience, and I really don't want to have to punish you."

Cal winced. It was the slightest little tic in his face, but I caught it. He'd suffered at the hands of this woman.

"Having you as a mother is punishment enough," he spat. "I've been living in purgatory my entire life."

"Watch your mouth." Raine suddenly looked furious.

"No!" Calvin yelled, and she seemed genuinely taken aback. "I am a grown man. All I'm trying to do is build a life with the woman I love. And your reaction to that is to kidnap her? To show up here with armed goons? What the fuck is wrong with you? This isn't normal! I can't live like this anymore!"

"We do not acknowledge that word in my world. Have you forgotten the basic principles of BestLyf already?"

"Normal! Normal! Normal!" Calvin shouted, going red in the face.

"That's it. I've had enough." Raine was starting to go red too, her perfect mask slipping. I could really see the resemblance now. An identical vein in their foreheads popped out as they shouted at each other. "I told you when you came to me yesterday that I was willing to let that woman live." She gestured vaguely in our direction, making a disgusted face. As if the mere mention of my mother tasted rotten in her mouth. I bared my teeth at her, gripping the poker tighter despite my shaking arms. "I've always been a reasonable parent, Calvin. I was willing to let you keep her as long as you understood that your place was by my side. But now I see just how far this insubordination has gone. How deeply she's dug her claws into you. She's corrupted you, my boy."

"She *saved* me," Calvin said, squaring his shoulders. "We are each other's salvation. You'll never understand what that's like—to have someone who truly understands you and accepts you for all your flaws. I pity you, Mother."

For a beat Raine just stood there, staring at her son, that vein in her forehead pulsing faster. I wanted to scream at him to stop antagonizing the homicidal megalomaniac, but the multiple guns pointed at me kept me silent.

Raine cleared her throat and completely ignored what Cal had just said. "As I was saying, I was willing to indulge you and let you keep her. But I've changed my mind, and now she, and that brat of hers, will have to die."

As if Raine had dropped a grenade into the little cabin in the woods, everything erupted into chaos.

My mom screamed and, with strength I didn't think her beaten body possessed, shoved me to the side to put herself in front of me. I stumbled but managed to stay on my feet.

Calvin dropped to his knees, clutching his mother's pants as he pleaded for her not to literally kill us.

Mom was yelling, threatening the people with guns, cursing out Raine.

Raine's lackeys got jittery and started barking instructions too. They glanced to Raine for guidance while closing in on us.

All logic fled my mind, and I went into pure fight or flight.

I swung the poker at the shoulder of the man closest to us, and it connected with a sickening crunch. He bellowed in pain and dropped his gun to the ground.

The others all sprang into action, diving for us.

I was shoved again. This time I fell to the ground with the wind knocked out of me. Someone kicked me in the ribs, and the pain was so intense I saw stars.

My vision returned just in time to see two of the lackeys smacking my mom down onto the couch. The man was shouting something while the woman punched her over and over and over.

A gun went off, the sound so loud it cut through the chaos already filling the small space.

Everyone crouched and looked around for where the shot had come from, but I didn't bother. I just stared at my mom's limp body.

"Mom," I wailed as everything started to go blurry. "Please . . ."

She wasn't moving, her face a bloody, pulpy mess.

From my position, I couldn't see if her chest was rising and falling. Every time I tried to drag myself closer, my vision would waver from the pain in my stomach and ribs, and I'd collapse back to the hard ground.

More gunshots went off. Boots pounded on the wooden floors. More shouting and violence.

It wasn't until Jet's face appeared in front of mine that I realized I'd been screaming hysterically.

I stopped screaming, but my overloaded mind still struggled to make sense of anything. Jet's mouth was moving, his hand stroking my head gently, but I had no idea what he was saying.

I used his steady gaze to ground myself. I focused on his dark eyes, then his lips, as everything around me started to register.

Cops swarmed everywhere. Raine's goons were either being handcuffed or prone on the ground—dead or knocked out? I didn't really care.

There was no sign of Raine or Calvin.

Mom.

So many people stood crowded inside the small cabin now. I couldn't see her between all their bodies.

"Hey, hey. Focus on me." Jet's gentle hands guided my face closer to his, and he locked his gaze to mine. "Eyes on me, princess. Just listen to my voice. We're gonna get you out of here."

"Mom . . . ," I croaked. I tried to look again, but he forced me to keep still.

"I know. There are ambulances coming. There are people with her. I need you to focus on you right now, OK?" He nodded slowly, and I found myself nodding along with him. "Can you tell me where it hurts? Did you get shot?"

I shook my head. "No. I . . . I don't think so." Panic welled once again, and tears started pouring down my face. "Fuck. Jet, did I get shot? Am I OK?"

I sobbed and he hushed me, stroking my head again and murmuring soothing things.

By the time the wail of ambulance sirens was so close it sounded as if they were inside, I'd managed to tell Jet I'd been shoved and kicked, and he'd poked at my ribs and run his hands over every inch of my body. He spoke to me the entire time, keeping my focus on him and away from the bustling activity where my mom's bloody body lay.

Even when the cops started clearing out the cabin, Jet still wouldn't let me look in her direction. He crouched right by my head, blocking my view with his body as two EMTs came to examine me.

The emergency workers whisked Mom out to an ambulance, and then the wail of the siren rent the air once more— this time getting fainter.

Not long after, I found myself in the back of another ambulance, Jet right by my side. As we prepared to leave for the hospital, I caught sight of Raine Clayton. She was leaning against a car, handcuffed, as she shouted something over her shoulder. Just before the ambulance doors slammed shut, she caught me watching and sneered.

Jet stayed with me through all of it, keeping me tethered to sanity with his touch, his voice, and his very presence.

Whatever the EMTs had given me seriously numbed the pain in my body. It made my head feel kind of fuzzy too, but the absence of pain made it easier to think.

"Jet?"

"Right here, beautiful." He gave my arm a squeeze.

"How did you know? I tried to call you so many times but . . ."

He smiled down at me. It didn't reach his eyes. "You have some very clever friends."

Donna had read between the lines of what I'd said on the phone as clearly as if I'd shouted the information at her. The rest was easy enough to guess. Harlow had tracked my phone, they'd gotten through to Jet, and he'd come to the rescue.

After a stretch of silence, I asked another question. "Is my mom going to be OK?"

When he didn't immediately answer, I tried to turn my head to look at him, but they'd put me in one of those neck brace things and I couldn't move an inch.

Maybe he hadn't heard me? But I knew he had—he'd started stroking my arm right when I asked it. He just didn't know how to answer.

I couldn't find the strength to ask again.

EPILOGUE

THE TEAL SILK FELT COOL TO THE TOUCH, DESPITE THE warmth of the day. I ran my hand over it, smoothing the fabric over my lap.

My ribs still hurt if I took too deep a breath, but I could sit up on my own and walk, and that was all I needed to cross a stage and graduate with the rest of my class.

Despite everything, despite how recent all the pain and chaos was, I refused to miss this. I refused to let that evil woman and her corrupt organization take one more thing from me. I was going to wear the silk gown and silly cap and graduate with all my friends if it was the last fucking thing I did. It wouldn't be, of course. I was going to be fine.

I had one cracked rib and some gnarly bruising, but I was OK otherwise. Unlike Mom . . .

A round of applause went up, and I belatedly joined everyone in clapping along to whatever Headmistress Perry just said. Once she started speaking again, I found the back of Donna's head, several rows in front of me, and focused on her perfectly smooth, short hair for a moment. Then I turned to look several rows behind me. Mena caught my eye immediately and gave me a small smile.

"OK?" she mouthed.

I nodded and turned back to the front.

The stage was set up in the middle of the football field, the bleachers packed with the graduating class's loved ones. My peers and I sat in alphabetical order, ready to go receive our diplomas.

Donna's last name—Mead—should've put her behind me, but she was seated in the front because she was valedictorian. Because *of course* she was. I was so proud of my friend.

Fulton being about as exclusive as you could get for a school, the graduating class wasn't massive. No one had last names that started with *F* or *G*, so Hendrix (Hawthorn) sat right next to me. As much as I was determined to be here for this rite of passage, it had been a rough few weeks, and it felt good to have someone beside me who knew what it had been like, who had been there for me right along with my girls.

He leaned sideways slightly and whispered in my ear, "You know, for a while I thought I'd never even finish high school, let alone graduate with half-decent grades."

I covered my mouth as we both chuckled.

"I guess you never know what life's going to throw at you," I whispered back. I was painfully aware we should've been too young to fully appreciate that sentiment. We'd seen too much. Experienced shit no one should have to.

"You'd think I'd be a bitter asshole after everything I've been through, everything I did." He shifted in his seat, his silk robe rubbing against my own. Hendrix was clearly in a reflective mood. I couldn't blame him. "But I guess I've also learned that life has a way of working out if you let it. Like, everything is OK in the end, and if it's not OK, it's not the end."

"It's because of who you are as a person deep down,

Hendrix." I kept my gaze forward. "You didn't let that shit define you, and you worked to learn from it. That's all any of us can do."

He cleared his throat. "Thanks, Amaya."

"You're not bitter." I shrugged. "But you're still an asshole."

I could see his grin out of the corner of my eye. "And you're still a bitch."

"Thank you." I let my grin break free and clapped along with everyone else as Ms. Perry finished her speech and walked off the stage.

More people spoke—inspiring words from former students, the class president, and of course, my valedictorian bestie. Donna's was the only speech I paid real attention to.

And then it was time. Guided by the teachers, my fellow graduates and I made our way forward in neat alphabetized rows. One by one, names were called, and students in shining teal robes proudly walked across the stage to accept their certificates and flip the tassel on their cap to the other side—a sign they'd officially graduated.

I cheered each one of them on, right along with the rest of the crowd.

Then it was my turn.

Ms. Perry called my name, and I took a breath as I stepped forward. I kept my gaze on my feet as I climbed the few stairs in my heels, then focused on Ms. Perry and reaching her.

I could feel all their gazes on the side of my head, hundreds of people staring at me and wondering just as many things as they already knew. It was all anyone in Devilbend had been talking about for weeks.

The tangled web of Raine Clayton's crimes was still unraveling, but it was clear to anyone she was done.

She had spent years perpetrating more crimes than I

cared to tally up—everything from tax evasion to straight-up murder. Because they'd caught her in the act of kidnapping and attempted murder in the cabin that day, the police had more than enough to keep her locked up while they gathered even more evidence against her, BestLyf, and multiple members of the organization.

She had immediately surrounded herself with an entire firm of high-profile attorneys, but even they couldn't get her out on bail. Due to her resources and connections, she was too much of a flight risk. But they were doing their damnedest to get her out of paying for her crimes. They had their work cut out for them.

Even if Raine somehow managed to avoid life in prison, she was ruined, along with BestLyf. The organization that had been growing since the nineties—one of the most powerful corporations in the country—was crumbling for the whole world to see, as if it had been constructed from dust and lies. TMZ was reporting on it constantly, sometimes hourly. With that many high-profile people involved, there was a constant stream of scandals, news, declarations of innocence, and scrambling to get distance from a ship that had already sunk.

The police had already gathered a good deal of evidence against multiple members of BestLyf, but recent developments had given them access to more information than they could realistically process in the short time that had passed. But even preliminary reports—the little that they'd speak about—made it clear they had enough to throw the book at Raine.

Jet had barely left my side at the hospital and had practically moved into my house when I was discharged. Since then, he'd relaxed his staunch rule against telling me anything to do with his work; I knew more details than anyone outside the investigation. They had enough to prove Raine had her hand in multiple horrific crimes. Most notably, she was aware of the murder of Chelsea—one of Mena's coworkers at the diner—who had gone missing and turned up dead. Raine had personally ordered the murder of Irene Richards in prison, and she had directly ordered my mother's kidnapping.

More broadly, she was well aware of all the illegal dealings connected to BestLyf—many of which Calvin had been in charge of. There was a massive criminal underbelly to Best-Lyf, a huge network of drugs, guns, and human trafficking. And she was behind it all, had built it all.

And now she was going to pay for it.

I knew the law was anything but straightforward and the process could be painfully slow, but I also knew in my gut Raine would not get away with it. She'd hurt too many people, and there was too much evidence to prove it.

Not to mention all the people suddenly willing to talk, to give evidence and even testify—most of them in an effort to distance themselves from this truly horrifying shit show. To save their own asses. High-profile people, like Nicola's famous actress mom, were falling over one another's designer shoes to speak against an organization that had been as useful to them as they had been to Raine Clayton.

I didn't care. As long as the real monsters paid for their evil deeds.

"Congratulations, Amaya." Ms. Perry handed me my high school diploma and shook my hand. I returned her smile and reached up to flip the tassel from one side to the other.

Then I reminded myself I didn't give a shit what all those people were saying or thinking about me, and I turned to face them with my head held high. I knew what really mattered to me, and their opinions weren't it.

I held my fists up in triumph, my diploma clutched in one, and everyone cheered a little harder. Maybe I'd been imagining some of the whispers and judgment. The whistling and clapping seemed to get a little more intense and last a little longer than it had for the students before me.

Maybe I was imagining that too, but whatever. I'd been through a lot to make it to this point, and I enjoyed the applause.

My focus zeroed in on a particularly rowdy group in the crowd.

In the first row of the audience, the people I loved most in the world—at least the ones not graduating with me—all sat together in the same section. They must've arrived extra early to grab those seats, although they were on their feet right now, whooping and cheering and clapping like crazy people.

Jet stood front and center, beaming at me as he held his hand up to his mouth and wolf-whistled. The sound carried over all the rest of the noise.

Turner was next to him. His graduation had been the week before, and we'd all gone along to support him, just as he was doing for us today. His dad and little sister were right behind him.

Harlow alternated between clapping and wiping away the tears streaming down her face. Easton had an arm around her while he cheered. Easton's brother, Ford, was on his other side, whooping as though he were at a football game and not a graduation. Harlow and Donna's parents stood next to Mena's mom and dad, and Hendrix's aunt and her boyfriend were beaming. His parents had come too, but they must've been seated elsewhere.

Calvin was at the end of the row, standing and clapping with the others.

The only reason he wasn't behind bars right along with his mother was because he was fully cooperating with the investigation. And because he'd been working with the task force for months before. He'd been serious about wanting to get out from under his mother's sick influence, to help stop her once and for all. The only time he'd wavered had been when Mom was kidnapped. He'd been terrified for her life and had done what he thought was the best thing to save her. He really did love her. There was no way I could deny it or question it anymore.

I was just sorry it had taken all this for me to really see it —to accept him for the genuine, kind man he was.

The only person not standing was my mom. She sat in a wheelchair at the end of the row, clapping and sobbing.

The doctors had kept her in a coma for several days, but she'd made it. She had several broken bones and horrific damage to her face, but she was alive. She was going to need a lot of plastic surgery to regain even a semblance of her beautiful face, and there was a strong possibility she'd never walk again. *But she was here*. She was here for me, and I'd never been more thankful for anything in my whole life.

I looked away from her quickly. If I didn't, I'd start sobbing as hard as she was, and I refused to let all these people see me cry.

The applause settled, and I moved to the other side of the stage to make way for Hendrix and all the students behind him. The rest of the diplomas were handed out, another speech was given, we threw our caps up into the air, and it was done.

Despite all the odds, I'd graduated high school.

The crowd dispersed all over the field, families searching out their graduates. People hugged and cried all over the place.

A body slammed into mine from behind, and Harlow wrapped her arms around me. She bounced and squealed at the back of my head: "I'm so proud of you!"

"Fuck, you're strong for someone so small." I chuckled, extracting myself from her just enough to spin around and return her hug properly. I didn't even care that it made my ribs ache.

Before we could separate, another set of arms wrapped around us, then another. Donna and Mena had joined us. We adjusted our grip so we were all hugging, then held one another for a long time as people milled around us.

"I love you girls so much," I whispered into our little bubble.

"Me too," Mena said.

"Me three," Harlow added.

"Me four," Donna declared, closing the circle of love.

"Come on, let's go get day drunk. We deserve it!" Harlow declared as we finally pulled apart.

"You didn't even graduate," her sister griped.

"So?" Harlow shrugged. "I survived this hellscape of a year, just like everyone else, didn't I?"

"She's got a point, D." Mena nodded.

"I don't give a shit what we do or where. As long as we do it together," I declared.

With our arms around one another, we walked toward the edge of the field and our waiting loved ones, our teal gowns and Harlow's pink dress billowing out behind us.

The girls teased me for being sentimental, but I just smiled because I knew they were only teasing. And I knew we would be just fine, as long as we had each other.

#DevilbendDynastyForever

THE END

———

Thank you for reading *Like You Know*. I hope you enjoyed this intense, angsty, emotional story. If you enjoy contemporary romance with twisty plots and a good dose of angst, you'll love Just Be Her.

If you could escape your life for one month, would you?

Alexandria Zamorano was everything I wasn't – sophisticated, ambitious, used to getting what she wanted. The only thing we had in common was...well, our face! It was like looking in a mirror when we collided. I don't know what I was thinking, agreeing to put on her pearls and step into her world for a month. Now, I'm stuck in the lap of luxury, trying to avoid an irresistible, persistent billionaire...the one man that's off limits.

And if someone took your place, would anyone notice?

Toni Mathers lived a life I could never have – uncomplicated, fun, never worrying about the consequences of wild nights. We looked identical, and I couldn't pass up the opportunity to don her tight pants and loose life for a month. The owner of the local dive bar, and the lead singer of the band, made all my escapist fantasies come true. Now, when I think about swapping back, it feels like I'll be leaving a part of my soul with them.

Our lives couldn't be more different....and when the secrets behind our identical appearance are revealed, neither of us will ever be the same.

One-click *Just Be Her* now - https://geni.us/JustBeHer OR keep reading for a sneak peak at the first chapter!

NOTE FROM THE AUTHOR

I really hope you enjoyed reading *Like You Know* and you'll consider leaving a review.

Want exclusive access to advanced copies of all my books? If you're a blogger, bookstagrammer, or reviewer, join my master list and never miss an ARC opportunity!

https://kaydencesnow.com/masterlist

ACKNOWLEDGMENTS

Firstly, to the man that always comes first in my life, my one and only, my very own HEA - John. I couldn't do any of this without you; and I'm not just talking about the books. Thank you. I love you.

Massive thanks to my friends and family for constantly reminding me what's most important, without even trying to.

Thank you to all the amazing, talented, supportive people who are integral to every step of this crazy process - my editor, my assistants, my beta readers, everyone who received an ARC and reviewed or helped to promote the book. THANK YOU!

To you, my readers, the most heartfelt thanks of all. The fact that people all over the world read my books still blows my mind! I would be nothing without you.

ABOUT THE AUTHOR

Kaydence Snow has lived all over the world but ended up settled in Melbourne, Australia. She lives near the beach with her husband and draws inspiration from her own overthinking, sometimes frightening imagination, and everything that makes life interesting – complicated relationships, unexpected twists, new experiences and good food and coffee. Life is not worth living without good food and coffee!

She believes sarcasm is the highest form of wit and has the vocabulary of a highly educated, well-read sailor. When she's not writing, thinking about writing, planning when she can write next, or reading other people's writing, she loves to travel and learn new things.

To keep up to date with Kaydence's latest news and releases sign up to her newsletter here:

kaydencesnow.com/#newsletter

Join her reader group here:
    facebook.com/groups/KaydenceSnowLodge

Or follow her on:

ALSO BY KAYDENCE SNOW

The Evelyn Maynard Trilogy

Variant Lost

Vital Found

Vivid Avowed

The Complete Evelyn Maynard Trilogy

Devilbend Dynasty

Like You Care

Like You Hurt

Like You Should

Like You Know

Standalones

Just Be Her

It Started With a Sleigh

Sand and Secrets

Reverie and Redemption

Expose Me